BROKEN BEAUTY

JACLIN MARIE

Editing Done by Antonia Salazar from AMS Editing
Physical Cover and E-Book Cover Done by Bobbi from
STARFALLDESIGNS

ISBN PRINT: 979-8-9881467-2-8
A-ISBN (E-BOOK): 979-8-9881467-3-5

BLURB

———

One bucket list.
Two strangers.
And many memories.
Ariella Madden spends her whole summer with Ash
Jones, a new boy in town who Ariella happened to run
into in a random bookstore.
Ash helps Ariella finish her summer bucket list before she
starts college.
The only rule she has for Ash is that after the bucket list is
complete they can never see each other again.
But what happens when Ariella ends up seeing Ash Jones
in her Psychology class the first day of school?

———

To the girls who love a broken beauty.

PLAYLIST

HIGH FOR THIS	**THE WEEKND**
WOO	**RIHANNA**
I LOVE YOU	**BILLIE ELLISH**
SPARKS	**COLDPLAY**
SOFTCORE	**THE NEIGHBORHOOD**
HOTEL	**MONTELL FISH**
1-800-273-8255	**LOGIC**
WHERE YOU BELONG	**THE WEEKND**
DO I WANNA KNOW?	**ARTIC MONKEYS**
DANGEROUS HANDS	**AUSTIN GIORGIO**
CAN I	**DRAKE**
GOOD FOR YOU	**SELENA GOMEZ**

Author's Note

Please note that this book is probably one of my darkest. I have never written anything with triggering topics that are mentioned in this book, and I have had a group of readers (Beta Readers) read it before I sent it to my editor because I wanted to find out what ways this might be triggering in order to provide a warning and confirm that I am not spreading any false information regarding the topics mentioned in this book.

I do write dark romance but not dark romance that contains topics like the ones that are mentioned in this book.

Before reading, I very much recommend that you read all of the trigger warnings and definitions that are in the next page. I don't care if you think you can handle it or already know the definitions; please, please read these trigger warnings and definitions.

I care about your mental health more than you reading my book. If you **CANNOT** handle any of these trigger warnings or topics mentioned, then **DO NOT READ THIS BOOK.**

If you do, however, continue to read this book after reading the trigger warnings, then I hope you enjoy Ash and all of his deviant tastes :)

Trigger Warning

This story contains mentions of physical and mental abuse. It also contains mentions of child abuse, drugs alcohol, etc.

PTSD:

A disorder in which a person has difficulty recovering after experiencing or witnessing a terrifying event. The condition may last months or years, with triggers that can bring back memories of the trauma accompanied by intense emotional and physical reactions.

Non-Consensual Sex:

Touching of intimate body parts such as genitalia, groin, breast, buttocks, or mouth or any clothing covering them, without consent; the removal of another person's clothes without consent; touching a person with one's own intimate body parts without consent; etc.

Domestic Violence:

Violent or aggressive behavior within the home, typically involving the violent abuse of a spouse or partner.

Rape:

Unlawful sexual activity, most often involving sexual intercourse, against the will of the victim through force or the threat of force or with an individual who is incapable of giving legal consent because of minor status, mental illness, mental deficiency, intoxication, unconsciousness, or deception.

Primal Kink:

A type of sexual kink or deviancy which involves becoming animalistic during sex. Can include scratching, biting, general brute force.

Self Harm:

the act of purposely hurting oneself (as by cutting or burning the skin) as an emotional coping mechanism

Bully:

seek to harm, intimidate, or coerce (someone perceived as vulnerable).

Child Abuse:

physical maltreatment or sexual molestation of a child.

ONE
ARIELLA

SUMMER

They say that dying feels a lot like living. I think of it as the complete opposite.

I personally think that living feels a lot like dying, especially when you have a life that feels like hell.

What's the point of living when you have to pay to live? You have to pay to breathe, eat, and have the absolute essentials.

In life, your body is slowly dying until finally, you crack.

The sound of a bell ringing makes me look up from the book and my eyes catch dark brown ones.

The door closes behind him and he removes his eyes from mine and walks away, towards the fiction side of the bookshop.

I look back at the book in my hands to try and start reading again but my eyes freeze on the page.

Damnit.

Why did you have to look at the door?

You knew you were going to get distracted.

I look at my watch and see that it's 3:30 in the afternoon.

I've spent a total of six hours here. I had to catch up on some work for extra credit.

It is the summer but I want to get school over with as soon as possible so I am taking summer classes.

After finishing some work for school, I walked around the shop and decided to reread one of my favorite books. The main character's husband is a serial killer and he has a list of people he has to kill, and at the end of the list he has his wife.

But earlier I found this book about some killer who goes on a killing rampage and it's a new release from a new author. I thought it was interesting so I read the first page and liked it.

But there are just some things that you read at home because this book has a lot of graphic scenes and I don't want to chance anyone looking over my shoulder to take a peek.

I'll have to ask Lo if I can take this copy with me.

I pack up my things and then head over to the front counter where Lo is reading a book.

I'm not surprised because what else would he be doing? I mean that is why he is the owner of the store.

"Ariella, what can I do for you now?" As I am about to ask if I can take the book home, Lo interrupts me saying, "Wait, let me guess." He looks away from his book and looks at me. "You want to take a book home?"

I give him a guilty smile. "I always bring the books back and you know I do."

"What book?" Lo puts his book down and I hand him the book I was reading. It's called "Right Behind You" by John Xander. Lo looks at the book and furrows his eyebrows. "I can't let you take this."

My eyebrows knit together. "Why not?"

"Because this is the only copy we have right now." Lo gives the book back to me. "Once I get more copies in, I can give you one. But for now it has to stay here."

"Can you let me know when?"

"I'll text you when we have some, Ariella. For now, you can put it in your hiding spot if you're so worried about someone stealing it." Lo says, giving me a look.

He knows I have a hiding spot that I keep all of the books in that I don't want people touching but that I can't take home with me.

I leave the front counter and go to the literature section of the store. Barely anyone reads literature and if someone were to find my little section they wouldn't dare pick up any of the books I have in that section.

I find my section on the top shelf. I feel a small smile lift on my lips as I see my shelf looks the same as the last time I put a book there.

All of my books on the shelves are covered by literature books. If you were to move a few out of the way then you would find my books.

I look around, trying to find a step stool. Usually I always keep one around here but I can't find it.

I walk around the literature area and still manage to not find it.

Damnit.

I get back to the shelf and I stand on my toes so that I can reach the top shelf.

As I try to reach it, my arm starts to hurt and I'm not even close to touching it. I reach farther and my body is pressed against the shelf as I try to get it.

I feel chills go up my spine when a warm chest presses against my back. I see a large hand with veins running up his arm and then tattoos crawling up his forearm and hand.

My stomach fills with butterflies as I imagine those hands touching me.

He grabs the book I was trying to reach for and I turn around and face him.

Dark brown eyes stare back at me.

It's the same guy that distracted me from finishing my favorite book.

Up close I can see his features more clearly than I did when he first walked into the store.

He has a sharp jaw structure, full lips, and piercing eyes. His dark brown hair matches his dark brown eyes.

"'Invisible Man'. You seem more like a 'Great Gatsby' kind of girl," he says while bringing his hand down and handing me the book.

"Last time I read 'Great Gatsby' was when I was a freshman. Safe to say that I wasn't interested."

His gaze dances all over my body and I feel hot when he stares at me with so much heat. His eyes then look at the shelf above me and I see a small smile lift on his face.

What is he thinking?

"Dark romance? That is more convincing."

I furrow my eyebrows at him.

How does he-

I turn around and see a dark romance book I hid there last time I came to the store.

Damnit.

"I wouldn't be judging my taste in books. I bet you're into one of those boring historical books or something."

"Now you're judging me." He tilts his head to the side and gives me a teasing smile. "I'm Ash."

"Ash." I say, testing his name on my lips. "I'm Ariella."

"So what books do you read, Ariella?"

As I roam my eyes down his body, I can tell he is full of muscle under the crewneck and pants he is wearing.

And as I look at him I realize how perfect he is for my plan this summer.

"I can tell you about it over dinner?"

Two

Ash

Summer

Never in my life would I think that spontaneously going on a date with a girl, who I only know the name of, would be something I'm doing on a Thursday night.

I'm not the type to go out and do things spontaneously.

I always have a plan.

I always do things by a plan.

I like having control over things. I like to have control of multiple situations where I'm included so that I don't get hurt.

But this girl Ariella, the way her eyes sparkled before she asked me what I am doing for dinner tonight.

The way her eyes sparkled with mischief as if she had a plan for me.

I liked it.

A little too much.

I smiled when she asked me.

She looks innocent but I just know that everything about her isn't pure.

God, I don't even know this girl's last name and I am going out with her.

When I first walked into the bookstore my eyes immediately went to her. She is hard not to look at.

And then I was walking around the entire store, trying to find this book that released by one of my favorite authors, and somehow I ended up in the section I saw her hiding a book in.

She definitely didn't look like the type to read historical fiction or classic literature.

But then I looked up at the shelf and I grabbed the book and saw another book with the title "Captured By You".

I already knew for a fact it was some dark romance book with erotica in it.

I look down at my watch and see that it's 7:15 pm.

Ariella is fifteen minutes late and I am trying to decide if I want to wait for another fifteen minutes or if I just want to leave and forget about her.

My patience is running thin right now and all I can think about is just going home and punching the mirror in my room until my hands bleed.

It's a good way for me to get any tension I have in my body released.

It feels good.

The pain.

Just as I was about to say 'fuck it all', I see Ariella sit down in the chair in front of me.

"I thought I was going to get stood up," I say.

Ariella's face turns a little red. "I overthink a lot and I just wasn't sure if I wanted to do this." I raise an eyebrow at her. "Like go on a date."

"Have you ever been on a date?"

Ariella nods her head. "Once but it was a while ago."

I nod my head and take a sip out of my water. "So why did you decide to ask me to go for dinner?"

Ariella sighs. "Because I want to experience a lot of things like dating for example and what happens on dates."

My mind immediately starts thinking dark and inappropriate thoughts. Thoughts that Ariella has no way to comprehend what exactly I'm thinking.

"What's your last name?"

Ariella's face pales. "We don't need to know each other's last names yet."

"Why not?"

"Because it's not important right now. In this moment, I want to learn more about you as a person." Ariella relaxes in her chair.

The waiter ends up coming to our table and takes Ariella's drink order.

"How old are you?" I ask.

"Eighteen, going to turn nineteen in December." Ariella answers. "What about you?"

"Turned nineteen last month."

"What did you do for your birthday?"

I almost laugh when thinking about it. My friends from New York threw me a party. So much shit happened but I was too high to even comprehend what was happening.

"My friends threw a party for me."

"Why the smile?" Ariella asks with a smile threatening to spill on her lips.

"'Cause it was a crazy party."

Ariella and I talk more as time goes on. We eat here and there but the food is forgotten as we keep talking.

I tell her about how I am visiting for the summer and that I live in New York with my father. She asks what brought me to LA and I tell her I am just hanging out with a friend. I just need some time away from my father but since meeting Ariella, I don't think I'll be going back anytime soon.

Ariella tells me that she is taking summer classes because she wants to be done with college as soon as possible. I guess she hates LA and wants to move to New York.

She wants to visit this summer but she has no one to go with.

As Ariella and I eat our food, I start to notice how lonely she is. She rarely talks about friends and if she does mention any friends she mentions Lo, who is the bookstore owner, and Bridgette who is Ariella's best friend that she has known since kindergarten.

"So about your choices of books," I state which makes Ariella blush. "If you could recommend any book to me to read, what would it be?"

"Do you like thrillers?"

I nod. "Happens to be one of my favorite genres."

"Well, there is this one book where the husband has a list of women he wants to kill off and at the end of the list his wife's name is there."

"Interesting."

"It's my favorite book."

"Does it happen to be by Jameson Hat?" Ariella smiles and nods her head. I love her smile, it's so genuine. "I have heard about the book but I have yet to read it. He's one of my favorite authors."

Ariella's smile brightens. "Same. I've been reading his books since his debut."

"Does he kill the wife?"

Ariella gives me a teasing smile and I swear I could go on my knees for her to do that again.

"If I told you it would ruin the book."

"Guess I'll have to finally buy it then." I give her a small smile. The waitress ends up coming back with the tab and I don't even think twice before giving her my black card. She takes it and Ariella just gives me a frown. "What?"

"I could have paid for mine."

"No. I'm having fun talking to you. Why would I let you pay if I'm having fun?"

"Because I can pay for my own stuff?"

"You don't need to when you are hanging out with me."

Ariella blushes again and I see her scratch her wrist. "I need to ask you something."

"Does this mean we should get some dessert?"

"If they have mousse cake then I think dessert is definitely a good move."

The waitress ends up coming back and I ask her to bring two mousse cakes to the table. I tell her to charge it on the same card and when she comes back with my card she also comes back with two mousse cakes.

"So Ariella, what is so important you have to ask me?"

Ariella scratches her wrist again and I see her throat move from swallowing. "I told you that I want to start experiencing new things."

I nod my head and take a bite out of the mousse cake.

Ariella does the same.

"That's right."

"This summer I made a bucket that I want to complete before going to college."

"Okay. What's on this bucket list?"

Ariella blushes but she grabs her bag and pulls out a piece of paper to hand to me.

2023 Summer
- **Go on a date with a stranger**
- **Kiss a stranger**
- **Go to a club and dance with a stranger**
- **Ask a hot person for their number**
- **Have sex with a stranger**
- **Go to New York**
- **Go watch the fireworks on the tallest hill**
- **Go star watching**
- **Go to the fair**
- **Spend the whole day at the beach**
- **Get a tattoo with a stranger**
- **Sneak into a movie theater**

"Interesting," I say while reading through the list. "And why are you telling me this?" I look up at Ariella but still have the bucket list in my hands.

"I need help completing it."

"And you want me to help you complete it I'm guessing?"

Ariella nods her head. "If you don't want to then that's fine but I just thought that maybe-"

"I'll help you."

Ariella looks shocked.

I am too, honestly.

Guess I'm not going home anytime soon. It's a good thing I have my dad's apartment.

"Really?" Ariella raises her eyebrows.

"Yes but there has to be a few conditions."

"Absolutely." Ariella agrees. "I can make the first one." I nod my head for her to continue. "After this summer is over I want us to have no contact. What's happening this summer leaves the moment summer is done and we are back in school."

"Agreed. One of the rules I had. I don't want to be committed to someone for that long," I explain. "One of the main rules I have is 'don't ask about my family'. That's the only other rule I have."

Ariella nods her head. "I don't want us to get too close. Because when this ends I don't want to end up hurt."

"I won't hurt you, Ariella."

"You won't mean to, but you will."

Ariella and I leave after we finish our dessert and I walk her outside the same time it starts raining.

On the weather app it didn't even say it was going to rain.

Ariella smiles as she looks around and watches people try and get to shelter.

"So is there a contract I have to sign?" I look down at Ariella and I watch as water covers her face from the rain.

She shakes her head while giving a small smile.

We stare at one another for a few more seconds before I feel the need to lean down and kiss Ariella on the lips.

Our wet lips meet and my eyes close from how good she feels against me. As we kiss, she opens her mouth and I let my tongue slip in. She breathes heavily and I feel her shudder against me when I touch her cheek.

Our lips move in sync with one another and it's like we have done this many times before. Kissing her feels like the world just stopped for us.

And I just realized that those voices are gone.

Everything is quiet.

I have no idea why I agreed to do such a stupid thing with such a beautiful girl.

She leans away and her eyelids are droopy.

"You okay?" I ask, wondering if she is going to faint or something.

"Why'd you kiss me?"

"To seal the deal."

Three

Ariella

Present

"Why won't you tell me anything about what you did this summer? I want to know!" Bridgette exclaims.

"Because nothing interesting happened. All I did was go to the beach."

Technically it's not a lie. I did go to the beach but she doesn't know that I actually went with someone.

"Yea, right." Bridgette rolls her eyes.

Bridgette and I have been friends since we were five. It all started when I found her stealing my bike. I left it on the front lawn the night before and then when I walked outside the next day I saw her trying to steal it.

Bridgette claims that she was just trying to make sure it wasn't her bike and after that we started fighting like two cats before I called her a liar and then she ended up crying. The next day she came by and asked me if I wanted to go ride bikes.

The rest is history.

I love Bridgette. She has been there for me for when I needed someone the most. She has seen me when I was on the brink of going down a dangerous path and I can't be grateful enough for her.

"You never tell me anything anymore."

"Can you stop being so dramatic? I literally told you that all I did was go to the beach. You were busy all summer too. Don't think that I didn't notice."

Bridgette's cheeks turn red and she ends up gathering her stuff before opening the car door.

I don't want to tell her that I was hanging out with Ash all summer because all he was, was a summer fling. Someone who I spent time with to experience new things.

Nothing more.

I get out of the car and she locks the door.

The school I go to is a private college that only has a select few attending. Most of the kids that attend this college are politician's kids, celebrities, or well known figures who don't want their kids to go to the other private colleges.

It's stupid that I can't go to a regular college like USC or UCLA but Dad said that he would rather me go to this school for the best education, even though it's basically similar to other colleges around the world, just nicer looking, a little smaller than most colleges, and more expensive.

My dad, Cal Madden, is a famous lawyer. He mostly does his work in New York but often visits California for me. He is always busy so I told him that I would be fine living here by myself. I'm eighteen, about to turn nineteen. I know how to handle myself.

I chose to stay here instead of living in New York with him because I feel closer to my mom over here, but I do eventually want to live out there.

I loved New York last time I visited. I think I just still feel comfortable here because of my mom. She will be in California forever and I just want to stay here for a little longer knowing that she is close by.

Bridgette's parents are a part of some world famous company and they decided to enroll Bridgette here so that she could get the "best education".

"You think Mr. Locke will make us do some stupid assignment again? He made us watch that stupid documentary about that one murderer who kills people in a clown suit." Bridgette says as we walk inside Mr. Locke's classroom.

We walk past his desk and my eyes meet his. I see a glint of mischief in his eyes making me turn my head away.

"I don't know. Everything he does stupid and unnecessary nowadays. I feel like he doesn't even try anymore," I say in a low voice, not wanting him to hear me talk shit.

Bridgette and I sat in our seats and we put our stuff in the chairs next to us so that no one can sit there.

My eyes can't help but look at Mr. Locke's, also known as Liam.

I was in his class a few semesters ago.

I chose to take his class because it said on the Rate My Professor website that he gives out extra credit. The thing I didn't know is that his "extra credit" was to give him a blow job in return for those points.

He asked me if I wanted to do it, I told him I wasn't interested and then I would just sit in the back of the class until the semester was over. I never spoke a word about that day because I was afraid of what would happen if I were to tell someone.

He asked me a few more times before the semester ended and for some reason, I still didn't mention it to anyone.

I don't want him to lose his job because of me.

Let's just hope this year it doesn't happen again.

The only reason I am in his class this semester is because Bridgette didn't want to be alone in this class. We both needed another psychology class and his class had two seats left so I joined Bridgette.

"Can you get your head out of the clouds?" Bridgette

says and I look away from Liam and focus my attention on her.

More students start to walk into class and Bridgette starts talking about how I barely called or texted her this summer while she was in London.

I know that she met a boy but she doesn't want to tell me about him. It's not unusual for her because Bridgette doesn't like talking about boys she likes with me or anyone.

She's shy about boys and I get that.

"As most of you know my name is Liam Locke but you can call me Mr. or Professor Locke. This class is a Psych 2 class. So if you didn't sign up for this class then I suggest you leave or come talk to me after class about signing up." Only one person leaves and Liam starts talking again but my attention gets pulled away from him when I see familiar dark brown eyes enter the room.

Last time I saw him was a few weeks before classes started. The words between us were filled with hate.

He found out who I was and from then, things between us changed.

Ash has issues. I won't ever forget about that.

So that's why after everything that happened, I stayed far away from him because I will only end up getting hurt.

"Damn," Bridgette whispers. "Who is that?"

Ash Jones.

Four

Ariella

Summer

I can't help but feel butterflies in my stomach as I wait for Ash's text saying that he's outside.

It's hard not to feel excited or nervous when an attractive guy is going to take you out and make you experience things.

> Ash: I'm outside.

I practically jump off my bed and run out of my house.

When I walk outside I see Ash leaning against midnight black motorcycle as he holds a helmet in his hand with a straight face while he looks around the street, at all of the other houses.

As I walk towards Ash, I admire him.

He is wearing an off white shirt with black trousers and then white shoes. I try not to stare at his biceps too much and how they bulge out of his shirt.

His hair isn't styled, just like how it was a few nights ago.

It's perfect.

"You look nice." Ash gives me a small smile and I can't help but smile back at him. I'm wearing a black summer dress that falls to my mid-thighs where my back is showing and I decided to curl my hair today. "I like your hair," Ash says while reaching out and touching a strand of my hair.

I try to ignore how hot my face feels as he admires my hair and looks at me like I am the most perfect girl in the world.

I keep my eyes on Ash and study how he looks at me. When his eyes collide with mine he lets go of my hair and I almost want to demand that he keep touching my hair.

"I like your bike."

Ash smiles and he looks at his motorcycle. "I got it right when I turned eighteen. I've always wanted one." He holds the helmet up to me. "You hair looks beautiful but I'm going to have to ruin it."

I smile at him because how could I not. I hope I'm not blushing.

Ash pulls me against him and puts the black helmet

on my head. "Where are we going?" I ask as he grabs the other helmet from his motorcycle compartment.

"The OC Fair. I've never been." He explains before putting his helmet on.

Ash explains to me how I have to hold onto him tightly as he drives. I have to swerve with him when he leans down and moves. He gets on the motorcycle and holds my hand as I get on behind him. I straddle him, tightening my legs around him as the motorcycle roars to life.

"Hold on, tight." He say before slowly pulling to the middle of the road.

We get to the fair quick.

Ash drives the motorcycle like he has been doing this his entire life. He went fast and it felt like we were flying. I kept tightening my legs around him whenever he would pass by cars.

And when he would stop at a light he would rest his hands on my thighs, softly caressing me, making butter-flies appear in my stomach.

I have to keep reminding myself that this is just temporary. I have to stop feeling like this before the summer comes to an end.

When we arrive at the fair, Ash parks in the first spot he sees and then once we are in line, he trails his eyes down my body, admiring my attire. I feel blush creeping up my cheeks.

"Can you stop looking at me like that?"

"Like what?" Ash tilts his head to the side while looking down at me.

His stare is so heated and filled with lust that I can't help but feel nervous under his gaze.

"Like you want me."

"I've wanted you since that day in the bookstore Ariella," Ash states while still giving me that heat-filled stare.

Damn him.

Ash pays for our tickets and despite me saying that I could pay for my own ticket, he refuses to make me pay for my own.

"What do you want to do first? They have a bunch of games and then the barn where you can pet goats and other animals."

"Let's go on some rides and then we can play games after so we don't have to hold the prizes and stuff," Ash answers and then I feel his hand slowly slip into mine.

Seeing his big hand with veins running down his arm holding my small one makes the butterflies in my stomach go crazy again. I feel heat burst in the pit of my stomach making me look away from our hands and instead look ahead and see some rides.

Ash and I go on three rides by the time he says that we should play some games.

We went on the bumper karts which were really fun. Ash and I kept bumping into one another or I should say, he mostly was bumping into me while I was laughing uncontrollably.

I wanted to go on the ride that swings you in the air. I couldn't help but make Ash take pictures of me on that ride. I am going to end up posting some of the pictures on my Instagram later on.

Ash and I went on this other ride that wasn't as fun as those two. As Ash starts walking us to where the games are, I see his head turn to where the maze is. He looks at me and I see a glint of mischief in his eyes and I can't help but feel excited.

"Let's play the games after this one."

"Okay," I say, while trying to ignore the heat in my stomach.

Once we are next in line for the maze Ash tugs on my hand making me look at him. "Want to play a game?" I can't help but smile and nod my head. Ash smirks. "You run and if I catch you, I get something in return."

"What do you get?" I raise my eyebrow at him and try not to get too excited.

"For two?" The maze guard says. Ash nods and shows him our wristbands. "Okay, you guys enjoy."

Ash looks down at me. "Whatever I want. You have ten seconds before I start running after you."

I let go of Ash's hand and run inside the maze. My lips lift in a smile as I run in different directions. I make multiple left and right turns before I end up in a room filled with mirrors and glass windows.

I reach out and try to find an opening where I can walk without bumping into a window.

While walking around and trying to find the exit, I hear a door open making me turn around and look the way I came. I don't see anyone enter the room making me feel shivers go up my spine.

I turn back around and I scream when I see Ash a few feet away from me. I turn around to head towards the way I came but I feel strong arms grab my waist and pull me into a hard, warm chest.

"Got you," Ash whispers in my ear, making me feel his lips graze my skin and his breath on the back of my neck.

I feel goosebumps run across my neck and I shudder against him.

"You got me," I say, trying to control my breathing.

I can barely make out the words he says from how husky his voice is. I never thought someone's voice could make my insides knot up with anticipation, but Ash's does. His words are direct and calculated. He knows what he does to me and I love every second of it.

I met him just a week ago and he already has such a strong hold on me.

He licks his lips before running his tongue on the inside of his cheek, devouring everything that I am.

His eyes find mine before he looks down at my lips. Is

he going to kiss me? Before I can prepare myself for his lips to touch mine, he leans in closer to me, slamming his lips against mine. He groans in my mouth—the sound alone makes my knees weaken.

Ash presses his hard body against mine just as I feel one of his hands hold onto my waist. His rough and calloused fingers dig into my skin as he grips onto the side of my body lightly. A sound escapes me as he guides my body closer to his.

His kisses are so aggressive it makes me out of breath and desperate for more of him.

His lips feel as soft as they did a few nights ago when he first kissed me. I like how rough he is right now, almost as rough as that night I had dinner with him. This kiss isn't soft or sweet, it's rough and hard, showing me how much he wants me. It's intoxicating and I devour every second of it.

This kiss explains who Ash truly is and I can't help but feel excited for when he will touch me.

"Ash," I moan as he starts to trail his hands to my ass and he squeezes, pulling me closer to him.

I feel the evidence of how much this kiss is affecting him through his trousers.

He grunts and then thrusts his tongue into my mouth. The glide of his tongue is soft against mine and my whole body feels like it's on fire from how rough and demanding his kiss is.

I love kissing him more than anything in this moment.

"Hey!" I feel the loss of Ash's lips but I can still feel the ghost of his lips on mine. "Get out of here! I don't want to be cleaning up any cum off of my floors."

I feel my cheeks heat up and I hide my face in Ash's chest. I feel Ash's chest vibrate making me assume he is laughing at me.

He lets go of me and instead grabs my hand. "We're leaving now!"

Ash pulls us out of the maze and once we are out I slap his chest and he laughs even harder than he did in the maze.

"That was so embarrassing!"

Ash grabs my hand. "It was fun. Don't be embarrassed. You won't ever see him again." He pulls me away from the maze and all of the embarrassment I felt washes away.

Ash and I go to where all the games are.

He picks the game where you can shoot balloons with a BB gun. Ash ends up hitting seventeen out of twenty balloons and he wins a brown stuffed bear which he gives to me.

After we play a few more games and he wins a bunch more prizes we leave the fair and start driving home.

I won a small pink panther for Ash and I told him that I want him to keep it. He lets me keep all of the other stuffed animals I won and he won.

As we ride back home, I hold the stuffed animals close to my chest as I hold onto Ash while he drives.

When Ash drops me off home, he walks me towards my door and then I turn around and look at him. "Thank you for tonight. I had fun. I haven't had that much fun in a while."

"We are going to be having a lot of fun together. I can tell," Ash says with that lust filled gaze.

Again my cheeks start to heat up. "I have to go."

Ash laughs softly. "I'll see you soon, Ariella."

"I'll see you soon, Ash."

FIVE
ARIELLA

"I told you this assignment was going to be stupid," Bridgette claims, as we walk inside Crowded Rooms. "He always gives us stupid assignments that never make any sense. Why is he even a teacher? He could be a model if he wanted to, so why a teacher?"

Bridgette continues to complain about Mr. Locke as we walk to our regular table. Crowded Rooms is a small diner that Bridgette and I found right when we started college. They have the best burgers, parmesan fries, Texas toast, milkshakes, and chicken tenders. In the mornings they serve breakfast but Bridgette and I always come during lunch or dinner because their chicken and parmesan fries are the best. We can never stay away from their food.

"If you think all of his assignments are stupid, then why are you in his class?"

"Because I need it for journalism. I want to be able to read people," Bridgette explains. "But also because Mr. Locke is definitely the hottest professor on campus and how can I say no to a hot teacher?"

I roll my eyes at her and shake my head lightly.

She is crazy.

"You can look at my notes if you want to," I offer.

"Thanks. Can we also talk about how hot that one guy who came in late was? I swear I would drop on my knees for him."

Ash Jones.

During the class he didn't talk at all. I would see him look at me a few times and when our eyes met I quickly averted my gaze.

Every time I would look at him I would remember the way his hands felt on my skin and the way his lips caressed mine.

What is he even doing here? Isn't he supposed to be in New York?

"Can you not be dramatic for once?" I raise an eyebrow at her, trying to ignore the butterflies in my stomach.

I really don't feel like talking about Ash. I don't want to remember any of the things Ash said or did to me this last summer. Even though it was possibly one of the best summers I had in a while, in the end, I only got hurt.

"I'm being dead serious, Ariella. He was so hot. You never see guys like that in California. I wish we had more guys like him."

"Guys like who?" a voice says at the same time I see a familiar person slide next to Bridgette and wrap an arm around her.

"Fuck off, Jace." She rolls her eyes and scoots away from him.

Jace Sanchez is another close friend of Bridgette and me. I met him through Bridgette because he was in her English class in high school and after he kept hitting on her he started to get close to me in order to be a part of our small friend group.

Bridgette tells me they don't have a thing but I swear they do. The way he looks at her and is jealous of any guy who comes her way shows how much he wants her.

Bridgette has a thing for him too but she doesn't like to admit it. I can tell she does because of the way she looks at him whenever he is close by or with another girl. She looks like she wants to pull the girl's hair out of her scalp when she sees them a foot away from Jace.

"Can you please stop playing games with me Bridge? I know you want me." Jace smirks at her and I see his finger caress her shoulder.

"Can you guys please not do this in front of me? I

want to be able to have the stomach to actually eat something today," I beg.

"Ask him. He is the asshole who is always trying to pull something." Bridgette looks at Jace. "Don't you have some other girl you can bother, Jace? Ariella and I are trying to have lunch."

"I am only here because I am meeting one of my friends. He said to meet him here."

I am about to call Jace out on his bullshit but then a familiar figure walks inside the diner and I can't keep my eyes away from him.

Ash Jones walks inside the diner, wearing black baggy jeans and a black zip up jacket.

I remember that jacket. One night I was cold and he gave me that specific jacket to wear so that I wouldn't freeze.

He walks in like he owns the place. I don't know what's more attractive, him, or the way he carries himself with so much confidence it almost makes you feel intimidated to be in his presence.

The whole entire summer, I was always intimidated whenever he would come a little too close to me or whenever he touched me, but I loved being intimidated by him because I always felt butterflies swarm in my stomach and chills would go down my back.

What I don't expect Ash to do is walk towards the table I'm sitting at with Jace and Bridgette.

What I definitely don't expect him to do is stop in front of our table and smile at Jace before shaking his hand.

Bridgette looks at me and widens her eyes.

I try to ignore how fast my heart is beating and keep my eyes on Bridgette, even when Ash makes an attempt to sit next to me in the booth.

"Ariella, stop being a bitch and let Ash sit," Jace says and I refrain from rolling my eyes and scoot down the booth, as far away from Ash as I can.

Even from being on the opposite side of the booth I still feel hot as if he is right next to me, touching me.

I hate how much he has an effect on me and I hate how much he knows he does too.

"Jace never told me that he has such a good looking friend," Bridgette says and I see Jace's jaw clench and unclench.

"Ash is originally from New York. He went to NYU, was it?" Jace asks Ash.

"Yea. I was living in New York with my father and moved out this summer."

Not what he told me.

"What are you studying?" Bridgette asks.

Psychology.

"Psychology," Ash answers.

"So why did you decide to move out here then?" I look at Ash and raise an eyebrow at him.

Ash's lips lift in a small smirk. "At first, I was just visiting for the first week of summer but then I decided to stay."

"There's nothing special in California. You should have stayed in New York."

"No, I'd say there are a lot of potentials in California."

Ash's eyes spark with that familiar mischief I always see him have. It makes the spot between my thighs ache.

I love the way he looks at me, even if it's filled with hatred.

I look away from Ash and at Bridgette.

"So how long do you plan on staying in California then?" Bridgette asks.

"Not sure. I am going to finish up my degree here and whatever happens next, we'll see."

I remember on one of our many dates last summer, Ash told me about how he wants to become a counselor for little kids. He wants to help them through life.

I loved that about him. How he wanted to help kids through talking and listening.

I don't know what happened between him and I.

I remember the night Ash and I last spoke.

It was with words filled with hate.

That whole night was a mess and I remember crying for days about it.

Boys shouldn't make you cry and I thought things

with Ash and I were going to end happily but that didn't happen.

I can never forget how mad he was and how much he wanted to throw me away. I hated how we spoke to each other but this is the way it has to be.

I can't be with Ash and he can't be with me. That doesn't mean I want to hate him though.

"I have to go. My dad is in town and I want to see him before he has things to do in the city," I explain before grabbing my stuff and making a move to get out of the booth but when I look at Ash, his heat-filled gaze is staring up at me. "Can you move?"

Ash shakes his head lightly before getting out of the booth and letting me leave.

Bridgette and Jace say 'bye' and I don't stay any longer to give Ash a chance to say anything. I practically run out of the diner and speed walk to my car.

I can't stay here any longer because if I do, I know Ash will get the chance to follow me and I don't want to face Ash by myself.

The moment I unlock my car and open the door, a familiar hand comes into my view and pushes my door shut.

I feel a sense of deja vu. The first time Ash and I met, something similar happened, but it wasn't filled with hate or disdain.

Shivers go down my spine as I feel his hard, warm

chest against my back.

"Madden." Ash says with disgust. "Ariella. Fucking. Madden." No, no, no, no, no. This can't happen. I can't face him by myself again. "Turn around Ariella."

I do what he says and turn around, pushing my back against the car as if that will help this situation. Ash's hands rest on either side of my head and I swear for a second he leans in closer to me and his eyes soften, only for a second before it's gone.

"Ash."

Ash's eyes darken and he leans in even closer. "Don't say my name like that."

"Like what?" I ask before my eyes quickly go down to his lips and then meet his eyes again.

"Like you want me when you know you shouldn't."

"Ash-"

"I only came out here to tell you this Ariella so listen carefully." Ash's lips are now maybe an inch away from mine and it's so hard to not just lean in and kiss him. I wish I could have him on top of me again and feel his hands on me and lips caressing mine. I can't help that my body misses him and a part of my soul. "Everything that happened this summer is gone. I don't care for you, I hate you. I will ruin you, Madden, and when I'm done no one will be able to save you other than me, but the fun thing about that is, I don't plan on saving you ever. I will fucking ruin you and then throw you away. That Ash you met this summer is gone."

"But I didn't know-"

"I don't fucking care," Ash cuts me off, eyes still dark and filled with hate.

"I won't let you treat me like a toy, Ash." I furrow my eyebrows at him and put my hands on his chest to push him away from me but he doesn't budge.

"Good. That will make this a whole lot more fun."

SIX
ASH

SUMMER

Today Ariella and I are at the beach.

One of her bucket list items is that she wants to spend twenty-four hours at the beach and that even includes sleeping there.

So I brought a lot of blankets and pillows for us as well as a tent we can use to sleep in.

I went to Ariella's house first thing in the morning and we used her car to drive to Venice.

This whole day I couldn't keep my eyes off her, even as she stares up at the sky, admiring the stars, I can't grasp how beautiful she looks.

Today Ariella and I walked around the beach, went in the water where I even managed to have a small water fight with her.

I definitely couldn't keep my eyes off of her while we were in the water.

How her skin looked when it was half naked and wet.

I swear no one is perfect and I have been told that by everyone, but Ariella is.

But that's not something I should be thinking about. This thing between us is temporary.

That's what we agreed on.

It hasn't even been a month since I met her and I am already obsessed.

"Do you ever wonder what stars mean?" Ariella says which makes me focus my attention back on her.

Right now we are in the tent looking at the sky. The tent I brought has a little sky view which is nice.

Ariella really liked it when she saw that the tent had that.

"What do you mean?"

"Like, I feel like stars appear whenever someone dies. And that's heaven for them."

"That's an interesting way to think of it." I smile at her and Ariella smiles back. Lately I have been smiling more and it feels good to smile again and feel genuinely happy. Not to mention that the voices are gone. "I think only good people are up there though."

"My mom is up there then."

Ariella smiles but it's not a happy smile, it's more of a

sad smile and I can't help but pull her closer to me and wrap my arm around her.

"What was she like?"

Ariella hasn't really mentioned her parents that much, only her mom. I learned she died when Ariella was sixteen due to heart failure. She told me when we were watching the stars on a hill. I know it was hard for her to talk to me about that but I could tell she wanted to.

I felt guilty about not telling her much about me but if I did then Ariella would run away.

Ariella turns her body so that she is resting her head on my chest and her arms are against my chest.

I hope she can't feel how fast my heart is beating.

It's been doing that a lot lately, too.

"She was the best. She would always cook and bake with me. One time we even made these weed brownies but I didn't know they were weed brownies until I made my own." I feel Ariella laugh lightly. "I miss her so much."

"I might be cliché for saying this but she is with you. She is taking care of you. I know it."

Ariella looks up at me and I swear her eyes shine when they stare at mine.

My eyes look at every detail on her face. I notice freckles that some wouldn't even notice if they looked at her from a few inches away.

My eyes go down to Ariella's lips and I see her automatically nip at her bottom lip. I look back up to meet her eyes and all I want to do is capture her lips with mine and make her lips bleed.

The blood in my body rushes down to my dick and I try to keep a groan in.

"Why do you keep staring at me like that?" Ariella asks softly.

"Because I want you but I'm also trying to be a gentleman."

From the moonlight shining down on us I notice her cheeks turning a shade darker but she doesn't look away from me. I can tell so many things are rushing through her beautiful head, filling it with wonders and thoughts about what she should do.

All I want to do is feel her lips on mine.

So I lean in and press my lips against hers.

Ariella leans in and excitement rushes through me. I feel her soft lips hesitantly kiss mine, almost like a baby deer's first step into the world.

Unsure and scared but also determined.

I open my lips up for her and kiss her back with urgency, taking over the kiss before I lean over her and hold her jaw in my hand.

Ariella's hands hold onto my neck and she kisses me back hard and rough just how I like it. I can feel how much she wants me through the kisses and the way she is breathing heavily.

I feel a breeze over us but we don't stop for a

second. We continue to kiss and nibble and I even nip her lip which makes her open her mouth wide and moan. I thrust my tongue inside her mouth and I feel her hips start to grind against my thigh that is between her legs.

Our tongues explore and our lips suck. Her chest pressed against mine makes me feel how hard her nipples are getting.

My hand travels down her stomach and I slowly slip my hand beneath her sweatpants.

"Ash," Ariella moans and she shivers against me. "Please-"

"You want to ride my fingers baby?" I ask against her lips. Ariella nods her head. "Ask nicely."

"Please touch me, Ash," she says against my lips and that's all it takes for me to take her lips into mine again.

I slide three fingers up and down her pussy and I get hard from how wet she is. She is so warm and wet and soft, softer than I thought she would be.

"God, Ariella, you're so fucking wet for me. Are you always this wet for me, baby?"

I can't get enough of her.

I kiss her harder at the same time I slowly push them inside her.

Ariella gasps inside my mouth. "Ash, more."

I rub my thumb on her clit making Ariella's hips lift and grind into my hand. Her lips part and I see her eyes open. They are glossed with wonder and staring at me with lust filled in her gaze.

I start my pace slow, making sure I only go halfway but circling her clit and moving my finger farther inside her. Ariella's eyes widen as I keep doing that movement slowly.

Ariella whimpers when I start to thrust my finger inside her faster. She cries as I play with her clit and I love the way lust takes over her face. She looks like she is up in the clouds.

Ariella and I have never gone this far. It's always just been grinding and kissing between us since I met her. I have never touched her until this moment and I don't think I will be able to stop.

I lean down and my lips attach to her neck. I kiss and nibble at her neck, marking her to show everyone that she's mine.

I only met this girl two weeks ago and she changed my entire outlook on everything.

For two weeks we have been with one another non-stop and it's so hard to not touch her but the wait is fucking worth it.

Ariella is making me goddamn feral.

Ariella clenches onto my fingers before she finally lets out a loud moan and releases all over my hand. Ariella moans and closes her legs, hiding her face in my chest.

I take my fingers out of her and I hold myself above her so I'm not crushing her.

Ariella wraps her arms around me and she brings my head into her shoulders.

A few minutes later Ariella's breathing is steady and I assume she is sleeping.

I get comfortable and lay down next to her, pulling her closer to me and she snuggles into my chest.

Last thing I see before darkness is Ariella.

SEVEN

ASH

That well-known feeling creeps into my soul, urgent to feel the sensation of the cracked glass broken into my fist.

It's strong and I haven't felt this need since before the end of the summer.

The last time I saw *her*.

As I look at myself in the mirror all I see is rage. I want to crack the mirror in front of me for feeling this way. I shouldn't feel the need to resort to these ways but it's a trained condition that my mother made me start doing.

Even though she's dead, I still think about her every day and I need it all to stop.

I just need to stop thinking.

I leave my bathroom before I do anything stupid.

The towel loosens from my waist when I reach for my briefs. As I slip my briefs on, the towel falls to the floor. I change into a pair of jeans at the same time I hear the front door open and close.

I pick up my towel and throw it in my laundry bin before leaving my room and walking downstairs where I see my father looking around my penthouse.

This used to be his but he ended up letting me stay here while I study in California.

It was a last minute decision, me moving here.

But after this summer I just couldn't leave.

Leaving would mean leaving her and I just couldn't let her go, not yet at least.

I could easily buy my own penthouse but I am trying to save every cent I have for when I am done with school.

Thankfully, I inherited my mother's business after she passed. Although I don't want to have anything of hers in my name, I am getting money from it and it will help me in the future.

All I do is sit back and watch the money grow.

Although she was a bitch, she was smart and ended up inventing some website for teaching kids which is ironic considering the past she and I had.

People were hungry for whatever she had to say. That website has got to be her stupidest idea to make money, yet she was drowning in it.

But at the same time she spent all of that money on

drugs and when she needed more, well that's where I came in.

I plan on changing her business when I finish my degree because this business and the money I am getting from her should be from something important and valuable, not worthless and fake.

"What can I do for you father?" I ask, walking past him and going to my kitchen.

"Jolie said she saw you at that diner I told you to stay away from, last week," my father states.

"Okay, so I'm not allowed to eat with friends?"

I grab water from the fridge and take a moment to look at my father.

Levi Jones is one of the most successful lawyers in New York. He has burned all of the other lawyers out of the state, well, except for one.

"Yes, but she told me she saw you were with Cal Madden's kid."

Fuck.

"What about her?" I raise an eyebrow at my father.

He hates Cal Madden's guts. I hate Cal Madden's guts too.

I can't fucking stand that guy and the fake persona he puts on. My father told me about how he threatened to destroy our family.

And Ariella Madden is his fucking daughter which made everything worse.

When I met her I knew nothing between us was going to end well because she is just like her father. I didn't see it until I figured out who she was.

Her father ruined everything for me and my father and I have never hated Cal Madden so much.

"You know what you are supposed to do, Ash. Destroy her. Her father is a menace and the only way we can destroy him is through her."

Part of my brain, the one that is irrational and only thinks with the dick, wants to forget about what my father is telling me and go back to Ariella. But then the other side of my brain, the one that is calculated and cold, the one who knows what we should be doing, wants to destroy Ariella and most of all her father.

My father wants to destroy Cal because he threatened to put me away. I also want to destroy him, but through Ariella.

It's just more fun that way.

"I am. You just have to be patient."

"Either you deal with it or stay the fuck out of it and leave her alone to let me handle it," my father threatens.

I'm not scared of him. I might be grateful for what he has done in the past but I for sure don't give a single fuck about his threats. I have thought about anything he could hit me with and I am prepared for the day I disappoint him.

It will be one of the best days of my life right after the death of my mother.

"Don't worry. As I said, be patient. Ruining someone takes time." I take a sip of my water and then put it on the countertop. "Other than trying to ruin lives, what are you doing here? Shouldn't you be in New York?" I raise my eyebrow as I lean against the counter.

"I have a few meetings here that I need to take care of and then I plan on going back to New York for a little bit and then come back for more meetings."

"What meetings?"

"Don't worry about it," my father snaps.

I'm used to his anger. I know what it's like to have to control that anger because I have to do it every day.

"Well I have things to do, so can you leave so that I can head out?" I ask, trying to not sound like a complete asshole toward him.

I walk past him to go back to my room.

"Where are you going?" my father asks, following me.

I look at him and smirk. "Don't worry about it."

When I walk inside my room I close the door and I hear my apartment door close making me know my father left.

I throw on a black hoodie before grabbing my keys and phone.

The drive to a familiar house is quick. It's pitch black

outside because of how late it is but that's perfect for what I am about to do.

I park a few houses down from Ariella's house so she doesn't hear the roar of the bike.

All of the lights in Ariella's house are turned off except for one which is where her room is. I sneak to the back of her house and put my hood up.

I know where she hides the key to her back door. She told me if I ever wanted to come in her room during the middle of the night to go through the back door. I remember that night so well.

I remember fucking her, making her scream into her pillows. Her legs were shaking while they were on my shoulders and I swear the bite marks on her skin were the most beautiful marks I have ever seen.

I unlock her back door and quietly push it open. I walk through her house with soft steps until I get upstairs outside her door. I hear her mumbling a soft tune.

It's probably something by Coldplay. She fucking loves them.

I slowly open her door and peek through the small crack. She is laying on her stomach facing her window and she has her laptop in front of her.

It looks like she is working on homework.

I can't help but stare at her legs and the way her toes curl. It reminds me of the times I would taste her in the morning and her toes would always curl right before she orgasms. She is so easy to read.

I stand in her doorway and watch her, just admiring the way she looks while she concentrates on her homework.

She is so beautiful that it fucking hurts to look at her.

I hate her father.

I hate her.

I open her door wider and Ariella turns around and I see her eyes are filled with terror.

Eight

Ariella

I see a dark figure as I am looking over Bridgette's notes and I turn my head and see him.

Ash has a dark look in his eyes and the black hood over his head makes him look sinful.

"Ash," I whisper as he walks closer to the bed and I turn my whole body around so that I am sitting up and facing him. "You aren't supposed to be here." Ash doesn't say anything, he only walks closer to me and puts his hands on either side of me. My heart is beating so fast that I can feel it thump against my chest, begging to be let out. Ash's lips are a few inches away from my neck and I feel a shiver run through my body. "What are you doing?" I whisper while not moving away from Ash.

His breath on my neck feels good and I can't help but feel the need to close my eyes.

"Why do you have to be so fucking tempting, Madden?" Ash asks and he still isn't touching me.

I want him to touch me so badly but I know it is wrong.

And as if answering my prayer, I feel Ash's lips on my neck.

My eyes close and my head leans back.

Ash's lips are soft against my neck and I feel chills and goosebumps spread on my arms. His soft touch on my skin feels like fire and his lips feel like a sin.

Ash trails his lips up my neck until they ghost over mine. "Ash," I say and our lips bump together but Ash makes no move to kiss me.

I want to strangle him for not leaning in closer and placing his lips on mine. "Quiet." Ash leans away from me and he keeps his knee on the bed between my legs, making me open my eyes. His hands glide over my skin and I want to close my eyes again but I keep them trained on him. "What am I going to do with you, Ariella?"

Next thing I know, Ash lifts my shirt over my head and the cold air hitting my nipples makes me shiver. "Ash." Ash pushes me on the bed and his hand brings my wrist over my head. His breath falls on my breast and my legs try to rub together but his knee stops me from moving. "Ash, please," I moan, sounding like a needy bitch.

I don't know what comes over me when it comes to Ash. He is the only person who has ever made me feel this way and I hate it. He always knows how to make me feel like I have no power and it sucks to feel controlled by Ash but at the same time it can feel so euphoric.

Ash's lips trail over my stomach and I breathe in and out harshly while moving my hips along Ash's knee. Warmth sparks in my stomach as I grind against his knee.

I feel like just surrendering myself to Ash.

My eyelashes flutter against my cheeks as they grow flushed when Ash finally latches his lips on one of my nipples. My back arches, feeling the need to have him closer to me. His hand trapping my wrist feels like hell because all I want to do is pull him closer to me and wrap my arms around him.

I feel Ash's teeth graze my nipple and my head goes to the side. His teeth pull at my nipple and I gasp.

I can feel how wet I am just from riding his knee. "Ash-"

I get cut off with a smack to my thigh. "Shut up, Ariella," he says before biting harder and then moving to my other boob.

"Ash, please. I'll do anything."

"I don't want anything from you." Ash bites my

nipple and he tugs on it harder. I try to move my wrists from his hold but he doesn't let me. Instead he moves his knee against the spot between my legs and I rub myself against his thigh. "I told you I would ruin you Ariella, didn't I?"

"No-"

Smack.

"What did I say?" Ash asks while moving his thigh against me harder.

I grind against him and keep trying to free my hands from his hold. My back arches and I feel my release slipping closer and closer, bringing me over the edge.

"Ash, I'm going to come. Please."

Smack.

"What did I say, Ariella?"

"Please-"

All of a sudden Ash's touch disappears from me and I feel cold and frustrated.

I want to kill him.

My body is hot and aching.

My thighs close automatically and I cover my chest as I sit up and look at Ash who is leaning against the wall near my door.

I'm shaking while maintaining eye contact with Ash.

Did he just fucking edge me?

That son of a-

"What's wrong?" Ash asks while tilting his head to the side.

"You-you just-"

"Edged you?" Ash lifts his eyebrow at me.

"Why would you do that?"

My face feels hot and I want to bury myself in my blankets and not face Ash.

"Because I wanted to."

I look around for my shirt but I can't find it.

Where did he put it?

"Why are you even here?" I ask, still covering my chest. "How did you get in?"

"Don't worry about it," Ash says before leaning off the wall and he starts walking towards me.

Ash grabs my hands and takes them away from my chest. I swear his eyes darken when they admire the marks he made on my skin. His fingers softly touch the marks and his eyes trail all over my chest until they stop at the spot on the side of my ribcage.

The spot where the tattoo lies feels hot and I just want the ground to swallow me whole.

It stays quiet for a few moments as I watch Ash touch the marks he made on me and caress the tattoo softly.

I can't help but sit still and admire him while he touches me. His features are soft and if you were to walk in you would never think that he and I have said hateful words towards one another. You would think that we are just two lovers admiring one another and showing their love when we are anything but.

After a few seconds, Ash stops touching me and looks up at me. "What are you going to do?" I ask.

"I'm going to break you piece by piece until there is nothing left for anyone to fix other than me."

NINE
ARIELLA

SUMMER

"I've never been to New York before," I admit to Ash. "My father works out there but he never once offered [to] take me there. I've always been afraid to go by myself."

"Well now you get to go and enjoy it." Ash give[s] [a] soft smile. "Don't you have friends who could [join] you?"

"I have Bridgette who I've known since I was a [kid]. She isn't here though. She is spending her summer with her parents in England."

I did call Bridgette the other day and she told me how England has been treating her well and how she never wants to leave. She started to talk about how hot English boys are and I couldn't help but laugh at her.

"You will like New York. I have a few plans for us when we get there," Ash says while caressing my hands that are between us.

Spending these last few weeks with Ash has been amazing. We have gone on all kinds of amazing adventures together and there have been a lot of kisses between us and stolen moments. I am trying not to think about how fast my heart beats whenever I see him but it's hard because of how my body reacts to him.

He knows exactly where to touch me and that makes my heart go crazy sometimes.

I keep trying to remind myself that this thing between us is temporary but then I also can't help but think, what if this can go on?

What if Ash and I were to stay together forever?

That's dangerous thinking.

"What kind of plans?" I ask Ash with a teasing smile.

Before Ash can answer, one of the flight attendants interrupts us. "Sir, looks away from me and at her. "We will be landing in fifteen minutes. They have your hotel room ready and all of the reservations for tonight are all set as well."

"Thank you." Ash nods for her to leave and she smiles before turning around and going back to the front of the plane. Ash looks down at me and I raise my eyebrow at him. "What?"

"What reservations for tonight?" I ask with a small smile.

"You'll see." Ash smirks before looking away from me and at the window to my right.

———

I don't know what exactly we are doing.

All I know is that Ash told me a car will be here to pick us up in a few hours and then he left because he needed to meet with his father.

The hotel room we are staying in is super nice. It has a small dining area and a living room in another room. The California King faces the beautiful city and this is possibly the best view that any hotel room might have.

You can see The Empire State Building and then Central park that is a bit further down.

I wanted to ask Ash how he could pay for all this and that me and him should go half but he left before I could ask him.

By the time it's dark, Ash is still not back and I refrain from texting him to ask him where he is. Instead I just decide to get ready.

I end up wearing a black skirt with a black cropped t-shirt. Since it's cold outside I decide to throw on an over-sized brown leather jacket. As I fix my hair and brush it out, Ash walks into the hotel room and he pauses when he sees me.

His eyes darken and I get chills down my spine as he looks at me like that.

I love it when he looks at me like that.

It makes me want to kiss him forever and not let go.

He walks closer to me and when he is close enough his hand automatically wraps around my waist and pulls me closer to him. "You look nice," he says while leaning down, placing his lips on the side of my neck.

I reach up and rest my hands on his neck. "Where have you been?"

Ash tenses under my touch and I almost want to pull my hands away. "With my father. He needed to talk to me." Ash's lips leave my neck and he looks down at me, still with that heated gaze.

"For four hours?" I raise my eyebrows.

"My father requires a lot of attention. I'm sorry I didn't text." He presses a soft kiss on my shoulder.

I don't ask him anything else about his father because I can tell by the way Ash's grip is around my waist that his father isn't someone he wants to talk about.

But from our agreement we also promised not to mention anything too personal about us for our heart's sake, more so my heart.

"So where are we going?"

Ash smiles and takes my hands off his neck and holds them in his. "The car is waiting downstairs."

"Can we use the subway? I've never been in one and I want to see what it's like."

Ash nods his head. "Of course. I'll let them know."

Ash and I walk out of the building and after he talks to the driver, he grabs my hand and walks to the entrance of the subway.

It's very hot down here and it almost feels like I can't breathe from how hot it is.

It's also very loud because of the subways and the tracks. It doesn't smell like I thought it would from what I have seen in the movies.

People make it seem like subways are the worst thing in the world but I don't see how.

"So what do you think?" Ash asks, looking down at me.

I scan around us and there are only a few people down here. It's a good amount of people but I thought it would have been more crowded.

"We haven't gone on the actual subway yet."

He smiles down at me and I reach up to place my lips on his.

One of his hands leaves my waist and grabs hold of my chin as he deepens the kiss.

Before I can tell him to stop and that we can't do this

in public I feel someone grab my ass making me flinch and look away from Ash and behind me.

I see a tall man, who is wearing a suit and has wrinkles on his face making me assume he is in his 50s or older.

I can smell the alcohol reek off of him from standing just a few feet away.

"If he's kissing you like that, I'd like to see what you would do to me."

I furrow my eyebrows and ignore him but Ash steps in and pulls me closer to him.

"What did you just say to her?"

"And now the boyfriend is getting mad." The old man rolls his eyes. "I said I'd like to see how the pussy feels, kid. Mind sharing?"

"Ash, just ignore him-" Ash leaves me and he rushes up to the man and pushes him to the floor before standing above him and throwing his fists into the man's face. "Ash!" Ash doesn't stop punching the man and people around us start pulling their phones out and recording. I take a peek at the older man's face and his eyes are swollen as he smiles and laughs. "Ash you're going to kill him. Stop! Someone stop them!"

Chaos is spreading through the subway we're in. People are cheering and yelling while others are jumping in to stop Ash from killing the guy.

I see Ash pull the guy's head off the ground before

banging his head on the concrete. A gasp falls from my lips and I feel chills spread throughout my body.

"Someone help me get this guy off before he kills him!" one of the guys who is trying to pull Ash away from the older man says.

Instead of someone helping him they all start to leave the scene. "Yo! Someone called the fucking cops!"

Ten

Ariella

PRESENT

"Bridgette, why do you always have to use my notes?"

Bridgette smiles at me and wraps her arm around my shoulder. "Because I want to make sure that your work is appreciated, and it goes to good use. And it will." She smacks a kiss on my cheek making me smile at her.

I wipe her lip gloss off my cheek and rest my head on her shoulder as we walk through the hallway.

I just got done with my American government class while Bridgette just got done with her writing class. I gave her my notes that I had from mine and since we have the same teacher, just different class times, I know that it wasn't a big deal or anything.

As we walk through the hallway, I see Jace leaning against a wall before he walks towards us. Bridgette groans and rolls her eyes before removing her arm from around my shoulder.

"Why do you always feel the need to ruin my day with your presence?" she says while glaring at Jace.

"Stop lying Bridge, you know you love me." Jace winks.

Bridgette laughs and looks at me, wanting my input.

I know Jace is secretly infatuated with Bridgette. It's obvious in the way he looks at her but obviously I am not going to say anything because it's not my place. I think if Bridgette knew that Jace secretly liked her, she would shy away and never speak to him again. When it comes to Jace, Bridgette is weird.

Usually she is very confident around men and knows how to fake it 'til she makes it but with Jace, something holds her back.

"We need to go. Ariella and I are planning on binging Vampire Diaries and then stuffing our faces with Canes."

"Why the fuck would you go to Canes when there is Crowded Rooms down the street from your house? You would really drive three miles instead of less than one for fried chicken fingers and some buttered bread."

Bridgette gasps and pushes Jace lightly. "It is not just buttered bread and you know that." I laugh and shake my head at them as we continue walking our way down the hallway to where the exit is.

Bridgette and Jace continue arguing as I hear what jabs they are throwing at one another.

Jace says that Bridgette is plain and boring and then Bridgette throws a jab about how he is a fuck boy and will forever be alone while fat and ugly.

Jace smirks and his eyes sparkle as we walk through the exit.

"Oh my god," Bridgette says, making me look away from Jace and at Bridgette's shocked expression.

Her jaw looks like it's about to break off and fall to the floor.

I look away from her and look outside. There are people surrounding my car and they are taking a bunch of pictures, cameras flashing and people snickering.

I run up to my car and push everyone out of my way.

The work *smack* is spray painted on my car.

The visual for everyone to see in a bright red color.

Everyone's snickers fade into the background as moments from the other night pop into my head.

Ash smacking me and me loving it so much I was about to orgasm from that.

That motherfucker.

My blood boils as I read the word over and over.

He is teasing me.

The other night, after he came into my room I had to finish what he started. The jerk didn't even have the fucking nerve to show up to class the next day, which I'm glad because, to be honest, what was I going to do?

Go up to him and cry and beg him to finish me off?

But he really has the nerve to spray paint my car with the word *smack*?

The fucking nerve he has. He is crazy. He is actually crazy.

Even though no one knows what it means, or at least the deeper meaning to it, I still feel embarrassed and my cheeks are burning and covered in red probably.

I turn to Jace. "Where is Ash?"

Jace bites his bottom lip, holding back a laugh. "He's at the diner."

"We're taking your car," I demand before walking towards Jace's car.

"Why can't we take yours?" Jace asks and I just know he is trying his best not to laugh.

He is lucky that I am saving all of my energy for Ash.

I feel like ripping his head off or just slapping him until he begs me to stop.

Jace drives out of the parking lot with Bridgette in the back and me in the passenger seat, clenching and unclenching my fists.

I can't stop visualizing that word over and over in my head while his grunts and dirty words mixed with my moans play in the background.

It's taunting me and I almost feel guilty for giving

myself to him so willingly again. I will never learn when it comes to him.

Bridgette is asking what's going on as Jace drives to where Ash is. I know she wants to know more; she has been wanting to know since Ash started hanging out with Jace a lot. She notices the small looks he gives me, but I keep brushing it off just because I don't want to talk about it.

I'll tell her eventually, just not yet.

When Jace parks the car I don't hesitate to get out. I hear Bridgette and Jace following behind me slowly. My heart can't stop racing as I rush inside the diner. I still can't process what just happened and if it was all a dream or not but I know that this is one of Ash's sick games that he likes to play with me.

My eyes roam around the diner when I push open the door and finally my eyes land on him, sitting at the very end of the bar with a blonde sitting next to him.

I am fuming and my head is in scribbles as I look over and see him laughing at something she is saying.

The fucking nerve he has!

I just can't believe him.

Who does he think he is? To embarrass me like that in front of everyone and now hangout with a girl knowing I would come and find him.

Ash has never been the type to push my buttons with other girls. Not until right in this moment, he has never touched or been around another girl when I was involved with him, or at least that's what I assume.

We aren't involved with one another but it hurts to see him with someone who isn't me.

Ash's eyes catch mine and he fucking winks like the douche he is.

I walk up to him and face the girl he is talking to.

She is pretty, but the poor girl doesn't know the kind of taste that Ash has.

"Hi, you were probably planning to eventually have sex with him right? Assuming that you didn't already?"

The girl blushes and I almost feel sorry for being so nasty but the way Ash makes me feel is crazy. I feel like a crazy ex-girlfriend even though we were never and never will be that.

I don't mean anything to Ash and this proves it. I am just a plaything to him.

"Um-"

"Let me save you the trouble darling. Ash, he has very aggressive tastes. He likes slapping, choking, degrading, all of that. You seem like such a nice girl and why would you want to be with a guy like that?" I say before I hear Ash snicker making me thrust my elbow into his stomach. "He also has chlamydia. Super serious case too. One of my friends caught it from him. Poor girl." The girl's jaw drops and she looks at Ash before looking back at me. "I'm so sorry. I'll make sure he is never around you or anyone else again. I'll get him the help he needs." I put a reassuring hand on her shoulder and she gives me a forced smile before getting her things and leaving.

I feel Ash's hand on my waist but I turn around and slap him across the face. "How dare you?" I yell and push his hand off of me. "You really have the fucking nerve to spray paint that on my car?"

"Oh come on, Madden, I know you like playing these kinds of chase and catch games." He smiles, despite the red hand mark appearing on his face from the slap. "You like my attention, any kind of attention I give you, you fucking crave it baby."

My body is shaking and I want to slap him again and scream at him, but he made me speechless. How does he always know how to make me feel so weak and below him?

Of course he admits he did it.

The fucking psycho admits it and is proud.

"You are sick! You are fucking horrible!" I push his chest and walk away from him. "I'll fucking ruin you, Ash!"

Eleven

Ariella

Bridgette wants to go to a party.

Usually I wouldn't be the type to go out and party but I feel like I need a night out to just forget about everything.

School is becoming stressful and I feel like all of the walls around me are closing in. That's the thing about anxiety, you can't stop it, with no amount of medication or other forms of therapy, my brain can't stop.

Bridgette said that we need to go out more since she hasn't gone out with me in a long time and I feel bad because I don't want to make it seem to Bridgette that I don't like hanging out with her, because I do.

I just need some time to myself to get my head straight.

"You are going to look amazing, Ariella. This dress looks better on you than it does on me," Bridgette says while admiring her red dress on me.

She also ended up straightening my hair and did my makeup. I told her I could have done it so that she could get ready but Bridgette loves cosmetology.

Bridgette is wearing a purple skirt with a black tank top. Her curly brown hair is slicked in a low bun.

She is gorgeous and I admire her confidence and how she carries herself. "You should have left your hair down," I tell her and Bridgette blushes and turns away.

She hates her curly hair and I don't know why. I love her hair. I wish I could have amazing hair like that.

"We have to hurry because Jace will be here soon." Bridgette puts on her shoes and grabs her bag while I check my phone.

It's 11:00 pm right now and the party started an hour ago.

This party we are going to is being hosted by one of the guys that Bridgette hooked up with last year. He is super cool but kind of a dick. I got mad at Bridgette when I found out she was talking to him again even though she said she was only talking to him so that she could get invited to one of his parties because they are the best as many people say.

I don't see what the big deal is about his parties. The only thing his parties have that others don't is a shit ton of drugs and a three-story house with a pool overlooking half the city.

This guy is super rich so I see how people would want to go to his parties.

Bridgette told me that he is a business major, and his father runs some billion-dollar company.

"They're here!" Bridgette yells before running out of my room and downstairs.

They?

I grab my bag and leave the room, following Bridgette downstairs. When I walk outside I see Jace's white Range Rover.

Bridgette sits in the front and through the window I can see a bunch of other people in his car.

I walk to Jace's side of the car and I look in the back and see Ash with two other people in the back with him.

Ash's eyes burn into my chest and then my mind goes back to a few nights ago when he was in my room edging me.

And then my mind goes to the other day when he spray paints *smack* on my car.

But a few days after that, when I woke up and looked outside, my car didn't have that word on there anymore. My car looked brand new. It was clean on the inside and washed.

Ash has been throwing me dirty looks and then

embarrassing me in class whenever he gets the chance by doing some stupid pranks.

When I opened my gym locker it was filled with a shit ton of condoms and all of the girls around me laughed and gave me dirty looks. He has also repeatedly made me fall on my ass whenever he bumps into me in the hallway. The jackass never stops and I don't think he ever will.

And my heart can't help but want to break whenever I see him with a girl around school or at the diner.

At our fucking diner.

He brings some dumb bimbo who looks like one of those moms in Calabasas that overdo their plastic surgery and end up looking like a damn frog.

I feel bad for talking bad about those girls because girls support girls but when it comes to Ash, I feel nasty and can't help but feel jealous. That doesn't mean I will show it though.

While doing all of this, he hasn't even said a full sentence to me since that day and it's frustrating the fuck out of me.

All he does is smirk at me and wink while pranking and embarrassing me.

Jace turns his head to look at me instead of gawking at Bridgette. "What's wrong?" Jace asks.

"Um, there's no room for me in the back. Where am I supposed to sit?"

"I didn't know I was picking Riley and Kyle up and

Ash decided last minute that he wanted to come." My eyes move to the back again and I see a girl and a guy who look almost like twins and then Ash who is still burning his gaze into my skin. "Just sit on one of their laps, Ariella."

I can either sit on a girl who is probably as small as me, a guy who I don't know, or Ash.

I let out a sigh and open the door to the back seat of the car and I see Ash who has his legs spread out.

Ash is wearing dark blue jeans and then a black shirt with a black and white varsity jacket with different patches on it. He is also wearing a familiar chain and it takes me back to when I first saw him wear it. Ever since he has been back, I haven't seen him wear that chain, until now.

"You coming or what, Madden?" Ash asks, raising his eyebrow at me.

I roll my eyes at him and ignore the heat in my stomach as I climb into Jace's car and place myself on Ash's lap.

All of a sudden I feel a thousand times hotter than I did outside.

Ash puts his hand on my hips. "Don't touch me," I hiss at him and try to move away from him but he shoves me back down on his lap.

"Sit still and don't move."

The car starts and Jace backs out of my driveway and starts driving in the direction of the party. Me sitting on Ash's knees feels uncomfortable so I scoot back making my back hit his hard chest. Ash's hands tighten their grip on my hips and I start to feel a bulge underneath my butt.

He's hard.

I squeeze my thighs together and squirm on his lap which makes Ash slide his hand up to my throat and he turns my head to look at him.

"If you keep moving, I'm going to end up putting my dick inside you as Jace drives. Stop fucking moving," Ash whispers in my ear as he puts his hand on my bottom lip. "When we get to the party, you're wiping that fuck-me lipstick off too."

What?

TWELVE
ARIELLA

Once Jace parks I don't waste time opening the door and getting off of Ash's lap.

During the whole drive, Ash kept gripping onto my hips, pulling me more into his chest and breathing harshly. I couldn't help but squirm on his lap as I felt his erection digging into my ass.

"Party time!" Bridgette says as she jumps out of the car and walks towards me. "This is going to be so much fun, Ariella. We haven't gone out in such a long time." Bridgette wraps her arm around my shoulders.

"Ariella looks like she needs a night out. She never drops that bitch act," Ash claims as he slams the car door and Jace stands next to him.

"Do you always have some remark to say about me? I

swear it's like you're obsessed with me or something from how much you talk about me."

"No, Ariella, it's just that you are so easy to hate on."

"You know what they say about haters, Ash." I give him a smirk before pulling Bridgette with me towards the front door.

"What's up with you and him?" Bridgette asks as we walk through the house.

Bridgette has been wanting to know more about Ash and I. She knows there is history between us because she isn't stupid. She knows I'm never this mean to anyone.

I have told her bits here and there but never the full story.

"Nothing. He is just an ass who doesn't have any manners."

Bridgette and I make our way towards the kitchen that holds all of the beverages and snacks. I pour myself a pink lemonade with vodka in it.

Bridgette pours herself a cup of whiskey.

When you look at her, you would assume that she is a girl who doesn't drink strong alcohol but Bridgette definitely knows how to handle her liquor.

When it comes to weed or anything like that, she is a total disaster.

"Make sure I don't do anything embarrassing. I want to get so drunk that I don't remember a thing that happened tonight." Bridgette says before she starts drinking her whiskey.

I chuckle and nod my head.

During the party, Bridgette and I dance a little bit, mingle with people who go to our school, and then decide to play a small party game.

Bridgette and I mostly dance though.

We let the alcohol drive us and slowly dance to the music sensually.

I feel eyes on us, more specifically me, as Bridgette and I dance together. I turn my head, my hair flowing through the air, and my eyes catch dark ones that are filled with lust and heat.

Ash.

He is staring at me like he either wants to kill me or take me into one of these bedrooms and make me scream in his neck.

Ash is sitting on one of the stools near the bar and his legs are a little spread making my eyes travel down to the spot between his legs. My heart swirls in my stomach as I notice the bulge underneath his jeans.

Slowly my eyes connect with his again and Ash is now smirking at me.

I don't know what it is about Ash but he always has a way of making me want to get on my knees for him.

How does he do it?

I look away from him before I start thinking those dangerous thoughts again.

I can't fall into his traps anymore. If I do then he will ruin me again.

"Let's go outside, I need some fresh air!" I yell to Bridgette which makes her nod her head.

Bridgette grabs onto my hand and she pulls us out of the dancing crowd and we make our way to the backyard where music is playing lightly and people are mingling and talking with other people.

"Hey Bridgette! I'm happy you made it," a guy says as he walks up to us. He has short blonde hair and dark brown eyes. He's the guy that Bridgette hooked up with, the one who is currently hosting this party as well. "Long time no see. How are you?"

"Joshua. Hey." Bridgette gives him a timid smile and grips my hands. I already know she wants to flee from the scene and not face him. Makes sense because he looks like a weirdo. "I'm good. Just hanging out with my friend."

Joshua moves his eyes to me. "Ariella, right? I've heard about you."

"Good things, I hope." I give him a small smile before pulling Bridgette away from him. "Well, Bridgette and I have to go meet up with our friends."

Joshua furrows his eyebrows and his hand grabs Bridgette's to pull her closer to him. "Oh, well, I was hoping that maybe Bridgette and I could talk some more. We haven't seen each other in a while."

That was for a reason dude.

"Yea, but you see we have people waiting for her and then her-"

"-boyfriend won't be too happy seeing her with someone that isn't me." A voice finishes the sentence which makes me look over my shoulder and see Jace standing behind Bridgette and I with Ash next to him. "So I suggest you get your hands off my girlfriend before I throw you in your own pool," Jace threatens.

Joshua sizes Jace up, contemplating whether or not he could take him or not. While Jace and Joshua have a 'Who's dick is bigger contest?' my eyes go to Ash who is staring at me.

The alcohol in my system makes my head buzz and I can't help but give Ash a smile.

"Okay man, I didn't know she was your girl. Last time I checked, she was single." I hear Joshua say before his footsteps leave.

My eyes leave Ash's when I feel Bridgette's hand leave mine. Jace grabs Bridgette by the waist and is holding her against him.

Wait, girlfriend?

"Um, last time I checked, she wasn't your girlfriend," I say, grabbing Bridgette's hand and pulling her to stand next to me.

"Shut up, Ariella." Jace grabs Bridgette's other hand and pulls her to his chest again.

I stop myself from raising my hand and slapping Jace across the face.

"Can you guys stop swinging me around? I feel like I am going to throw up if you keep doing that," Bridgette complains. "And I'm not your girlfriend, douchebag. Get that out of your head." Bridgette pushes herself off of Jace before walking away from us and towards the house.

Jace follows her with his jaw clenched.

I am about to follow but then Ash blocks me from following. "Move out of my way before I connect my fist with your face."

Ash chuckles and his hands rests on my hips. "Your threats mean nothing to me."

"I'm serious Ash, leave me alone. You've done enough for a lifetime." I try to move out of his hold but all he does is pull me closer making our chests press against one another.

"No, I still need to have a little more fun with you."

I can feel how hard and fast his heart is racing with his chest against mine. It almost sounds like music to my ears.

I lay my hands on his chest and reach up so that my lips are a centimeter away from him. "You always suck the fun out of things," I whisper, my lips close to his.

"Oh yea?" Ash smirks but he doesn't move his face closer or farther from mine.

It's almost like slow sweet torture, not being able to kiss Ash.

"Why won't you kiss me anymore?" I ask, begging to know the answer.

I know that if alcohol wasn't in my system then I wouldn't find the courage to do this and I know for a fact the next morning I will be regretting this.

"Because you taste like shit, Ariella," Ash says before I feel freezing cold water around me.

I feel myself sober up and I open my eyes and see that I am at the bottom of the pool.

Fucking jackass, he threw me in the pool.

I should drown on purpose just so I could ruin his life and haunt him forever.

It's peaceful down here anyways. Might be more peaceful in heaven now that I think about it. I wouldn't be able to hear Ash's annoying fucking voice ever again or be reminded of the haunted memories between us.

I never thought about killing myself, not when my mom died, not when Ash wasn't in my life anymore, not when I got bullied in high school, and definitely not when my dad was found with another woman who wasn't my mom a few weeks after her death.

But my head sometimes can't take it and it's so peaceful down here now that I think about it.

Might be the alcohol talking.

I'll just blame it all on that since it's easier.

I feel arms wrap around my waist and next thing I know I can breathe again and goosebumps cover my entire body as I shiver against a warm chest.

"God fucking damnit Ariella. You aren't that drunk, I've been watching you." Ash's voice fills my ears and I wipe some water off my face and open my eyes seeing Ash's face against mine.

"I hate you." I push his chest to make him let go of me but he doesn't budge.

"Hate you too, Madden."

Thirteen
Ash

Summer

Ariella and I quietly walk inside the hotel room.

It's the middle of the night and I feel like shit for ruining our night. I wanted to take her to this rooftop bar where a famous DJ was performing.

The view would have been amazing and it sucks that me fighting in the subway ruined everything.

I had to call my dad to get me out of jail. He wasn't happy when I was talking to him on the phone.

I couldn't even concentrate on him. The only person I was concentrating on was Ariella and how she was basically alone in the city without me while I was detained.

I was scared for her because I know that the city is a big place.

But when I saw her in the police station as the officer was taking the cuffs off of me I was shocked.

I'm surprised she found her way here and not the hotel to wait for me.

By the look on her face, she looked like she was relieved to see me. I can't forget her screams and how she yelled at me to stop and was trying to get people to get me off of the guy before I pummeled him into the ground.

Sure I may have overreacted but the way he was saying those things to her made me want to end his life.

I got that familiar feeling creeping up my neck at that moment and the next thing I know, I couldn't stop myself.

The way my fists connected with his face gave me so much adrenaline that I couldn't stop.

I didn't want to stop.

"Sit down so that I can clean your hands," Ariella says as she puts her jacket on the chair.

I sit down on the bed and rest my hands on my lap and look at Ariella who walks towards the bathroom.

Probably to get the first aid kit.

I look down at my hands and see cuts all over them.

I get flashbacks of moments from me punching the glass mirror in my bathroom. The way the shards of glass would enter my skin and make me bleed.

I was always fascinated with the way the blood ran down my hands.

"I found this first aid kit but it doesn't have a lot of the stuff we might need to make sure it's not infected," Ariella says while walking back into the bedroom. She drops the first aid kit on the bed and kneels in front of me. She takes my hands in hers and she inspects the cuts. During the drive home she wouldn't talk to me or look at me. My father had a driver come and get us. Despite him being mad, that douchebag cares about me. "God, Ash," she whispers before letting go of my hands and looking through the first aid kit.

I stare at her as she tends to the cuts on my hands.

She's so beautiful.

I have always thought that Ariella was beautiful but every time I admire her I can't grasp how beautiful she is.

Since we started hanging out more I noticed how much I want to always be around her.

I feel like shit knowing that I ruined our night.

It was supposed to be a fun night out. I was supposed to make this day special for Ariella but I ruined it.

It's all my fault.

"I'm sorry. I feel like shit for ruining your night." Ariella doesn't say anything which makes me lift my head and look up at her. "It was supposed to be special and we were supposed to have fun but I ruined it and I should have never punched him. I just didn't like the way he was talking about you, Ariella."

"It's not your fault." She wipes dried blood off of one of my knuckles before looking up at me. "I appreciate you standing up for me but I have never seen something like that before. I was scared for both you and him because you looked like you were almost about to kill him, Ash."

"Because he was fucking-"

"I know what he did." She looks back down at my hands. "But he shouldn't have to die for that. I was terrified that you were going to kill him and luckily your dad was able to help you get out."

"Did you talk to him?"

"No. But I know he got you out because of the police officer I was speaking to. He also had to do an interview with me about what happened but your dad helped you a lot. Without him you probably would have had charges, Ash." She stops wiping the blood off my hands and puts all of the materials back in the first aid kit. "You're so lucky you have people who are there for you, Ash. Don't take advantage of it."

She stands up and leaves the room to go back into the bathroom.

I look back down at my hands and clench and unclench my fists. I already know they are going to be bruised tomorrow.

It's not like I'm not used to it.

Ariella comes back inside the room and she has a towel in her hands. It looks wet and I see steam coming off the towel. Ariella gets on her knees in front of me and all I am thinking in this moment is how I want to bring her closer to my lips and claim her.

I feel my pants tighten to the point where it's almost uncomfortable.

"Stand up."

Ariella looks up at me, just as she is about to wipe my hands with the towel.

She furrows her eyebrows. "Why?"

"Just stand up, Ariella." Ariella glares at me and she looks down at her hands but she freezes. "Can you listen to me and stand up?"

Ariella places the towel on the bed next to me and slowly she places her hands on my thighs and looks up at me. "You're hard, Ash."

Her eyes are filled with innocence and wonder. I want to ask her if she ever had a guy's dick down her throat and just thinking that she might've makes the possessive side of me want to come out and demand who, so I can kill that motherfucker.

"Yea, and if you don't stand up and stop looking at me like that I'm going to shove my cock down your throat."

Ariella ignores me and she slides her hands up my thighs and one of her hands touches my belt before looking back up at me. "Can I?"

"Just stand up, Ariella. This is your only way out."

"I want to," she says, before unbuckling my belt and unbuttoning my jeans.

She reaches into my pants and my eyes roll when I feel her fingers graze my cock. "Fuck, Ariella." I rest my hands on either side of me and lean back so that I can watch Ariella stare at my cock in wonder. She caresses me through my briefs before slipping her hands between the fabric and wrapping her hand around my cock. Ariella moves her hand up and down and I look down at her and see her look at my cock in awe. It's like she's never seen a guy's dick up close before. "Baby, wrap your hand around me tighter." She squeezes me in her hand and she moves her hand up and down while looking at me with those innocent fuck-me eyes.

Ariella pulls me out of my pants and I look down at her tiny hand wrapped around my cock and almost cum at the sight. It's red and swollen while her hand is squeezing the base. I look at her and she looks like she is trying to figure out what to do next.

"I've never done this before."

"What?"

Ariella's cheeks turn red and she smiles shyly. "You know, this."

"A blow job or a hand job?"

"Both," she states.

Oh Ariella, you are in so much fucking trouble.

I knew I wanted to ruin her from the moment I laid my eyes on her, but now I know for a fact that I will ruin her.

"Wrap your lips around my cock. Put your hands on my thighs and breathe through your nose, alright?"

Ariella nods her head and she lays her hands on my thighs like I asked her too and then leans down to wrap her soft lips around my cock.

The first contact of her lips on me makes me roll my eyes and I hold myself back from making her take all of me down her throat. If I were to do that then I would scare her.

My hand reaches down to grab her hair, I guide her up and down my cock, slowly, so she gets the hang of it.

Ariella digs her nails into my thighs and my breathing gets harder.

I don't go far down her throat, but I move her head up and down, slowly thrusting my hips against her face.

I feel my eyes getting heavy but I don't want to close my eyes. I want to watch Ariella take my cock and then swallow my cum.

I want to fucking mark her.

Ariella rubs my thighs as I feel myself coming closer and closer to my release.

I run a hand through my hair, getting hot everywhere in my body.

Ariella sucks harder and scratches my thighs as I feel my release rush through my body. Ariella keeps her mouth on me as I release inside her mouth. She grips onto my thighs and my hand tightens in her hair.

My breathing comes out harsh and my eyes feel like rolling back and just staying closed forever while having Ariella's lips on me.

Once I finish, Ariella sucks every last drop off of me which I didn't expect her to do.

I open my eyes and grab her cheek to make her look up at me once she is done. "You have no fucking clue what you have done, Ariella."

FOURTEEN
ARIELLA

SUMMER

This morning I felt soft kisses on my neck and smelled a cinnamon and vanilla-like steam in the air and it made me realize that Ash got us breakfast. When I rolled to my side and opened my eyes, I saw Aslı who was looking at me with a soft look in his eyes.

They were filled with adoration and I wanted to believe that Ash and I could fall in love someday, but that's not possible and it can't ever be possible.

Ash and I had cinnamon toast for breakfast and some fruit. There was also coffee with vanilla creamer. Ash then told me that he is going to take me to all of his favorite places in New York today and then later on he wants to take me to his favorite club.

I laughed when he told me that he was going to take

us to a club because we aren't over 21 and he told me that it wasn't going to be an issue.

I don't know what his plans for the club tonight are going to be or what they include but I also can't help but feel really excited to see what happens.

I like spending time with Ash.

These past few weeks have been a dream and I can't help but feel free with him.

I've known so many people, boys to be exact, like Jace, but I have never felt this free and excited like I do with Ash. It's amazing and euphoric to feel like this.

As Ash and I walk the streets of New York I can't stop staring at all of the towering buildings everywhere around us. I like the vibe of New York from what I'm seeing.

"So I'm thinking that we just walk around until you see something you like or want to try," Ash says as he looks down at me with a soft smile that makes my insides turn.

I nod my head before looking around where we are walking.

Right now we're near Central Park. Ash is holding my hand and I am trying not to die from the heat.

I swear New York's weather is ten times worse than California. If it's hot in California then it's ten times hotter in New York to the point where it's humid and sweat is running down my arm pits. I am praying that Ash doesn't smell the B.O. or notice how I am sweating.

Today I decided to wear jean shorts and a black

cropped shirt. I tied my hair in a messy ponytail and decided to wear my white tennis shoes.

Ash is wearing black jeans and a white shirt with his classic chain necklace. He also decided to wear a hat today which makes it hard to take my eyes off of him.

My eyes catch a tattoo shop and I pull Ash towards the shop. I look at Ash and see him smirking while his eyes roam around the shop before they go to me.

We walk inside the tattoo shop and it's almost dead in here. There are only two people getting a tattoo done. Some employees are sitting on the chairs scrolling through their phones as music plays throughout the shop.

"Hello." My eyes catch the guy at the front desk and I smile and walk towards him. "How can I help you guys?"

I look at Ash. "Get a matching tattoo with a stranger."

"Are we still strangers?" Ash smirks and I blush before looking at the guy.

"We want to get tattoos together."

"I'll have to ask the artist. Is it something complicated or small?"

"Small."

"Okay, just pull up what you want while I go talk to him. Give me a second." The guy walks away and I turn my head to Ash.

"I hope you are fine with getting one because if not then this will be a total fail."

Ash laughs and he slides his hands around my waist to

pull me closer. "I'll get one with you. Do you know what you want?"

"I have an idea. I kind of thought of this last minute," I say, giving Ash a small smile while my cheeks start to heat up. "I was thinking of getting the Roman numerals for 2023."

"I like it. I've always wanted to get a Roman numeral tattoo."

"I want to get it right here." I point to the spot under my boob on my left side.

"That might hurt. Is it your first tattoo?"

"Yea."

I know that Ash has tattoos. I've seen glimpses of them when he is undressing or when we went to the beach for that whole day.

I never asked what the meaning of them is because I know that's too personal. Plus, I'm always reminding myself that what's happening between us is temporary.

"Okay. I'll get it in the same spot."

"Matching tattoos with a stranger." I smile up at Ash.

"Kind of stranger."

The guy comes back, this time with the tattoo artist. I tell him about the tattoo and where I want it and then I explain how Ash will be getting the same tattoo as me.

He brings us to his room and then preps the area where the tattoos will be.

I'm going to get mine first.

I feel nerves explode in my stomach and I can't help but overthink.

Should I do this? Is this a good idea? Am I crazy for getting a tattoo with someone who I have only known for a few weeks? Will I regret this?

I probably will regret this but whatever.

When the artist first touches my skin with the gun I squeeze Ash's hand and my eyes catch his. He smiles at me before looking down at the tattoo gun meeting my skin.

"You doing okay there, Ariella?"

I nod my head and rest my chin on my elbow while staring at him. "It doesn't hurt as much as I thought it would."

"As you get more tattoos you start to not feel it." Ash shrugs.

"When did you get your first tattoo?"

"Seventeen."

"What is it?"

Ash laughs and I feel him stroke my hand lightly. "Lips."

I furrow my eyebrows. "Lips?"

Ash laughs again and nods his head. "My friend dared me to go get a tattoo of his lips so he had to put bright red lipstick on and then kiss a paper for the artist to tattoo that on me."

I try not to laugh because I know it will ruin the tattoo. "That's a very random way of getting a tattoo."

"Yea, but it's a good story to tell people about my first tattoo."

The artist finishes up my tattoo and then he does Ash's. Ash decided to get it in the same area as I did.

While he's getting his tattoo I can't stop staring at the way his muscles flex and his shoulders tense up. He keeps his hand on my thigh as I watch the artist tattoo him. I can't stop smiling at Ash when I see the tattoo on him.

Even if I ever do regret getting this tattoo, it will be an amazing story to tell people. I know that I don't want to forget Ash or how he made this summer amazing. I love that he is doing this with me and that I get to have the privilege of knowing him.

I just really hope my future self agrees with that.

FIFTEEN
ASH

"What is it about her that makes you never stop looking at her, Ash?" Jace asks at the same time he leans against the wall near me.

He just got back from his business class. Jace always tells me to meet him next to the exit of the school so that he can talk to me about what happened in his day. He sometimes reminds me of a girl because of the way he always wants to be talking about what happened during his day, how things went with Bridgette that day.

The dude says I'm obsessed with Ariella while he never even stops talking about Bridgette, which is fine.

I don't care.

I think his relationship with Bridgette is interesting

and as I see them hanging out more I am always trying to figure out what exactly is going on between them.

I look away from Ariella, who is talking to a girl in one of her classes. Ariella is giving her a small smile and nodding her head while talking to the girl.

Today Ariella is wearing a white sweatshirt and blue jeans. Her hair is tied in a ponytail and it makes me able to see all of her features clearly. Her high cheekbones and plump lips make me not want to look away from her.

"Don't worry about it," I look away from Ariella and my eyes travel to Jace.

"No. I'm curious. Ever since you met her at the diner you have been different, more on edge if anything."

"How about you mind your own business Jace? This doesn't concern you."

I have known Jace for a while now. I met him when I was visiting a few summers ago with my dad and long story short, my father and Jace's father were partners for some business and after we met we just started hanging out more.

I like Jace, even though he can sometimes piss me off a lot.

"It does if you plan on hurting my friend. I'm serious, Ash. Ariella's dad will fucking destroy you," Jace says and I look away from him and instead look at Ariella who is waving bye to the girl at the same time Bridgette walks over and smiles at the girl while she leaves.

Ariella and Bridgette talk while they are both smiling softly at one another.

I feel like sometimes when I look at Ariella, she is just faking her smile so that she doesn't worry Bridgette.

Bridgette is a good friend and I know that if Ariella were to tear down that stupid wall of hers and show it to Bridgette, Bridgette would do anything in her power to make Ariella feel like she is on top of the world.

Ariella tore down those walls with me once, she told me about her mom and how she still thinks about her all the time and wishes that her mother was still in her life instead of her dad.

She told me about all of the things she wished she could change about herself and how she would do anything to make herself perfect in other people's eyes.

She also told me that she would rather live in a book than reality because reality was too fake and negative.

At the time I told her that was because all she read was romance books and everything in romance books turns out okay, most of the time at least.

That night, we talked a lot. I felt bad not telling her about myself but at the same time I know that if I told her about the real me, she would run away and never look back.

Ariella's head turns towards me, and her smile drops. She is completely ignoring every word that Bridgette is saying and all of her attention is focused on me.

The sudden urge to smile at her fills my veins.

She doesn't know that I am the one who fixed her car and I'm not going to tell her either.

Sure, what I did was stupid and probably a douche thing, but I just needed to tease her a little bit.

It was an easy fix and I just decided to wash her car and clean the inside.

Sometimes I find myself wishing things between us could go back to normal, but I know it never can because of our dads.

"Ariella! Bridgette!" Jace calls them over.

Bridgette looks at Jace and frowns while Ariella looks away from me and has the fucking audacity to smile at Jace.

That fucking brat.

Ariella grabs Bridgette's elbow and they walk towards us. Ariella keeps her eyes on Jace while I stare her down, trying to make her look at me.

"Hey, Jace."

"Ariella." Jace smiles and then he looks at Bridgette. "Bridge." He smirks, trailing his eyes down her figure. "Are you guys busy tonight? Ash and I were thinking about going to the new club downtown."

I furrow my eyebrows and look at Jace. "I didn't know you made these plans."

"Wow, is Ash turning down a chance to pick up girls at the club? Shocking," Ariella says while rolling her eyes.

Now all I want to do is wrap her hair around my fist and shove her against the lockers to show her how shocking I can fucking be.

Or maybe slap her ass until it's fucking red and she is aching.

"Don't be a brat."

She glares at me. "I'm not being a brat. Just saying how shocking it would be that you are turning down the chance to get your dick wet."

"Who said I go to clubs to get my dick wet?" I raise my eyebrows at her.

"Let's just say I know someone who was unlucky to be at a club with you."

"Are you sure that person wasn't you, Madden?" Her cheeks turn a bright red and my hand reaches out and pinches her cheek. I lean towards her and my lips ghost over her cheek. "I remember New York very well, Ariella. Stop being a brat or else next time I come inside your room, I won't give you that release that you are still desperately trying to get," I whisper in her ear before backing away from her.

"Screw you." Ariella scoffs and I chuckle.

"I'd like to see you try, Madden."

"My dad will destroy you, Ash. Start treading carefully."

Oh, I'll destroy Ariella's dad while destroying her in the process.

Sixteen

Ariella

The club we're at just opened up a few days ago. Jace knows about it because one of his friends got a job here as a bouncer.

Thankfully, we were able to get in for free and Jace also got us a table. Bridgette and I got ready at her house because she wanted me to raid her closet and choose something to wear from there.

I told her that her style and my style are completely different but she wouldn't take 'no' as an answer.

So now I am wearing a tiny black dress and white heels.

I'm not used to wearing heels and Bridgette wanted me to wear heels that were even higher but I told her that I need her smallest heels.

Jace ended up picking us up and when we walked outside I saw Ash sitting in the front.

Even though he was in the car I could feel his eyes burn holes in my chest.

I hate how he has this effect on me. It's strange that he is the only person to ever make me feel like that.

He didn't say anything to me when I sat in the back with Bridgette. Only Jace was talking to us the entire time.

Ash has been quiet since we arrived at the club. He hasn't said a word to me and he has only looked at me twice.

When we got to the club he opened the door for me and he gave me his hand before skimming his other around my waist.

For a second I pretended that Ash and I were something more and that we never even knew who our parents were.

Ash and I were just us.

For a second I believed that Ash and I could be real.

"Can I get you ladies anything to drink?" the server asks, making me break out of my thoughts and look at him.

"Can I just get two Manhattans and then two shots of your best vodka?" I ask and I look out of the corner of my eye and see Ash glaring at me.

I fully look at him while Bridgette orders. My eyes go down to Ash's hands and I see that they are formed in fists while he is glaring at me, giving me those murderous brown eyes of his.

"Thank you," Jace says, making the server leave.

"I think we should get a few drinks in our system and then dance," Bridgette says, looking at me. "I want to make sure I'm a little drunk for dancing."

"You're not fucking dancing with that skirt on," Jace demands, but Bridgette ignores him and rolls her eyes.

"Jace, let her have her fun. She will be fine," I assure Jace.

"And what about you, Madden? Gonna need someone to clean up your mess again?" Ash says, which makes me look at him.

My eyes turn into slits as I glare at him. "If you're going to be a fun killer then you might as well leave. No one wants to hang out with a bore."

Ash laughs and shakes his head lightly. Seeing him do that puts butterflies in my stomach.

"Careful, Madden."

The server comes back with the drinks before I can say anything back to Ash.

Bridgette and I take the shots together while the boys just watch us while sipping on the drinks they got.

Jace got some kind of mule and Ash got straight whiskey.

Bridgette and I talk while sipping on the drinks we got for ourselves.

I downed the first Manhattan and when I looked at Ash I saw him giving me a warning glare, which I ignored.

If he doesn't want to have fun, fine by me, but he will not ruin my night.

"Let's go dance now."

I pull Bridgette to stand up and she cheers before downing the rest of her drink.

"Don't embarrass yourselves!" Jace yells while Bridgette and I walk towards the dance floor where people are dancing against one another.

The song "I Feel It Coming" by The Weeknd is playing and everyone is dancing and swaying their hips to the music.

I wrap my arms around Bridgette and close my eyes while dancing with her. She is yelling out the lyrics to the song like a crazy person and wanting to jump up and down.

Bridgette and I dance very differently. She is a crazy, fun dancer while I like to dance slowly until I feel the music burn into my bones.

I love how we are so different yet so alike.

"God I hate it when you dance slow Ariella! Dance faster!" Bridgette yells.

"Just slow down and feel the music, Bridge. The club or song aren't going anywhere."

"You're no fun." She pouts and I laugh at her and remove my arms from her.

"Dance by yourself then. I'll have fun dancing by myself."

"I love you! Don't forget that!" she says before dancing up and down to the music.

While dancing I close my eyes again and softly hum to the beat of the song.

My hips sway side to side while I slide my hands down my body slowly.

Every song by The Weeknd always gets me in the mood. It's definitely not the right time for that.

Especially when he is here.

"Thinking about me, Madden?" I feel strong arms wrap around my waist and I lean my head back against Ash's shoulder. "Why are you always a temptation?"

I smile. "Because it's fun."

"You know what this reminds me of?" Ash asks while his hands lower to my hips, one of his hands grazing the skin below my dress. I feel chills run down my back and goosebumps explode on my skin. "That night in New York," Ash whispers in my ear. "My hands on you, feeling your soft skin while kissing your neck, Ariella." Ash places his lips on my neck and I feel sparks explode all over my body.

His voice against me feels like a sin, traveling down my body, filling me with shudders and excitement as I go back to that night.

Ash's hands on me feel like heaven.

The song playing is "I Feel It Coming" by The Weeknd. Listening to this song while having Ash's hands on me feels euphoric and makes me want to close my eyes as he touches me sensually.

"You like my hands on you, Ariella?" Ash whispers in my ear and I lean my head against his shoulder.

The song is slow but sensual and closing my eyes makes me feel the music in my bones.

My fingertips softly graze Ash's arm around me. "Yes," I whisper, moving my hips against his. Ash turns me around so that I am facing him. I laugh and wrap my hands around his neck. I lean towards him so that my lips are only a centimeter away from his. "You want to kiss me, Ash?"

"You don't ever have to ask me to put my lips on you," Ash says before smashing his lips on mine.

I kiss Ash like I need him, like I'd cease to exist if his lips were to stop kissing mine.

Kissing him was like a whole body feeling. My stomach erupted in butterflies, my heart melting in his hands, lips.

And like a craving finally filled, his lips kept caressing mine. There wasn't a care in the world except for his hands gripping me and holding me against his body. The longing and tension in the air.

He was mine and I was his.

There wouldn't be a thing to ruin that.

Right?

Seventeen

Ash

SUMMER

The thing about Ariella and the reason why I like her so much and feel so free around her is mainly her smile.

It's genuine and it's fucking beautiful. Seeing her smile is like a breath of fresh air and then her telling me to continue kissing her makes me feel the happiest I have ever been since I was a kid.

It feels good knowing that someone like her likes someone like me and actually wants to be around me.

I mean when we were at the club, Ariella and I didn't have one sip of alcohol and it feels like we both are just drunk off each other.

Euphoria is rushing through our veins and begging us to be closer to one another.

I remove my lips off of Ariella's making her whimper.

"I can't concentrate on unlocking the door if you keep kissing me like that," I say, my voice filled with lust.

"Like this?" Ariella whispers in my ear before placing her lips on my neck.

I hurry up and unlock the door as fast as I can. Once we are inside the room I grab Ariella by her thighs and wrap them around my waist as I walk to the bed.

She grinds against me once before moaning and removing her lips from mine so that she can look down.

She notices the bulge in my pants.

"This is what you do to me, Ariella. You make me fucking crazy." I rest my face into her neck. "You make me needy and desperate. I'm so fucking desperate to have you."

"Then have me," Ariella whispers softly.

I lean away from her neck and look at Ariella, her eyes are filled with that drunken look that's combined with lust. She looks almost breathless while staring back at me.

I walk towards the bed and place Ariella down. I take off her clothes one by one, taking my time to admire every inch of her body.

She is so beautiful that it almost hurts to look at her.

I kiss her while trailing my hand down her stomach. Ariella's legs rub against one another and her eyes fall closed.

I spread her thighs with one hand and straddle her hips. My hand slowly makes its way to her pussy. I run my finger down her folds and she moans in my mouth. Ariella is wet and hot. She is so wet, just like every other time I have touched her. I slowly thrust two fingers inside her. Ariella thrusts her hips into my hand while moaning. Her teeth bite my bottom lip slowly and I smile into the kiss.

She is just as fucking rough as I am, I bet.

I take out my fingers and rub her clit in fast circles. Ariella moans and her hips move against my hand between her legs.

She removes her lips from mine and her moans fill the air. She throws her head to the side while her chest rises from how hard she is breathing.

Ariella comes around my fingers, moaning and thrashing on the bed.

Seeing Ariella come on my fingers makes me feel so satisfied and hard at the same time. I want to fucking consume her and never let her go.

"Ash," she moans.

I press a kiss to her lips before getting off of her and backing away from the bed. I slowly take my clothes off and put a condom on while Ariella bites her bottom lip and crosses her legs.

Once I have all of my clothes off I walk towards Ariella and spread her legs and hold them against the bed.

"Don't hide from me Ariella, I want to see you." I say when she tries to cover her chest.

"I'm shy." Ariella's cheeks blush that cute pink color.

"Is this your first time?" She blushes and tries to hide her face. "I need to know, Ariella, so I know how hard I should go on you."

"You want to go hard on me?" Ariella widens her eyes and I nod my head.

I want to hurt Ariella. I like the thought of hurting her but only if it's bringing her and me pleasure.

Hurting myself and others has always brought me pleasure but I never acted on it because people would think I'm crazy, which I probably am a little crazy thanks to my bitch of a mother.

"I won't if you're a virgin, Ariella. So are you? Answer honestly." Ariella nods and I nod back at her. I release one of her legs and trail my hand slowly up her thigh. I feel goosebumps rise on her skin and she squirms against my hold making my eyes move to her face. She is watching my hand slowly trail up her thigh and to the spot between her legs. I cup her and she tries to force her legs shut but I don't let her. "Keep your legs open for me, Ariella." I run a finger in between her folds. "God, you're so wet for me, Ariella. Did you think about the different ways I would fuck you on the drive here?"

"Yes," Ariella moans as I rub her clit slowly.

Ariella squirms again and tries to move herself against my hand. I feel butterflies in my stomach explode as I watch her do that.

I swear that's the hottest thing I've ever seen anyone do.

I slide my fingers out of her and then trail my fingers up her body until they rest on her throat. I lean down and press my mouth on hers. Our bodies are sticking together and I can't help but grind against her.

Ariella's eyebrows furrow and she closes her eyes and leans her head back. I stroke her throat and then reach down with my other hand to gather some of her wetness and put it on my cock before pressing my hand against the mattress as I slowly slide inside her.

"Oh-oh, my god." Ariella moves her face to the side and her hands grip onto my shoulder, nails digging in my skin, getting me harder.

I push inside her slowly and then lean down to press our lips together again. "You feel-" I thrust inside her a little more, slowly going closer and closer, "so-" I thrust into her again, "so fucking good," I say before slamming the rest of me inside her.

Ariella screams and she wraps her legs around my waist. "Ash!"

I thrust in and out of her slow and deep, making her feel me but also making sure I'm not going too hard on her.

Ariella's moans fill the room making me smile and press my lips against hers.

I don't want everyone in the city to know what Ariella sounds like when she comes.

Her pussy is fluttering around me so fucking perfectly that I never want to leave.

"God, Ariella, you have no clue what you do to me. You fucking ruin me." I say, thrusting faster inside her.

I bring my hand that was on her throat to her breasts and play with her nipple, making Ariella arch her back so our chests meet.

Ariella wraps her arms around my neck and removes her lips from mine so that she can bite down on my shoulder.

She arches into me making me thrust deeper into her. I hit a spot that makes Ariella gasp and moan while she bites onto my shoulder even harder.

"Good girl," I say while hitting it, again, and again, and again, and fucking again.

"Ash-"

"Just a little bit longer baby."

I pull out all the way before thrusting back in harder. I reach my other hand down to her stomach and push down on her pelvis as I thrust in a few more times.

"Ah!" Ariella screams as she releases around me and I pull out and rip the condom off before releasing my load on her breasts.

Eighteen

Ariella

Bridgette and I have a psychology exam next class so we're studying in the library. We were going to go to Bridgette's house to study but what was the point if we were just going to drive back here?

Bridgette has a hard time studying so I am trying to help her concentrate but she just keeps looking around the library as if someone will come out and start shooting the whole place down.

She is a little nervous about the test but I told her she has no reason to worry because I know she will do amazing.

I mean, if I'm being honest, I'm having a hard time concentrating too.

After the club last night with Ash and Jace, my brain

hasn't been able to focus. The moment between Ash and I on the dance floor with his hands around me, touching me, caressing me, and his lips lightly kissing my neck keeps popping into my head and every time it does I can't help but blush at the moment.

I can't get Ash out of my mind and that's a huge problem because he is distracting me when he shouldn't be.

I shouldn't be thinking about him or how I want him or how much I missed him touching me and kissing me.

I can't help but wish he was touching me and kissing me right now.

That night I had a dream of him and me.

In the dream, he told me how much he wanted me and I swear I had a little flashback of the night we spent in the sheets after we got home from the club.

My first time.

He made that night so special and I miss him and what we had.

After that moment between us on the dance floor, I went back to the table while Ash went outside and I didn't even get to see him the rest of the night. He just up and left without Jace, Bridgette, and I. I haven't seen him since.

I hate how I am subconsciously looking for him too.

"Wait, I think that they might have a book here on these terms," Bridgette suggests.

She left her book at home and I never got the chance to buy one so I have been using hers for the semester.

When she told me she left her book I got so pissed because we had to use what we knew from our notes, which isn't really anything because Mr. Locke likes to mainly use class time for worksheets and not lectures or reviewing the book.

I roll my eyes at Bridgette and stand up. "I'll look for it. You keep writing down those definitions."

Bridgette rolls her eyes and I leave her alone and go to the section of the library that has all of the psychology books. The rows and rows of books are long and feel like they go on forever as I try to look for the book that Bridgette left at home.

I scan the different rows of books and look for the familiar green spine.

I turn the corner and start scanning the other shelf when I feel a tall and dark presence behind me.

It's familiar and I can't help but feel excited as I feel the presence's hands skim my back, trailing their fingers down my spine. Chills go down my spine and I want to rest my head against the shelf.

"Miss me, Madden?" Ash whispers in my ear, and I feel his warm, hard chest against my back and the vibration of his heartbeats.

I turn around to face Ash and when I do, he has a small smirk on his face while looking down at me.

Once upon a time, that smirk would bring me to my knees and I would do anything for him. Things between him and I are different though and we can't keep doing this.

"You need to stop, Ash. We can't-"

"We can and I will. Don't tell me what I'm not capable of, Ariella, because you know very well I always get what I want. I don't care how far I have to go to get it."

"If our fathers-"

"I don't care. Tell your father what I'm doing to you Ariella and I swear I'll ruin his life too. If I have to, I will go through my father to ruin his life."

"You can't do that."

"What did I say about you telling me what I can't do?" Ash asks while leaning into me and resting his hands on the shelf, burning his eyes into mine and making me want to surrender to him.

It's hard to not feel intimidated by Ash because his whole aura screams power and confidence. He knows he's the shit and he doesn't care about anyone who might be a threat to him.

"Are you going to hurt me, Ash?" I ask him, looking up at him while trying not to get scared and wanting to look away from him.

I hate how vulnerable he makes me.

Ash reaches down and skims his finger along my jaw while admiring every little freckle and detail on my face.

"I'm going to do more than hurt you, Ariella."

Ash trails his hand down my neck, lightly running his fingers down the valley of my breasts until they rest on the top of my skirt.

The way he is touching me reminds me of the times he used to touch me in the summer. Soft and caring even though Ash is anything but.

Ash has very violent and devious aspects about himself and I learned to love it throughout the summer. Sometimes I got scared but I also couldn't help but feel excited at the same time.

Today, I am just wearing a black tennis skirt and I wish that I wasn't because as I look into Ash's eyes I already know exactly what he is thinking about doing to me against this shelf in the library.

"Not in the library, Ash," I whisper while resting my hand on his.

He looks at me for just a moment. I can tell that it's more of a warning glance to tell me to let him do whatever he wants to do with me or else he won't let me have that release he knows I am desperately waiting for.

"So if we weren't in the library you would let me touch you?" he asks, raising his eyebrow.

I was about to answer but I shut my mouth. What the hell am I going to say?

Lie and make him touch me even rougher and more aggressively or just say yes and tell the truth about how I want him to touch me so badly, just not in public. I am scared of getting caught but at the same time, the thought of it thrills me.

"If you don't answer I am just going to end up fucking you instead of just putting my fingers in your pussy so pick, Ariella."

The butterflies in my stomach swarm and it makes me want to punch my stomach to make them go away.

How does he do it? I need to know how he can make me beg for him and want him like I am desperate.

Since I don't answer fast enough, Ash shrugs and he puts his hand down my skirt making me yelp.

"Okay, yes. Yes, I would."

"Yea?" Ash says while looking down at his hand in my skirt.

His hand is cupping me and I feel him squeeze my pussy making me close my eyes and rest my head on Ash's shoulder. "Yes, Ash."

I feel Ash's lips press against my neck, lightly sucking the skin. My eyes roll back and I wrap my arms around Ash's neck to hold him for support. My legs feel like they are going to give out any minute making me fall down.

"You're mine, Ariella," he says before thrusting a long finger inside me. Ash keeps his face in my neck as I form an 'O' with my lips. I buck my hips against his hand, forcing him to move his finger inside me farther and give me some sort of relief. "You're mine to touch." Ash is just using one finger and all I want to do is feel relief. "Mine to fuck," he says, rubbing my clit at the same time while thrusting in and out of me with his finger. "Mine to ruin."

"Ash, fuck," I whimper before he thrusts two more fingers inside me.

I grip his hand as he moves his fingers in and out. "And mine to own," Ash says before pinching my clit, making me release all over his fingers.

Ash rubs me until he gets my release all over his fingers, while also making me want to beg him to do more.

How is it possible for me to finish that fast?

With Ash out of all people?

He gets his hand out of my skirt and what I don't expect is for him to put all three fingers that were inside me, inside his mouth.

He sucks my release off his fingers, not even sparing a glance at me as he does it.

My legs feel weak as I watch him do that. Now all I want him to do is take me in the library.

I don't even care who watches.

Oh my god.

I push Ash away from me and look around to see if there is anyone around us in the walkway. Luckily there isn't but that doesn't mean someone didn't hear us.

"Stop being embarrassed and get over here, Ariella."

"No. You are seriously insane," I say, pushing away from Ash and walking towards where I came from.

"You didn't say that when you were coming all over my hand!"

I ignore him and walk back to the table where Bridgette is still waiting.

I fix my skirt, hair, and shirt while walking toward her.

When she sees me, she furrows her eyebrows. "What took you so long?"

"I was having trouble finding the book."

"So you didn't find it?" Bridgette looks at my hands in front of me.

I hide my hands behind my back. "'No, I wasn't able to," I say before sitting down next to her.

Bridgette was about to look away and focus on her notes but I see her eyes go to the side of my neck. "You have a little something, Ariella," she says, pointing to the side of my neck.

I feel anxiety cripple inside me and I reach my neck to feel what she is talking about but I don't feel anything serious.

Bridgette shakes her head before pulling out her phone and snapping a picture of my neck before showing it to me.

He gave me a fucking hickey.

Nineteen

Ariella

My eyes trail all over Ash's face. I still can't understand how calm and soft he looks when he is sleeping.

The way his eyes sometimes flutter, making me assume he is dreaming about something. One of his strong, muscular arms are wrapped around my waist while his other arm is resting on his pillow next to his head.

The sheets are down to his waist making his v-line pop out. My stomach fills with butterflies once again knowing that what is lower was inside me not too long ago.

For the past five or so minutes I have just been admiring him. He is too beautiful to not look at.

I honestly don't get how someone can be real and sleep in bed with me while looking like him.

After three rounds, Ash decided it was time to go to

bed. I didn't know that he would have that much stamina. After the first time, I felt like that alone was enough but then he said, "Want me to show you some real fun?" and then he thrusted inside of me again and again until I came for the second, third, fourth, and fifth time.

My legs were shaking by the time we were done.

Ash is relentless and never took a break to even catch his breath. This man could spend hours pleasing me and I wouldn't even be able to catch up with him. He explores places that have never been touched before by anyone and it was special to me.

This was never supposed to happen.

This wasn't a part of the deal.

We broke the deal.

The feel of hands on my cheek makes me focus back on Ash who is now awake and has his eyes on me. He looks tired as he stares at me with those soft eyes.

"Morning," Ash says in a deep, husky voice that makes me feel vibrations down between my legs. "How'd you sleep?"

"Good," I mumble. Ash and I stare at each other for a few minutes more before I decide to break the moment and say, '"We shouldn't have had sex last night."

"Do you regret it?" Ash removes his hand from my cheek making me yearn for his touch some more.

"Yes-well no, not really-"

"Well, whatever you're overthinking about doesn't matter."

"Ash, after this summer is over we can't be together anymore. I thought you knew that. That wasn't a part of the deal. I was suppose to have sex with a stranger, not you."

Ash sighs before moving the sheets off of him so that he can get out of bed. My eyes land on his butt and I can't help but admire the toned muscles in there and down his muscular thighs.

"Is that what you were thinking about the whole time I was inside you?" Ash raises his eyebrow at me while leaning down and grabbing his briefs on the floor.

"No. I loved last night." I sit up and hold the sheets to my chest. "It's just I have to think about what happens after, Ash. You aren't emotionally available, you told me that and then I told you that I am not trying to get hurt and that I just wanted someone to experience firsts with me."

"Ariella, you were never a temporary matter for me. I did this with you because I liked you as a person," Ash says, getting more and more frustrated. "I kept doing this with you because I fucking like you, Ariella. Not because you were part of some dumbass plan that you are thinking about in your fucking head!"

"Ash-"

"I know that you are trying to protect your heart, I get

that, I do, but I also know that last night is something I do want to keep doing with you."

"I can't keep having sex with you. It will make leaving you just as hard."

"Are you not listening to anything I'm saying?" Ash says and I look down at his hands and see them forming into fists.

"We still have the rest of the summer left. What happens when it's done? You are going to stay here and I am going to stay in California. Long distance won't work. I don't want to do that."

"What if I told you that I am going to stay?" he says before crossing his hands over his chest, making his biceps ten times bigger.

I laugh.

I can't help but laugh.

He can't just stay with me in California.

"You need to stop joking around."

"I'm not."

"Ash-"

All of a sudden Ash is on me.

Ash's hand is on my throat, not choking me, just keeping his strong hand on my throat. His legs are around mine and my back is against the bed.

"You're mine, Ariella. I meant what I said last night. Now that I have you, I'm not letting you go. I don't care about your stupid deal or your stupid overthinking. I don't even care about your fucking past relationship trauma because none of them can measure up to me, even if they just gave you a first kiss or make-out. You're mine and I'm not letting you go. Understand?"

Some girls would find this possessive act very concerning and would probably run for the hills but I can't help but want to cross my legs after hearing everything he is saying to me.

So instead of running away and squirming in his hold I wrap my arms around Ash and pull him down so that his lips can meet mine.

Ash's tongue licks my lips before biting down and thrusting his tongue to slide against mine.

His hand on my throat tightens lightly before he removes his hand and trails it down my body.

"Yes," I moan.

Ash slides his hand beneath the covers and his hand rests against my stomach. "Glad we understand each other." He rips the covers off of me and I gasp and remove my lips from his. "I say we spend all day in the hotel room, order food, and then we can do some of your crazy bucket list items tomorrow."

I smile at Ash and nod my head before I feel his lips smash against mine.

TWENTY
ASH

Watching her dance with guys to make me jealous is working. If she was trying to accomplish just that then its most certainly fucking working.

I feel like breaking glass with my knuckles and then watching blood run down my arm from that.

And it's all because Ariella Madden feels like pushing my fucking buttons.

Jace invited me to some stupid party and at first I told him to fuck off and that I just felt like staying home, but then he mentioned that Ariella and Bridgette were going to be there.

I had to go. If Ariella was there, I just had to go and watch her. I need to see how she acts when I'm not around.

Right when I walked inside the party my eyes immediately found her in the living room with Bridgette as they talked to these guys. I didn't show I was pissed when she looked over but Bridgette was smirking while watching Jace get pissed off.

I don't know how long they are going to play this game for.

After getting drinks from the kitchen I noticed Ariella started dancing and that brings us to this moment. Me watching her dance with some guy she thinks is going to make her forget all about me. But I see the way her eyes go to me every once in a while.

The way her thighs would press together when her eyes trailed down my body. I love the way she looks at me. She looks at me like she wants me to own her entire world and she is probably thinking she is looking at me like she hates my guts and wishes I was dead.

I see the guy's hand trail down her thigh and I try to focus on the way my fingernails dig into my skin. I can't go over there.

Not yet.

I'll let her have her fun for a little bit before I punish her in one of the rooms upstairs.

"You're a lucky guy." I turn my head and look at a guy with long brown hair.

He looks like the guy from Scooby Doo with weird messy hair. "Excuse me?"

He nods his head to the dance floor where Ariella is. "That's your girl?"

I turn my head to look at Ariella who is still dancing with the guy. "Yea."

"Seems like whatever she is trying to do it's working," he comments.

"She likes playing games with me." I look back at the guy as he brings a beer bottle to his lips.

"I can tell, even though she's dancing with another guy, that she belongs to you. It's obvious in the way she keeps looking over at you."

I look away from him again and see the guy she is dancing with, whispering in her ear. A flash of fear appears in her eyes and I don't spare another minute getting out of my chair and walking past the crowd of people to get to her.

When I walk up to her, her eyes meet mine and her head tilts up. The guy stops traveling his hands down her body and he raises an eyebrow at me.

"Sorry, can't you see I'm kind of busy?"

"What you're currently touching, belongs to me. I'd like it if you stop touching her now."

The guy furrows his eyebrows. "Sorry man but she came onto me."

"Did she?" I look down at Ariella and see her force her eyes to look anywhere else but me. "Well, I'm here now so I'm going to take her off your hands," I say before pulling her out of his hold.

Ariella's hands immediately grip my shirt when she crashes into my chest. I ignore the guy's yells as I walk out of the crowd.

"Ash-"

"Shut up," I say while making my way towards the upstairs.

Ariella stays silent the entire way upstairs. I don't know where Bridgette is or where Jace is and I don't care.

All I care about is getting Ariella to understand that no one touches her but me.

I eventually find a door that's unlocked. When I walk in, it's dark and the only light that is visible is the moonlight shining through the window. I let go of Ariella and make my way to the bed before sitting down.

"Why do you always ruin things for me? You know I was having fun?"

"Yea I could tell," I say, sarcasm laced in my tone. "Come here."

She furrows her eyebrows at me and crosses her arms over her chest. "No."

My jaw clenches and I nip at my bottom lip.

I fucking love our arguing and how we fight. It turns me on but sometimes I wish I could strangle her to make her understand.

"I said come over here. I won't ask very nicely again," I say in a low tone, still demanding and rough.

"Ash-"

"Get over here before I drag out your punishment for making someone touch something that's mine."

Ariella leans against the wall and sets her eyes on me.

Ariella is a good girl, you can tell from the way she speaks to you or shows off her smile. But when it comes to me, she can be so fucking cruel and bad. I know she is trying to appear confident and strong but I also know, secretly, she is so innocent and way too good for the kind of person I am.

I get up from the bed and my eyes trail down her legs. Her legs that look so perfectly bare and shaven. They are glistening from the moonlight because of the kind of lotion she puts on. She is so perfect.

Even when she pisses me off.

Ariella keeps her eyes on me the entire time I make my way to her. When her head lifts up to make eye contact with me, I see a challenge and innocence mixed.

I place my hands on her waist and press my hips into hers.

She'll get her punishment in another way.

I lean in and press my lips softly to her neck. Ariella lets me and she melts into putty when I trail kisses all over her neck, slowly and gently. I lick my way up to the spot below her ear. Ariella moans and her hands go to grip my t-shirt.

"Ash," she says, breathlessly.

I lick her skin and then suck at the spot below her ear. She raises one of her legs around my waist, which I go to grip.

It's perfect that she is wearing a skirt.

I trail one of my hands towards the inside of her skirt and I feel the fabric of her underwear. While still kissing and sucking on her neck I unwrap her leg around my waist and pull down her underwear until they slide down her legs.

"Are you wet, Madden?" I whisper in her ear before kissing her soft spot.

"Ash-"

"Answer me," I demand, running my hands down her waist to touch her thighs.

Her head leans back and hits the wall. "Yes, please touch me," she whimpers.

One of my hands dances towards the spot between her thighs and I run a finger in between her folds. She's soaked and so fucking warm.

I could slip three fingers in and it would be so easy to make her come.

With my other hand I undo my belt and unbutton my jeans. I pull out my cock that's already swollen and hard, wanting to be inside Ariella.

Not yet, though.

I stroke her between her folds as I rub the head of my cock, back and forth. The same motion as I'm stroking

Ariella. She forces her hips closer to mine, making my cock make contact with her wet cunt.

"Ari, stop moving," I say while keeping my eyes trained on the way my fingers play with her pussy.

"What are you doing?" she says as I see her look down at what I'm doing. "Put it inside, Ash. Please."

I lick my lips before leaning closer to her. I rest my forehead on hers and direct my cock in between her folds. I nip my bottom lip, concentrating on the way she feels around me.

I'm not even inside her and I already want to come and mark her.

I lean down and press a kiss to the spot below her ear. "If you move one inch, I'm going to pull out."

She nods her head but the way her eyes flutter under her closed eyelids tells me she can't even concentrate on what I'm saying.

I thrust my hips against her slowly, rubbing my cock along her folds. The way her silky wetness covers my cock makes me want to bust inside her. I grunt as I keep moving inside her, rubbing my cock against her wet and warm pussy. I play with her clit with my cock making Ariella moan and shift her hips against mine.

"What did I say?" I hiss, grabbing Ariella's throat. "You want me to pull out?" I ask, tilting her head to make her look up at me.

Her face shows pure ecstasy and I'm not even inside

her. Her mouth is open and she is panting hard making me even harder.

All I want to do is push inside her and make her scream.

I want to show everyone at this stupid party that she's mine.

I squeeze her throat lightly. *Mine.*

I've always been a selfish motherfucker, but when it comes to Ariella, I'm so selfish that I'll kill anyone who fucking touches her like this.

Which reminds me that I need to take care of that sorry fuck downstairs after I'm done with her.

I thrust against her fast and by the way Ariella moans and grips onto me I can tell she is close.

I force myself a foot away from her and I grip my cock in my hands, stroking myself harshly. I squeeze myself tightly and as I feel my release coming closer, I point my cock towards Ariella's pussy, shooting my load on her.

My hands slow as my release shoots out to Ariella.

I hear her gasp and breath harshly, slowly realizing that I just edged her again.

I grip my cock in my hands, slowing down my breathing. I open my eyes and look at Ariella who looks like she just got fucked thoroughly even though I barely even touched her.

With my hands at least.

"Why did you do that?" she asks, slowly coming back to reality.

I smirk and let go of my cock. "Because I felt like it." I walk towards her and pick up her underwear from the floor and put them in my pocket. "Besides, that was your punishment for that stunt you did downstairs. You're lucky I didn't take out my anger on your ass, Madden." Her face turns a shade darker. I fix my jeans and my belt. "Next time I see someone touch you like that again, I'll fucking bring them inside a room and fuck you in front of them before banging their head against the ground so they forget seeing you naked and coming around me."

I don't wait for her shocked response. Instead, I leave her in the room and make my way downstairs to where that motherfucker was.

I go to the kitchen and once my eyes land on his, I don't hesitate to walk closer to him and swing my fist into his face.

TWENTY-ONE
ASH

Tonight, Ariella is holding a little hangout at her house. She invited Jace and Bridgette over so that they could all watch a movie and then Jace ended up inviting me over.

He told me that he was going out tonight and I asked him where he's going and he wouldn't tell me so I threatened him with Bridgette and that guy spilled that he was going to Ariella's house for a movie night.

Ariella obviously didn't tell me anything because I know that I am definitely not her favorite person right now.

I don't care that she didn't invite me over.

Sometimes I think that Ariella forgets who I am and what I'm capable of.

After Ariella's punishment during the party the other night, I beat the hell out of the motherfucker who touched her.

I remember Jace and a few other guys pulling me off and then Jace telling me to go home before someone called the cops.

Ariella was on the top of the staircase watching me walk out of the house.

During the past few days after that, I tried to avoid her. I just needed some space from her before I saw her again.

Ariella makes me do irrational things.

It's good she didn't see me punching that guy. I wouldn't have wanted her to see me doing that. I never liked Ariella seeing me in that kind state. I would hate to see how she would react if she were to ever find out what I do to the mirrors.

It's quiet when I walk inside her house. I used the backdoor instead of the front door. Jace told me that he and Bridgette are on their way.

While walking through the hallway towards the living room, my eyes scan the portraits on the wall. A lot of the pictures feature Ariella and Bridgette posing. Some of the pictures show Jace wrapping his arms around Bridgette and Ariella.

Most of the pictures show Ariella when she was a

toddler and then an older looking woman who looks just like Ariella.

I have never seen pictures of Ariella's mom before but I'm assuming that this is her.

Ariella's mom has long golden-brown hair and her eyes are hazel with specs of blue. I know Ariella got her eye color from her father because her eyes remind me of his cold gaze which shows no mercy to anyone.

In a few pictures I see her father but most of the pictures she has with her parents are when she was younger.

I study another picture of Ariella and her father standing side by side, smiling.

They have the same fucking smile too.

I hate it.

I feel the need to drive my fist into the wall and ruin all of these pictures that contain Ariella.

I want to erase the need that I have for her and put it all into a single punch.

"What are you doing here?" I turn my head and see Ariella leaning against the wall with her arms crossed over her chest making her breasts pop out a little bit.

I straighten my back and walk away from the pictures. "I was invited. You didn't know?"

"No, because I am the one who did the inviting, Ash. I didn't invite you over. Leave."

I walk towards Ariella until our chests are just a few

inches away from one another. "I think I'll stay," I say before brushing past her to walk towards the living room.

"You can't be here!" I hear Ariella yell from behind me.

"Ariella, last time I checked you don't have any authority over me," I say as I sit down on her couch and lean into the cushions.

Ariella comes into my view, blocking the TV, and still crossing her arms over her fucking chest.

"You have no right to be here, get out."

I take my time to admire Ariella.

She is wearing gray pajama shorts with a white tank top. Her nipples are poking through the thin material of the shirt.

I feel blood rush down to my cock and the jeans I'm wearing start to suddenly feel tighter.

All I want to do is pull her on my lap, rip that shirt off her chest and then suck and lick her breasts until they are bruised.

"How about you stop being such a brat and treat your guest with some respect?"

"You aren't a guest." She glares at me and raises one of her eyebrows, basically telling me to get my ass out of here.

Like fucking hell.

I'm going to have some fun tonight.

Ariella and I stare at each other for a few minutes and

in those few minutes it feels like time stops between us and we are back at the hotel from last summer.

I feel my eyes soften as I look at her. All of that tension and the feeling of violence leaves my body as I look at her.

Her eyes that are filled with heat and hate staring at mine calm me. Ariella in general calms me.

She could be in a room filled with thousands of beautiful people and my eyes would never leave hers.

"What's up motherfuckers!" I hear Jace yell, making the moment between Ariella and I break. I stop looking at her and turn my head and see Jace walking inside Ariella's house with a bottle of his favorite vodka and a big bag of chips. Jace looks between Ariella and then me before looking at Ariella. "Shit."

"Did you invite him?" Ariella asks while pointing her finger at me.

"He's my best friend Ariella, plus I have a good reason," Jace says, trying to explain himself.

"Like what?" Ariella raises her eyebrow and tilts her head to the side trying to appear more intimidating towards Jace.

Jace's eyes go to me before going back to meeting Ariella's. "Why are you guys so intimidating?"

"Jace?"

"I'm here so there's no point in trying to get rid of me, Madden," I look back at Ariella and then get comfortable against the pillows and then spread my legs. Ariella's eyes trail down my body before moving up to meet my eyes. Heat is filled in her eyes and I just wish that she could fucking act on her lust. "So, are we going to spend the whole night bitching or are we going to watch a movie?"

Ariella scoffs and then she walks away.

Bridgette arrives around fifteen minutes later.

Bridgette puts her stuff in Ariella's room while Jace and Ariella prepare all the snacks. They put them on the coffee table in front of the couch.

We all agree on a movie, DareDevil starring Ben Affleck and Jennifer Garner. Jace gushes over Jennifer Garner and how hot she is in this movie while Bridgette rolls her eyes and sits as far away from Jace as possible on the floor.

Ariella is about to sit down next to Bridgette on the floor, far away from me, but instead I grab her wrist and make her sit on the floor between my legs.

She glares at me before trying to move but I force her to sit down. She keeps squirming so I lean forward, and my lips touch her ear.

"If you keep being a brat tonight, I'll bring you over my lap and smack your ass until it's red and burning, Ariella."

Ariella glares at me but she doesn't squirm anymore. Instead, she relaxes and rests her body in between my legs.

While watching the movie I keep looking down at Ariella.

Every time I look at her, all I can see is her that summer.

I feel like she is the same girl I met that summer but then I also hear my father yelling in my ear about Ariella.

I sometimes don't even know what to think anymore, in moments like this for example.

Twenty-Two

Ariella

Summer

Ash and I got back from New York a few days ago and those past few days I have just been locking myself in my house.

I am ignoring Ash's text messages because I am too scared to face him. I just feel like things are different now that we are back in California.

Ash has been calling me and sending me messages since he dropped me off home from the airport. I'm surprised he hasn't barged in my house and demanded answers from me.

Ever since I had sex with him, I feel different. I don't know if it's a good different or a bad different.

It's definitely not a bad different now that I think

about it but it can't be good because then feelings get involved and that's what I'm trying to prevent.

We only had sex that one night but the rest of the nights we did other things, and kissed.

We kissed a lot.

And I can't help but like it a lot.

He makes me feel needy and desperate for more and that's a scary thing for me.

I have to remember that he wants more, not just a stupid summer fling anymore like when we first started this.

But I can't help but try my best to keep my guard up. I want to have more with Ash but I'm scared.

Bridgette managed to call me last night and tell me how her summer is going. She told me all about her England summer fling and how hot he is. She found out that I went to New York and she was begging for me to tell her who I went with.

I'm definitely not giving her any of that information.

She is having fun in England though. Her parents are taking her to the soccer game that they are holding out there. I'm not much of a fan of soccer though.

I was always into volleyball.

The sound of banging on my door makes me lift my head from my pillow and look at the window across from me.

I get up and wrap my throw blanket around my body as I stand near the window and look outside.

My eyes widen when I see a familiar black motorcycle parked in the front.

"Ariella! Get your ass down here and unlock the fucking door!" Ash yells loudly. I squeal and run out of my room, downstairs and in front of the locked front door. It's locked. Thank God. "Ariella! If you don't open the door, I swear to God I'll break it down!"

Thank God my father isn't home.

He's been in France for the past month because of some vacation he is taking with some mystery girl who happens to be the girl he spent the last few weeks of my mother's life with before she died.

I rush to open the door and when it's wide open my eyes go straight towards Ash whose eyes are filled with darkness and heat.

So much darkness and heat.

"Ash-"

"Three fucking days, Ariella," Ash says before taking one step inside of the house. "Three days, no call and no text from you." Once he is fully inside of the house, he closes the door behind him and he rips the blanket away from my body and turns me around so that he can pin me against the front door. "Three fucking days, Ariella. Tell me what you were doing in those three days and why you didn't text me or call me once. Why?"

Seeing Ash like this, with his whole body tensed and his eyes filled with a darkness I've never seen before. His jaw is clenched and his hands in fists.

I notice the scratches and cuts on his knuckles making my eyebrows furrow.

It makes me want to kiss every single inch of his body and caress the tense muscles that are probably aching.

I reach down and take his hand in mine, inspecting the small cuts. "What did you do to your hands?" I ask but Ash takes his hand away from mine making me look up at him.

"Fuck the hands, Ariella. Answer the fucking questions."

I glare at him and cross my arms over my chest. "I needed some time to myself alone. You are crowding my space and my mind. I just need to breathe Ash."

"So, you just ignore my texts and calls? At least fucking tell me that you want space from me Ariella, not just ghost me." Ash's hand cups my cheek softly and he lifts my head to make me look up at him. "Is it because we had sex?" I feel my cheeks heat up and I try to turn my head to not look at Ash but he doesn't let me. "Tell me."

I sigh and rest my head against the wall behind me. "I just- I'm scared," I admit. "I've never done this before and I just don't want to get hurt. That's the whole reason why I decided to do the summer bucket list with someone I won't have to see ever again."

Ash sighs and shakes his head lightly as he caresses my cheek with his fingers.

Overthinking has always been a big problem for me. I've never been the type of person to think about things rationally because I try to prepare myself for the worse. I'm used to bad things happening to me ever since mom died.

And one of the things my mother always told me to guard myself around was boys because they are the most dangerous type of hurt.

They can wreck your heart and tear your soul in half without even realizing.

My mother and father have always had a good relationship but it took them a while to get there. My mom got hurt a lot in the process but she told me that she wouldn't change a thing because she loved my dad with all her heart.

I know my father loved her so much. He loved her entirely and truly. Ever since she died, he lost a big part of himself. I lost him.

What she said about boys scared me and I have always tried to steer clear of them, even though they are nice to look at, it's better to just admire them from afar.

Ash takes his hand off my cheek and he pushes away from me. "Get dressed. I want to take you somewhere."

He tells me he will wait outside while I get ready.

I decide to wear a pair of jeans with a black muscle

shirt. I pull my hair in a ponytail and then run downstairs while grabbing my bag and then locking the door before walking towards Ash's car.

"Where are we going?" I ask Ash as he hands me his helmet.

"Be patient. You'll see."

After the helmet is one, I sit on the back of his bike and hold onto his waist.

As Ash drives my eyes go down to his hand on my thigh.

I notice the bruises and the small cuts on his knuckles. All I want to do is bring them to my lips and make him feel better.

I don't want him to hurt.

There is a darkness in Ash that I haven't met yet. I know that I will probably be scared of it and that this darkness inside him will probably destroy me.

I can see that darkness in him when he looks at me whenever he is mad or frustrated. I saw it the night he went to jail and the night he was talking to me a little bit about his dad. I see it whenever he is touching me with rough caresses and then dirty words.

But I know that I won't see it until it's too late.

I'm scared but I know I have to be patient for him to peel back those layers and show me that darkness.

By the time Ash parks his bike it's dark outside.

The sun was setting about the same time we were leaving.

I look around us and I see a bunch of greenery and trees.

Goosebumps rise on my skin and I try not to freak out as I overthink about what Ash could have brought me out here for.

He's going to kill me.

"Come on."

Ash is about to get off the bike but I stop him. "Wait." Ash looks back at me and he furrows his eyebrows. "Why are we here? Why did you bring me here?"

"Because I want to show you something." Ash says before getting off. Ash holds my hands and helps me get off the bike. I look around me and you can't see anything other than the trees. He takes off the helmet and rests it on the handle. "Come on," Ash says, offering his hand to me.

I grab his hand and he starts walking forward. We walk up steps and Ash tightens his hold on my hand, making sure to hold me close to him.

"Ash, where are we?"

"You'll see," Ash answers while still walking up the steep steps that are filled with dirt. When Ash finally does stop, I look up and see a huge tree with stairs around the trunk. "Come on."

Ash walks forwards, towards the tree.

We walk up the steps, with steady feet. Ash makes sure to not let me go as we walk up slowly.

When we get closer to where Ash is walking, I see a door come into my view.

A tree house.

Ash opens the door and he lets me walk through the front door first. I look around the house and admire the old wood and the little knick knacks.

I walk around the house while Ash just leans against the door and watches me admire it.

"What is this place?" I ask before moving my gaze to the view outside.

I walk towards the open window that showcases the beautiful lights of the city and then the acres of land in front of us.

"I found this tree house a few years ago when I came to visit California with my mom and dad."

That's the first time I've heard Ash mention his mom.

I can't help but wonder why he doesn't talk about her.

"How did you find it?"

Ash stands next to me with his hands resting on the window seat. "I needed some time away to clear my head from what was happening at home so I found his house and just slept here for a few days before going back to the hotel."

My eyes don't move away from his hands. I want to

take all of Ash's pain away and hold onto it so that he doesn't have to hurt anymore.

I reach over and touch Ash's knuckles with my finger. Ash looks down at our hands and watches how I trace every cut and every line.

The cuts he had from New York are almost healed. He didn't get a lot of damage from punching that guy but these cuts are different.

They look deeper and I just know that a lot of blood was coming out of Ash's hands.

"What happened Ash?"

He takes his hand away from my finger and turns around so that he can face me. "Ariella." He says making me look at him instead of his hands. "You never leave my mind. All I think about is you and I can't help but not feel something for you."

My heart beats hard against my chest.

How is he able to do it?

I take a step towards Ash and wrap my arms around his neck and pull him closer to me so I can hug him.

"Just don't hurt me, Ash. I need my heart to be intact."

"I promise Ariella."

TWENTY-THREE
ARIELLA

PRESENT

The smell of weed fills the air of my kitchen as I mix the weed butter into the brownie batter.

Thankfully everyone is upstairs sleeping.

Bridgette is sleeping in my room while Jace and Ash are sleeping in the guest rooms upstairs.

I couldn't sleep and I ended up finding a stash of weed in my room so I just had the random idea to make weed brownies.

The others will enjoy them tomorrow and they can take them home with them.

Bridgette fell asleep on the floor so Jace took her upstairs to go to sleep. After the movie we all kind of just went into the rooms. I showed Jace and Ash where they could sleep and then I joined Bridgette in the room.

I was reading on my phone for a good hour before I got bored and decided to bake when I found the weed.

My mom taught me how to bake stuff with weed in it. It's one of my golden memories with my mom. She always loved cooking and one time she found a small baggy in my backpack and then decided to use that to bake brownies with weed in them.

It became a thing me and mom did once every other month when dad would leave for business trips. But if I wanted to do the weed brownies with her, she told me that I had to not do any drugs or smoke weed without her. She told me she didn't want me doing that because she wanted me to focus on my school and that drugs can become a huge distraction.

Along with boys.

"Smells like you're having fun."

I turn my head to the entrance of the kitchen and I see Ash leaning against the open doorway.

I managed to find Ash's sweatpants and shirt that he left here once during the summer.

I really didn't want to give them to him because the sweatpants are really comfortable and the shirt is one of my favorite shirts to sleep in, but I wouldn't tell Ash that. So, I just gave them to him.

Ash isn't wearing the shirt though, just the sweat pants.

I try not to ogle his chest and abs for too long.

His body looks like it was sculpted by God's specific hands. God took his time on Ash, one look and that's obvious.

My eyes go to the familiar tattoo on his ribcage and my stomach once again fills with butterflies as I stare at the tattoo. All of a sudden, the tattoo I have on the side of my ribcage starts to burn.

I know Ash can feel me staring at the tattoo but he won't bring it up, because if he did then we would have to actually have that conversation that we both don't want to have.

"Weed brownies." I say before looking away from Ash and going back to mixing the batter.

I hear Ash's footsteps come closer until I feel his body right next to mine. His natural body heat against my bare arms makes me want to curl into his chest and hug him forever.

His embrace might be one of the safest places I have been. He always felt so safe and even now I know that he won't let anything hurt me.

Whenever I am with Ash, I know that he will protect me from anything except himself, which I sometimes don't mind because I have always felt the pleasure rush through my veins and excited when it came to Ash.

"I remember you telling me about how your mom and you used to make baked goods with weed in them."

I can't help but smile.

Yea, I remember telling that to Ash. I loved talking about my mom with Ash because he just listened and asked questions. He never pushed me too far about her or her death. He never made me feel uncomfortable when it came to talking about her.

I stop mixing the brownies and start to put the mix into the baking dish.

"Cooking makes me feel closer to her. I feel like cooking and doing things that I used to do with her, makes me feel like she is here with me."

"I know. I remember you told me," Ash says. "I remember you telling me all of the bakery desserts you used to make and then the adventures you went on. I know you made that bucket list for the summer so that you can somewhat feel closer to her and like she is actually here with you, experiencing those some of those things."

I look away from the baking dish and focus my attention on Ash.

I can't believe he remembers all of that.

I have to remind myself that he doesn't care though and he never will.

That's not who Ash is.

"I didn't think you would remember all of that." I put the mixing dish down and then put the baking dish inside the oven.

"I remember every little detail about you, Ariella. I just don't show it."

"Why not?"

"Are we both ready to have that conversation right now?" Ash says, making me look up at him. He is leaning the side of his body against the counter and his arms are crossed over his chest making his biceps appear ten times larger. "Stop eye fucking me and answer the question. Are we both ready to have that conversation? Because I will gladly start talking."

I look away from Ash and move to put the mixing dish inside the sink. "No, we're not."

"How do you know?"

I turn around and face Ash. "Because you have this stupid grudge against me and you want to, and I quote, 'ruin me' when I have done nothing wrong."

Ash walks up to me until his chest is pressed against mine. The thin tank top I'm wearing fails to hide how hard my nipples probably are and how hot Ash's chest is against mine.

His hard, rippled body pressed against mine, making me want to curl inside of him and never leave his embrace.

"My plan has always been to ruin you, Ariella, but I was never meant to hurt you."

"They are both still the same thing."

"No, not to me." Ash leans in a little closer to me. "You were never meant to not be mine, Ariella. I knew from the moment I saw you in that bookstore that you and I were always meant to be together."

I can't trust him.

He is a boy who will break my heart and tear my soul in half like my mom said. Ash is the one guy who I, out of all people, should have no reason to be near.

He will just bring darkness in my life.

"Well, I'm not going to be. Not when you are having a grudge against me. And let's also not forget about how you have your own demons and darkness to fix before we talk about last summer and what happened."

Ash's lips turn in a smirk. "I thought you liked my darkness, Madden?"

Ash leans close and his lips ghost over mine. The way his breath is hitting my lips makes me want to lean into him and close my eyes to absorb him.

But he only brings trouble and heart break. That's what Ash does.

I push Ash away from me. "Leave me alone and don't touch me."

"You can only control this thing for so long, Ariella."

"We'll see about that Ash," I tell him before I see a ghost of a smile on Ash's lips.

I just hope I don't fall into his trap again like I did last summer, because if I do, then it's game over and he will ruin me like he wants to.

TWENTY-FOUR
ARIELLA

PRESENT

Liam's eyes haven't stopped looking at me since I entered the classroom.

Almost no one is here, and I just got a text from Bridgette that she can't come today because she woke up with a cold.

I cursed at her through the phone, wishing that she could come today.

Usually, I meet Bridgette in class early so we can talk or she picks me up from my house and we just chat while driving to school. I decided to drive myself today because after classes I have my annual appointment with my gynecologist.

I always have these appointments. Ever since I started my period, I've been seeing her. She makes sure I am healthy and we always catch up when I see her. Her and my mom went to school together so they were pretty close and I trust her a lot.

"Ariella." I lift my head from my hands and see Liam looking at me. "Can you come here for a quick second?" Liam asks, which makes me wipe the sweat from my hands on my thighs and stand up.

I walk towards his desk and stand in front, putting my hands to my side.

"What's up?"

"Your grade." Liam turns his computer around and I furrow my eyebrows when I see a 62%. *That's impossible, I just turned in an essay last week.* "You need to do better."

"But I just turned in an essay last week."

'"Which you didn't do very well on. You also don't do much class participation."

"I have been present in class though."

"Yea but not participating." He turns his laptop around and rests his arms on his desk. "I want you to do better Ariella, and I know you can. What happened?"

I think this through.

Liam probably wants me to do extra credit again. I'm not doing that but I want this grade. "Of course, sir. I-"

"Ariella." That familiar voice that irritates me but makes me feel so relieved, calls my name making me turn my head to the doorway. Ash's eyes are filled with that same darkness and I look down at his hands which are in a fist. "Come on."

I smile at Liam. "I'll bring up my grade. Thank you for letting me know," I say before turning around and walking towards Ash. I feel Liam's eyes burn deep holes in my back. "Thank you."

"Why do you look scared of him and why was he talking to you?" Ash says while wrapping a possessive arm around my waist as he walks me to where I sit.

The feeling of his arm feels so natural and familiar that I can't help but lean into him and feel his warmth.

I have never told Ash about Mr. Locke and it was a good choice that I made because Ash would go ballistic on Liam.

I know it.

"It's nothing. I just had to talk to him about homework."

"That didn't look like nothing based on your face. Tell me the truth Ariella," Ash demands.

I didn't expect Ash to act so possessive or caring towards me and I definitely didn't expect Ash to sit right beside me.

Since the other night in my kitchen, Ash has been acting less like an asshole. The little pranks he was doing stopped and the teasing remarks that he would say to try and hurt my feelings stopped.

He still calls me a brat and we still argue but it's not as much since the night in my kitchen.

Something shifted between us that night and I just have a feeling that things are going to get worse from this point on.

Last summer's memories keep appearing in my head and I can't stop thinking about Ash and how he keeps consuming my every breath and thought. I want him out of my head.

"It's nothing, Ash. Don't worry about it." I look away from him and open my laptop. Liam starts talking once almost everyone is here. He talks about a project that he wants us to start today with a partner and when he says that, I see his eyes travel to mine. Liam looks away at the same time a heavy arm rests on my shoulder. I look at Ash and see him glaring at Liam. "Stop." I try to shove his arm off of me but he leans down and I feel his lips touch my ear.

"I can easily make you agree to anything I say with just one finger, Ariella. Don't make me show your fucking teacher who you belong to."

"I don't belong to anyone." I turn my face and look at Ash with determined eyes.

"Is that so?" Ash smirks and raises one eyebrow.

I glare at Ash and he just nods his head and looks at Liam.

Ash clears his throat which makes Liam look over at

him. I turn my head to look at him so that I can ask what the hell he is doing but then I feel a pair of warm lips smash onto mine.

It's so unexpected that I freeze.

This is the first time we have kissed since last summer and I don't know whether to push him away and slap him or if I should pull him closer and enjoy this moment between us.

He tastes like the cinnamon gum that he always chews and he smells like the woodsy cologne he wears.

I kiss Ash back. It feels nice to kiss Ash again and I feel like I'm breathing so hard while kissing him because I need to somehow get more of his air.

I know what he is doing right now, he is showing Liam that he claimed me and that I am his. He doesn't care that the whole class might be watching and for the moment I don't care either because I just want to feel his lips against mine for the first time since last summer.

Ash tastes so intoxicating that I don't want to stop kissing him.

He slides his hand onto my throat and gives me a warning squeeze before ripping his lips off mine and looking at Liam.

My head rests on Ash's shoulder and I don't even dare to look at Liam and see how he is glaring holes in mine and Ash's chests.

"Sorry to interrupt you Mr. Jones and Ms. Madden

but if you want to do those kinds of activities, I would expect you to do that outside of class," Liam lectures but I don't look at him.

My cheeks feel like they are on fire.

"Apologies, sir. My girlfriend just can't keep her hands off of me," Ash says and I can hear the playfulness in his voice.

I punch the side of his stomach but Ash doesn't even flinch.

"Next time you do that, I will kick you both out of my class and don't even bother coming back. Is that understood?"

"Understood, sir." Ash rests his arm around my shoulders and then leans back in his chair while still staring ahead.

Liam goes back to talk about the project and I slowly take my head away from Ash's shoulder.

I wish that Ash would have kissed me where it was just him and I. It would have been special so that I know I hopefully mean something to him, but I'm just a game.

This is all just a game.

"Why would you do that?" I whisper.

"Because you're mine," Ash says while not taking his eyes off of Liam.

TWENTY-FIVE
ASH

My hands ache against the hot water running down my hands and I look up to meet my dark eyes in the cracked mirror.

I cleaned up the glass from the floor so that Ally doesn't have to touch the glass and clean it up again. I feel bad for making her clean up all of the other shit in my house when I'm not able to but she said she would rather make sure I am taken care of than living in a pigsty.

She never scolds me about why I always punch the mirror; she never gets mad. Instead, she always shakes her head lightly and says my name softly, almost with sadness.

This is the fifth time this month that I have cracked a mirror but I can't help it. It's a release I need to be able to forget about the haunted memories from last summer and years ago between my mother and I.

She and I look so much alike and I hate it.

Today I have to meet Ariella for the project that Liam assigned us yesterday. It's due next class and since Bridgette wasn't in class today, I forced Ariella to be my partner.

Once class ended yesterday, she bolted out of the classroom with flushed cheeks and I texted her later on that I would be coming over for the project. I didn't get a reply but I know she saw it because of the read receipt.

I wipe the blood off my hands and then put ointment on the knuckles before leaving the bathroom.

After I put a shirt on, I leave my room and lock the door, even though Ally will easily be able to get in and see the mess so that she can clean it.

The drive to Ariella's house isn't long. When I am parked in front of her house I look up at her window and see her walking around the house with a white tank top and pink underwear.

That fucking tease.

She is holding her phone and talking, probably to Bridgette.

I get out of my car and lock the door before walking towards her house. I knock on her front door and a few minutes later the door opens and I see Ariella with her phone in her hand and she is still wearing that fucking pink lacy underwear.

I'm going to strangle her neck and fuck her until she chokes for dressing like that and opening the door. "Cute," I say before meeting her eyes and seeing a challenging glare hidden.

I step inside her house and she closes the door behind me. I walk upstairs towards her room and I hear her small footsteps trailing behind me.

Her room is cleaned, unlike the last time I was in here. Her bed is made and all of the shit on her desk is organized.

My eyes go to her book shelf which is filled with many, many romance books. Some of the books on her shelf are flipped so that the page side of the book is showing instead of the spine.

Most of the books on that shelf are from me.

"Your room hasn't changed much."

"Don't act like you weren't here for almost the whole summer, Ash." Ariella closes the door and I turn around and see her leaning against the door crossing her arms over her chest.

The tank top is made with very thin material making me see her nipples like I did the night she hosted movie night.

"Stop being a tease and let's start the project, Ariella."

"So, for the first time you don't want to touch me?"

Ariella raises her eyebrows at me and she pushes her chest out a little bit.

"If you keep acting like this, I'll fuck you so hard your dad from across the country will hear you scream his enemy's son's name so how about you be a good girl for me and sit on the bed so we can do this assignment." Ariella's cheeks turn red and she walks to the bed and pulls the throw blanket she has over her lap. My lips lift in a small smirk. "Where's your laptop? I didn't bring mine."

"On my desk." I go to her desk and sit down on the chair.

I open the laptop and click around and find the email that Dr. Locke sent everyone.

In this assignment we have to ask our partner these questions and see what their reactions are to the questions.

"Okay I'll ask you the questions first and then you can do the same." I look at the first question. "How old were you when you realized that you have experienced trauma?"

Ariella's eyes are filled with vulnerability and I am probably the last person she would want to bare her guards too.

"Sixteen. When I lost my mother," Ariella admits, refusing to look at me. I think if she did then it would feel more intimate and real to her. "What about you?"

"Six." I have never told Ariella about the things my

mother would do to me or the kind of trauma she put me through. The only people who know are Ally, my father, and Cal Madden. I think that's why I feel like I owe them something sometimes. Because they know my deepest, darkest self and helped me out of that state, kind of. Well except Cal Madden. He can go to hell and choke on fucking fire for all I care. Before Ariella can ask a question about who or why, I go on to the next question. "What is the one thing you are looking for?"

"Strength," Ariella answers. "What is the one thing you are looking for?" she asks while keeping her eyes trained on me.

"Relief." I am always desperately searching for a relief, whether it's punching things until my fists are bloody or just touching Ariella. It's one or the other. "When was the last time you genuinely felt happy?"

Ariella's eyes freeze on mine. "Um, a few months ago." Last summer. I smile at her. "What about you?"

"A few months ago." I look away from her so that I don't have to see her reaction. "When did you realize that you felt pleasure through something you shouldn't have?"

I look up at Ariella and I see her blushing again. "I'm not answering that."

"It's on the assigned question list, Madden, I'm afraid you have to."

Ariella smiles shyly and she looks at the ceiling while saying, "The night you scared me in the mirror maze." Ah, the mirror maze from last summer. One of my favorite memories from that summer. I felt the excitement in her kiss when I pressed her against the mirror. I have never been so turned on in my life as when I was kissing her in that moment. I know I have deviant fantasies and fucked up morals sometimes but I have never acted on them because I don't want to scare people away. I have only got a taste of them. Like from the other night when I scared Ariella in her room while she was doing homework, God that felt so fucking good but I needed to teach her a lesson and I couldn't go forward because it was all part of the game. "You remember that night, don't you?"

"Of course, I do."

I feel heat in my blood as I look at Ariella. I know she was made for me. That darkness is in her too. I know that because of the way she melts under my rough touch and the way my hand wraps around her throat or the way I whisper dirty things to her. She is just as dark as me.

"What about you?"

"Scaring and hurting you."

Ariella licks her bottom lip but she keeps her eyes on me. I look at her hands clenching the blanket and the way her throat bobs up and down.

I put the laptop on the desk and walk over to Ariella. She looks up at me with those innocent eyes. I want to tarnish her soul, mark her skin, and then rip her heart out to make it mine.

It is mine.

Ariella Madden is mine.

I lean down and rip the blanket from Ariella's lap.

Her legs are crossed and her hands immediately hold onto her thighs. "What are you doing?" Ariella whispers as I move closer to her.

My breath hits her lips and I want to devour her in that moment. "Getting a relief." I whisper before licking her lips and then forcing my tongue inside her mouth while kissing her.

My hands fall to Ariella's thighs as I open them and nestle myself between them. Her legs wrap around my torso and I press my hips against her. I groan against her lips when I feel her kiss back.

I squeeze her thighs in my hands before sliding them up her body and then under her shirt to hold one of her breasts in my hand.

I squeeze her breast and Ariella moans and arches her back. "Ash." I glide my other hand down and then trail it all the way to the spot between her legs.

Ariella is warm and I can feel how wet she is from pressing my hand against her soaked underwear.

She is always bare. "You're so wet," I whisper against her lips.

"Please," she begs, trying to grind against me.

"Were you hoping to get fucked today, Ariella? Were you

hoping I would fuck you and make you scream my name?"
Ariella bites my bottom lip when I move her underwear to the
side. I smirk against her lips and lick them before breathing
her in. "God, you taste like hell Madden and it has never been
this sweet." I lick her bottom lip before biting down on it.
Ariella moans and she grinds her hips into my hand and one of
my fingers grazes her clit. "What do you want, baby? Tell me."

"I want you to touch me, Ash," she breathes.

"But you hate me," I say before thrusting a finger
inside her and pressing a hard kiss to her lips again to
swallow the moan she lets out.

"No, Ash."

"No, you don't hate me or no, you want to stop?"

"I-"

I thrust the finger inside her harshly while rubbing her
clit with my thumb. "You what?"

Ariella's chest rises and falls against mine and my hand
on her breast squeezes and pinches.

I kiss her lips, inhaling her and getting lost in her
touch. Her tongue brushes against mine and she drags her
fingers along my back, marking my skin.

"I don't hate you; I never have," Ariella whispers
before taking my lips again.

I thrust another finger inside her and rub her clit
aggressively. "You can never escape me, Madden."

Ariella clenches on my fingers and she breathes hard

against my lips before I feel her sticky release around my fingers.

Ariella trails one of her hands down my chest and I grunt and remove my lips off of her when I feel her hand touch me over my pants.

"Take them off and have me," she says and I rest my head on her shoulder. She tightens her legs around me. "Please, Ash."

My hand leaves the spot between her legs and moves out of her shirt. I wrap my hand around her waist and flip us so that she is on top of me with her hand still holding my swelling cock.

"Not yet." I take her hand off of my cock and put it on my chest. "Not right now."

Ariella understands and instead of getting off of me she stays still and presses a timid kiss on my lips before closing her eyes slowly and resting her head on my chest.

TWENTY-SIX

ASH

PRESENT

Right when I walk through the front door of my apartment, I look at the clock on the stove.

It says 1:53 am.

Ariella and I didn't end up finishing the project. Instead, we talked and kissed and then she tried teasing me again and because of that I smacked her ass and fingered her until she was coming again and again.

When she fell asleep, I watched her silently and I felt content where I was. Ariella's breathing against my chest was calming and it felt good watching her sleep like everything in the world was okay.

She was sleeping on me as if I wouldn't hurt and ruin her.

After I watched her sleep for a good hour, I fell asleep

with her in my arms and woke up to the sound of my phone ringing.

Ally was calling me and asked me where I was. Usually, I am home at night. I rarely go out and when I do, I am with Jace who invites me to bars or parties and I only go if Ariella is there.

Every reason why I go or stay out late is because of Ariella.

But Ally and no one else needs to know that.

I put my shirt and shoes back on and then pulled the blanket up to cover Ariella's shoulders.

She snuggled into her pillows more and as I think about it, I feel a small smile lift on my face.

Damnit.

I walk into my dining room to put my keys in the bowl but I stop when I see my father sitting at the head of the table with a crystal glass filled with what I am assuming is whiskey.

"What are you doing here?" I walk towards the kitchen that is connected to the dining room.

"Where were you?"

"I asked the question first," I say while going towards the cabinets to grab a crystal glass. "Why are you here?"

"I heard that you have been talking to Ariella Madden."

"Yea, we already talked about this-"

"Yea but what we didn't talk about was you getting

close to her and kissing her in front of everyone in class."

I freeze.

He wasn't supposed to know about that.

How does he know about that?

Fuck, how does he know about that?

"Last time I checked, I'm an adult," I say before walking towards my father.

I grab the bottle of whiskey and pour some of the liquor into my glass.

"Yes, and last time I checked, we had a deal, Ash."

I sit down on the chair near him. "You don't have to worry about it. I'm handling it."

Kind of.

With Ariella, all of my plans for her went down the drain the moment I touched her. I knew I shouldn't have touched her.

"Handling it by doing what exactly?"

"Dad-"

"No, Ash," he cuts me off and slams his glass on the table. "I don't want you near her anymore. I'll handle Madden's daughter and take care of her."

I place my hands on the table and lean towards him. "You're not going to fucking touch her."

"I'll do anything I want, Ash. And what I want is for Cal Madden to go down on his knees for me. I will ruin him by ruining his daughter. I don't care if I have to ruin you too in the process."

"You don't have anything to worry about. Will you just let me handle it for fucks sakes?"

My dad shakes his head lightly and sighs.

He knows that I need his word.

If I don't then I'm in deep shit. I was almost close to getting caught last summer when I went to jail and if that were to happen again then I would be fucked, especially without my dad's help.

And he knows it.

"One more chance Ash. One more or else you're done." My father gulps the rest of the whiskey in the glass before placing it down and standing up. He places a hand on my shoulder and squeezes. "Remember what's at stake Ash. That is what drives you and what always will drive you."

He pats my shoulder twice before walking away and leaving out the front door.

My hand around the glass squeezes until it shatters in my hand.

Glass sticks to my hand but all I can do is look forward and not move a muscle. The glass in my hand stings but it's a good sting.

It gives me relief and a way for me to focus on something other than that moment from when I was seventeen. It makes me focus on something other than how I fucked up in so many ways that night.

Twenty-Seven
Ariella

Music busts through the speakers in the massive living room as Bridgette and I walk toward the kitchen to get something to drink.

Some song by Jay-Z is playing and most people are just dancing while some others are grinding against one another. I look away from the living room and instead pour myself some vodka and then lemonade to top it off. Bridgette pours herself the same thing except she mixes her vodka with orange soda.

Bridgette pulled me to this party that one of her classmates is holding. He has a pretty big house and a big backyard with a pool outside.

I was thinking about just staying home and watching a

movie or finishing this one thriller book I started but Bridgette begged me to come.

She is not sick anymore, obviously.

The bitch is perfectly fine and is ready to dance her little ass off while probably making Jace jealous and want to punch every guy here for staring at her.

Bridgette is wearing a blue mini-dress and she decided to curl her hair. She wanted me to wear a mini skirt that I am sure will be going up my ass a lot tonight.

"Can you stop glaring at everyone and act like you want to be here?" Bridgette says, which makes me look at her.

"I'm not glaring." I furrow my eyebrows at her.

"Yes, you are." She takes a sip of her drink. "You seriously need to stop being a party pooper and start having fun."

"Who says I'm not having fun?"

"Your face," Bridgette says, then starts to gulp down her drink.

I take one sip of mine while looking around the house and my eyes catch familiar dark ones.

Of course, my eyes had to find his. He and I always seem to know when the other is in the room.

It's been a few days since he made me come all over his hand and then left me.

For the past few days, he has not acknowledged me

once and I am starting to get pissed off. He looks at me and then glares before turning his head.

I thought things between us were going to be normal after the night we spent together. Ash spent the night, or at least I think he did because when I woke up he wasn't there. His lingering scent was there on my pillows and I stayed in bed that morning for an extra ten minutes closing my eyes and smelling my pillows.

I can't get enough of him and it's an issue.

When we are at school, he looks at me and glares before not looking at me for the rest of the class.

He is getting on my nerves by going back and forth.

That night it felt like old times, him holding me while I fell asleep, and then when he kissed me it felt like I was flying and that everything seemed right.

It felt like summer all over again.

But of course, Ash being Ash, he has to go in and ruin it by being a major dick and ignoring me.

If he wants to play that game then fine by me.

My eyes leave him and they go to the dance floor where I see a guy who is wearing a white shirt and just a regular pair of jeans, looking at me.

He is fairly attractive.

He looks like he is around maybe 6 feet which is good just in case he has to go up against Ash.

I bring the cup back up to my mouth and take a few sips. "I'm going to go dance," I tell Bridgette after finishing my drink and then walking towards the living room.

I walk past the guy with the white shirt and smile at him.

I dance my way to the middle of the crowd. The song playing is "Woo" by Rihanna. I sway my hips from side to side, matching the rhythm of the song. My hands are roaming down my body at the same time I feel a pair of hands come around my waist. I turn my head and see the white-shirt guy.

Finally.

I close my eyes and rest my head on his shoulder. "I knew you wanted me," he whispers in my ear but I don't pay attention to him.

I couldn't give two fucks about him.

The guy's hands touch my stomach and my hips, not going any lower, thank God.

My eyes open and I look straight ahead and see him.

Ash is sitting on the couch with Jace next to him. Two girls are sitting with him. One near Jace and another sitting next to Ash.

Ash's jaw is clenched and I look at his fists and try to ignore the way my heart beats when I see scratches and bruises on his knuckles.

Don't feel sorry for that bastard, he is with another girl and left you.

I slide my hand down to hold the guy's hand. I trail his

hand down my thigh to place it there and then wrap my other hand around his neck.

"Tell me 'bout your picture-perfect love, tell me how you think without the drugs, maybe you just need to send for me..."

"Put your lips on me," I say to the guy while keeping my eyes closed, blocking out the outside world.

When he puts his lips on my neck, I imagine Ash's touch but it doesn't feel like him.

His hands and lips don't feel like Ash's even though I try desperately to imagine it's Ash who is touching me.

"I don't even really care about you no more (no more), I don't even really care about you no more (no more), I don't even really care about-"

The song fades into the background when I feel the guy's hands and lips get ripped off of me.

I'm not surrounded by someone who isn't Ash, instead, I open my eyes and turn around only to see Ash straddling the guy on the floor while pounding his fists into his face.

The music eventually stops, and people are yelling around the house, telling Ash to get up.

I see Jace jump in and try to pull Ash off the guy but he fails miserably. Other guys join in to get Ash while everyone is still cheering and yelling.

Everything is rushed and chaotic and I don't even know where to focus. Instead of helping I just stand back and watch Ash as he struggles against people trying to pull him away.

"Come on, Ash. Dude, it's not worth it," Jace yells while getting Ash off of him.

It takes a total of three guys to pull Ash off and then other guys cover the guy in the white shirt, protecting him in front of Ash.

The guy wearing the white shirt has a bloody face and his nose looks like it's broken. His white shirt is covered in some blood and his eye also looks like it's swelling up.

Jesus Christ.

I look at Ash and see has no marks on his face. I look down at his hands and I see they are bloody and still bruised, maybe even a darker purple than how it looked before he punched that guy.

Ash pushes Jace and the other guy off of him before leaving the crowd and going toward the front door.

Jace looks at me and then where Ash left before looking back at me again.

Fuck.

I remove my eyes from Jace and instead walk towards the way Ash went.

The front door is open and when I walk outside I look around and see Ash leaning on his motorcycle with his head down.

I cross the street and walk towards his car. When I get

close enough to his car, I take slow steps toward Ash until I'm a few feet away from him.

"Ash," I say and I'm about to say his name again but he lifts his head and turns his body to face me. He is staring down at me like he wants to inflict pain and make me scream. *Fuck, what did I do?* "Are you okay?"

"That's a really fucking stupid question." He takes a step towards me but I don't dare move. "Get on the bike, Ariella."

I furrow my eyebrows at him. "No."

"Ariella-"

"No, I came with Bridgette and I am going to leave with her."

"Do as I say and get on the bike," Ash says before taking another step towards me.

I cross my hands over my chest and look up at Ash. "No. You can't boss me around and be a dick. I didn't do anything wrong. You are acting like a fucking maniac, Ash."

"Ariella-"

"No-" I get cut off when I feel Ash smack his hand on the car behind me before grabbing the back of my neck.

He pulls me towards him so that our bodies are glued together. "Get on the fucking bike Ariella or so help me God I'll make sure everyone at this stupid party knows you are mine."

TWENTY-EIGHT
ARIELLA

SUMMER

"Every time we go out, I want you to wear a dress with me," Ash says as his finger lightly rubs my thigh.

I blush. "Why?" I ask, while trying not to smile so hard but it's hard when it comes to Ash.

Every time I'm with him, I feel like smiling. No one has ever made me feel this happy before. Ash makes me feel like I am blind to everything around me and it's just me and him stuck in the world.

I hate feeling like this somehow will end soon.

Today he wanted to get ice cream so he came over and we took my car to the ice cream shop because afterwards we plan on going to the beach for a little to hangout.

"Because I like knowing I can touch you whenever I

want." He gives me a small smile before turning his head to face the road.

I smile and look out the window so he can't see how red my cheeks probably are and how big I am smiling from what he said.

The things he says just seems to make things harder for me to resist him. I wish I could touch him but I don't have the guts to say or do that.

When Ash pulls into a parking lot I look to see where we are. There are little shops around us, an ice cream shop, toy shop, and some more restaurants and food places.

"What are we doing here?" I ask, looking at him as he parks the car.

"We're getting ice cream."

"That's not on the bucket list though."

Ash smirks and says, "I know," before getting out of the car and closing the door.

I hurry and get out of the car and Ash is already on my side. He holds his hand out for me to take. I smile and take his hand as he closes the door behind me.

We swing our hands as we walk towards the ice cream shop.

When we get inside it's freezing cold and I get shivers down my spine. We walk up to the counter and look at the ice cream selections. While looking at the selections I feel a jacket being placed on my shoulders making me look up at Ash, who isn't wearing his jacket anymore.

He isn't looking at me, instead he is looking at the ice cream selections as if they are the most interesting thing in the world while I am looking at him like a puppy in love.

"Hi." I hear, forcing me to look away from Ash and look at the girl who is standing behind the counter with a white cap on her head with the name "I Scream!" which is the name of the shop. "Have you guys ever been here before?"

"No, first time," Ash says as he looks at the ice cream selections. He grips my hand which makes me look at him again. He is looking down at me and his head is tilted a little bit making me admire the way his jaw is structured and how strong it looks. I get flashbacks of the nights in New York when I woke up with his face between my legs making me hold onto his hair as he made me see stars when it was so bright outside. "Ariella," he says, making me come back to reality.

"Huh?" I ask him, feeling heat cover my cheeks once again.

"I asked, what ice cream do you want?"

"Oh." I smile and look at the girl who is waiting. "Can I just have cookies and cream please in a medium cup?"

She nods and scoops the ice cream. Ash tells her that he wants rocky road which I grimace at. He notices and shoves my shoulder with his.

Ash pays, despite my efforts to make him let me pay.

He has paid for every single thing every time we go out. I tell him it's not fair and he tells me to shut up and that he doesn't mind paying for me and that he would pay for the whole world if it meant I would be happy.

What he said made my heart beat so fast I thought it was going to burst out of my chest. The way he says things that hold such meaning to me, will never make sense. He has the ability to ruin me and he has no clue.

We sit down at an empty table, next to one another. I sit in the corner while Ash wraps his arm around my shoulder making me lean against him.

"Where do you see yourself in the future?" I ask him while eating my ice cream.

Ash takes a bite out of his ice cream before licking his lips. "Probably living in New York and working as a counselor or for my father's company."

"What does your father do?"

"He's a lawyer. He is a criminal defense attorney."

It's funny how Ash's dad is a lawyer and so is mine.

I wonder if his dad knows my dad or if they have ever worked together. My dad does work in New York a lot and he wants me to move out there but I feel closer to my mother here in California and I don't want to leave her just yet.

"You should be a lawyer. Lawyers are hot," I say while taking a bite of my ice cream.

I look up at Ash and see him smiling down at me. "Oh yea?"

I nod my head. "You should give me your dad's number. Maybe I can take a swing at him-" Ash pushes me against the wall lightly making me laugh. "I'm just kidding, I'm just kidding. Your dad is probably old and wrinkly and ugly."

"He is."

"But you also look like him so he can't be that bad looking-"

He shuts me up by pressing his lips against mine. I can taste the chocolate flavor of his rocky road ice cream making me moan into the kiss.

Ash takes my ice cream and puts it on the table making me slide my hands up his chest and wrap my arms around his neck. His hands grip my waist and I whimper against him.

"You taste so fucking good, Ari," he mumbles against me.

"I guess rocky road isn't that bad," I mumble back before licking his lips and kissing him back.

"So, you're going to buy it next time?"

I push him off of me and laugh. "Just because it tastes good on you doesn't mean it tastes that good."

Ash backs away from me and sits down taking his ice cream as he has a small smile on his face.

You wouldn't be able to notice it from far away but I see it.

And that's all that really matters.

Twenty-Nine
Ariella

Present

Ash parks in front of a tall building that looks like it reaches the clouds.

I can't stop looking out the window, even when Ash parks the bike.

It looks like a luxurious, tall building that only the elite would probably live at.

I turn my head and look at Ash, "Where are we and why are we here?"

Adrenaline rushes through my bones and I feel excitement in my blood. I can't help but feel scared of what Ash might do. Ash is impulsive whenever it comes to me, I've noticed that now.

He doesn't think strategically or rationally.

I don't know if that's a good thing or a bad thing.

I feel a pair of hands grab my waist and pull me of the bike. I yelp and hold on to Ash as he pulls me out.

"Ash-"

Ash pulls me away from the bike and we walk inside the tall building. "What is this place?"

"You'll see, now shut up."

My lips stay closed as I take in the lobby. Ash pulls me with him until we are in front of the elevator.

It dings before opening. There is a small group of business-looking men, all wearing navy blue suits with a tie. I blush and look at Ash.

He wraps a possessive arm around my waist and walks inside the elevator, going in the back.

"You are insane."

"Watch your mouth." He leans closer to me and his lips touch my ear making me shudder. "You're getting on my nerves and if you keep acting like a fucking brat like you did at that party, I swear I'll make you get on your knees in front of these guys in the elevator. After they watch me face fuck you, I'll fucking punch all of them until they go blind. Understand?"

I swear I make that gulp sound that people do on TV. My hands fist by my side and I feel heat run up my neck.

My thighs press together and I try not to focus on the uncomfortable ache between my legs.

One by one, the floors climb and I feel stuck in this elevator with Ash and all of these men.

One of them looks at me and I smile but Ash tightens his hold on me and glares at the guy. "Keep looking at her and I'll rip your eyes out." The guy immediately turns his head while all of his buddies snicker and look at Ash.

Finally, we stop and I look at the floor we're on.

Five floors below the top floor.

The elevator opens and one of the guys turns their head and looks at me. "Good luck tonight, lass. You'll need it with this one."

"Hurry up and get out, Richard, before I threaten you."

"Wouldn't want to catch a lawsuit with you, boy." Richard and his buddies walk out.

Ash and I follow them out, but he turns a corner and walks all the way down to the only door in this hallway.

Oh God.

Ash unlocks the door and he pushes it open before walking in, holding the door open for me to walk in.

I walk in slowly and my eyes trail over the windows that overlook the city with the beach in the background.

"Is this your apartment?" I ask as Ash closes the door behind me.

The view he has outside his window is so appealing. You can see all of the city lights and then the dark sea. The city looks alive in the dark. I've never been to a view this high before to look over the city.

"Yes." Ash takes his phone out of his pocket and he

tosses it on the couch near us as well as his keys. Ash turns around and faces me. "Do you know why I'm mad?"

Fear and excitement creep up my neck and I take a step back. "Because I danced with another guy."

"Because you let another guy put his fucking hands on you, Ariella." Ash takes a step towards me. "I've been trying so hard to leave you alone and let you be but you keep pushing my limits." Ash takes another step closer which makes me take another step back. It's like a little game between him and I. Who will win between the two of us? "I've had enough and I've given you so many changes. I'm done."

"What are you going to do?" I ask, trying to stay calm.

He won't hurt me.

But at the same time, that's what Ash likes doing. He likes to hurt people.

He likes that feeling of distress. He gets off on it.

And I have a feeling I am going to be enduring a lot tonight.

"I'm going to make you scream."

My heart is beating hard and fast against my chest. Adrenaline is still running through my veins.

"Ash-"

"Run, Ariella. If you leave the apartment without me catching you, I'll leave you alone and move back to New York."

"And if you catch me?"

"Then you are quite fucked, Madden."

I don't waste any time.

I turn around and run towards the dark hallway near his front door. Chills run up my spine as I dash through the hallway.

Multiple doors come in my view but I keep running and turning to different corners.

I should have gone upstairs.

I open one of the doors and run inside.

There is no lock but when I turn around and see the room I'm in, I am filled with shock.

It's dark in here but I notice the rows and rows of bookshelves that fill in the room. In the center there is a floor to ceiling window that showcases the moonlight.

I hear heavy footsteps outside the door.

I take a left and run down one of the rows.

My chest is tight and I have an urge to give up and fall asleep. I rest my back against one of the shelves and rest my head against the shelf.

My breathing is shaky and my heart feels like it's about to explode out of my chest. I close my eyes and try to calm down my breathing but then I hear the door open making me freeze.

Even though he is probably feet away from me I feel him everywhere.

I feel him in my bones, soul, and it's like he is stealing all of my breath and taking away the ability to breath.

It's not possible but I wish I could freeze my heart. I feel like Ash can hear how fast my heart is beating.

This whole experience feels like the time when Ash was chasing me in the mirror room at the fair. I get a sense of déjà vu and a small smile makes its way to my lips.

That was one of my favorite moments with Ash and the fact I'm experiencing it again excites me.

I stand up and run towards the other side of the bookshelf but instead I am faced with eyes filled with darkness and a small sadistic smirk plastered on Ash's face.

"Got you."

Thirty

Ash

My arms are wrapped around Ariella and I can feel how she shudders against me. Her heart is beating so fast that I feel the beats against my chest.

It's fascinating to see her this way. The way she melts against my hold. The way her lips part and she leans into me, hoping for a kiss.

"I'm giving you one chance. If you don't say anything, I'm going to take that as a sign to do whatever I want to do."

Ariella keeps her mouth shut, her eyes are filled with lust. She looks at me like she wants to consume me with everything she has, and I am more than happy to give that to her.

I reach down to grab her thighs, wrapping them around my waist. My lips smash into hers.

Ariella's hands travel up my body. She grip onto my hair and tilts my head back. She trails her kisses down my neck and I take that as my cue to leave the library.

I walk out and Ariella continues to kiss and lick down my neck as I walk to my room upstairs. My cock feels like it's going to fall off with how much it strains against the zipper of my pants.

It's been aching since the moment I gripped Ariella's neck and told her that I was tired of her bullshit and to get on the bike.

She has been begging me to fuck her since the moment she started dancing with that asshole.

Ariella nips at my skin at the same time I stop in front of my bedroom door. My eyes close and I hold Ariella against the door. Our hips are pushed against one another and she starts to grind against me. The way she moves against me feels dangerous and all I want to do is rip her clothes off and show her she's mine.

Ariella is mine.

My lips smash onto her again. I don't ever want to stop kissing her. It has to be my favorite fucking thing in the world.

Her heavy breaths hitting my lips make me tighten my hold on her thighs and Ariella sighs into my mouth when I thrust my tongue in between her lips.

I kiss her like I've never kissed before. My lips feast on hers until she is gasping and her whole body is filled with adrenaline.

Our tongues glide against one another as I rub small circles on her thighs. Her nails dig into my neck as she keeps breathing hard into the kiss.

I remove my lips from hers and open the door.

"Take these fucking clothes off of you," I demand as I put her down.

Ariella, slowly but sensually, takes off her clothes one by one. The skirt goes first and my eyes travel up and down her legs. Next comes her tank top and she isn't wearing a fucking bra underneath.

My jaw clenches and then my eyes go back to her pussy that's covered with pink lace underwear.

Ariella slips her fingers beneath the lace and then she sensually pulls down the material.

Ariella is bare and the way her legs press together confirms how turned on she is by this.

Me demanding her.

This whole experience has been very different from the moments we had sex.

It's raw and real. Not that when we had sex it wasn't real or passionate but I was hiding that darkness inside me that I know Ariella wants to see so desperately.

Now she will.

At least some part of it.

She has pushed my limits so it's only fair that I push hers too.

I walk up to Ariella and my hand goes to her jaw. I press one of my fingers on her lips, which makes them part automatically.

"What are you going to do to me?" Ariella whispers and my eyes finally connect with hers for the first time since we left the library.

I let go of her and put some distance between us.

I have to go slow. It's all about the pace.

"Get on the bed. Hands and knees, ass up, and face against the mattress," I demand. Ariella's eyes widen and I see the excitement in her eyes. She looks at the bed and then me. "Don't make me do it for you. I won't be nice about it."

Ariella does as I asked and she gets on the bed, her bare ass in the air and her head against the mattress.

I strip, taking my shirt off and then pants and briefs.

I forget about the condom because since the first moment I was inside of her, I've always wanted to feel her bare, and I don't care if she isn't on birth control, I'm going inside her bare.

I don't want there to be a barrier between Ariella and I anymore.

I walk up to the bed and I look at her pink pussy that's glistening from how wet she is. I place one hand on her ass, which makes her flinch. My other hand makes its way to her pussy and rubs a finger up and down her folds.

Ariella moves her hips in a circular motion against my hand and moans, "Ash." I thrust a single finger in before ripping it out and slapping my hand against her pussy. Ariella jolts her body forward and moans. "Oh."

"You're getting ten slaps for what you did at the party."

"W-What-"

My hand makes contact with her pussy again and she jolts forward. "Count. If you miscount, I'll start over."

"Ash-"

Slap.

"We're still on one."

"O-One," Ariella whimpers. *Slap.* A sob tears from her throat. "Two. Oh my god!" She yelps.

"You don't look at anyone else." *Slap.* "You don't fucking touch anyone else." Slap. "And you don't ever, ever, use another man to make me jealous." *Slap.* "Because I swear, I'll kill anyone who dares to touch what's mine." *Slap. Slap. Slap.* "You're fucking mine, Ariella."

"T-Three, four, five, six, s-seven," she says while shaking against me. Her legs are trembling the more I slap her sensitive spot. "Ash-"

I slap her two more times before thrusting my fingers inside her. She moans loudly and tries to move away from me. I get on the bed, mounting her.

My finger thrusts inside her at a fast pace and her heavy moans fill the air. "Am I understood, Ariella?" I ask, still shoving my fingers deep inside her.

"Ash-"

I cut her off with a slap to her ass. "You still don't fucking get it yet, do you?" My hand connects with her ass and I take my fingers out and replace them with my cock. Ariella cries and her pussy clenches against my cock. "Fuck Madden, you're strangling my cock, baby. Did you miss me that much?"

"Yes," she mumbles against the mattress.

One of my hands holds onto her shoulder as I thrust in and out of her. "You've only been with me haven't you baby? This is my pussy, isn't it?"

"Yes," Ariella moans against the bed.

"This pussy belongs to me. No one else has touched my pussy."

"No Ash, please," she moans as I rock into her faster and harder. My hand comes down on her ass and red marks paint her skin. "Don't stop."

"Don't plan too." My hand connects with her skin more than once and my hips slam against her again and again and again. "I love how you take me so well, Ariella. You can be so good when you want to be."

"Ash-" I pull Ariella up by her hair and her back is pressed against my chest. I continue to move inside her as I place my lips on hers. Ariella cries against my lips and her hands hold onto one of my arms that's holding her against me. My other hand connects with her ass more than once until I feel her shake against me and her pussy clenches around me. "Ash, oh-"

"Fuck, baby. Come around me like a good girl." My lips meet her throat as she comes with a moan.

I push her back down on the bed, she is limp with her lips parted as she screams. I thrust into her fast and hard, not taking a second to stop. I know my fingers are bruising her skin but I don't care.

I want my marks on her.

"Ash, stop. I can't-"

"You can and you will." I say, pressing her hand back to the mattress to muffle her screams.

I wrap an arm around her hips, my hand finding her pussy. I rub fast and hard on her clit making her try to move away from me but I keep a hold on her, not letting her go.

She comes again with a scream.

Soon I follow after her, biting her shoulder, leaving my mark as I come with a grunt.

THIRTY-ONE
ARIELLA

SUMMER

It has been a few days since Ash last came over. He took me to the bookstore and bought me every book I touched, even if I didn't think I would like it, he still bought it for me and said that if I don't like it, I can return it or donate it.

I scolded him and told him he didn't have to do that before he pushed me against the bookshelf and started kissing me. Lo caught us kissing and then told us to stop and go do that outside. Ash laughed and he kissed me one last time before letting me go and walking away, leaving me breathing heavily.

After the bookstore, we went to the beach to hang out. We laid on the sand and I read one of the books he got me while he listened to me read out loud. When the sun started to go down that's when we left and Ash just dropped me off home. He told me he would come back later because he had to meet his dad which I was fine with.

I didn't know that he was going to not text me or call me to tell me he wasn't coming.

I didn't smell his scent on my pillows or see the outline of his body on the side of my bed.

Since that day I haven't gotten a call or text from him. I haven't texted him either because I'm too scared. I never like making the first move but I'm so tempted to.

Is he okay? Is he ghosting me? Is he not interested? Does he not like me anymore? Was he just using me?

So many questions and so few answers.

My father flew here from Paris the other day and he visited me right after Ash dropped me off that night. We had dinner and dad told me about how things are going for him. He asked me about college and how I am doing in all of my classes. He told me that Bridgette is having a lot of fun in England. He knows Bridgette's dad and they talk a little bit. I asked him about the girl he is seeing and he just said things are good and that's it.

I close my book and toss it on the floor.

I can't concentrate.

All of a sudden, I feel overwhelmed and my over-thinking is getting the best of me.

I need to sleep and stop thinking about Ash.

I need to stop thinking about the word I want to say or admit. It's a scary thing.

Love.

It's terrifying and the way it makes people do crazy things makes me scared of what I might do for Ash. This whole summer was supposed to be a temporary thing.

What happened?

He is consuming my thoughts and it's not healthy at all.

I was about to turn off my lamp but then my door opens. I am ready to scream but then I see Ash leaning against the door frame. He looks like he has been there for a while but is now just showing himself.

"You scared me," I say and then get off the bed to walk towards him. I manage to look down at his hands and see they are scarred again and have bruises on the knuckles. "Why do you keep doing this? What do you do to yourself?" I ask as I reach for his hand to inspect the cuts. He lets me, he always does when I notice his hands are like that. What does he do to his hands to make them look like this? I look away from his hands and meet his eyes. They look empty and deranged. He looks like he wants to smash every piece of furniture in my room. I put my hand on his jaw and furrow my eyebrows as I look at him. "What happened? Talk to me." Ash takes my hands off his face and he looks down at my hand. "What's wrong?"

Ash looks up to meet my eyes. "Ariella fucking Madden."

My brain is filled with questions.

How does he know my last name? I never told him.

We never exchanged last names.

"What's the matter? What?"

"Cal Madden's only daughter."

Even more questions.

How the hell does he know who my dad is?

"How do you-"

"You're a fucking cunt, Madden." He lets go of my hands and almost forces me away.

Even more questions run through my head as I try to not let tears form in my eyes. "What's the matter? Why are you mad?"

"Cal Madden's fucking daughter happens to be the one I am fucking around with."

"Why does that matter? What are you even talking about?"

"Levi Jones', Ariella. You are fucking Levi Jones' son," Ash says with a straight face.

My eyes widen and I feel panic and shock run through my bones.

Of course, he had to be Levi's son.

I mean Ash did say his dad was one of the most powerful lawyers in New York other than my dad. How did I not see it?

Ash looks almost emotionless as he looks at me. He looks like he hates me and would rather see me die than touch me again.

But all I want is for him to say he's joking and then touch me. I need his reassurance that this isn't real.

That he isn't the one my dad was trying to put away. "Ash-"

"Don't say a fucking thing, Ariella."

"Ash, I didn't know-"

"I have spent a year of my life trying to defend myself against your father. My father has spent an entire year trying to protect me. What will your dad think when he finds out I'm fucking you?" I hate how Ash is calling this relationship we have 'fucking'. He knows it's more than that. "My dad was having a fucking fit when he found out."

"Your dad knows?"

"Of course, he does. He was my fucking lawyer, Ariella. He had to know that I am fucking the prosecutor's daughter. This will land me in so much shit if someone were to find out."

I don't know much about Ash's case but I know it was something bad. I know it had to do with his mom and now all I am wondering is what the hell happened. Nothing about his case is a public record because his dad kept it all under wraps for him and away from the media.

Now it all makes sense.

But now that I know Ash is Levi's son, I want to throw up. It can't be true.

That's why Ash doesn't talk about his mother. I know she is dead from what I heard from my dad but how? Does it have to do with Ash's dad? Does it have to do with Ash? What happened to Ash's mother?

That's all I can think about and how Ash is Levi's son. This can't be happening.

"Ash we can work this out-"

"No."

Tears are threatening to spill from my eyes. This all is so overwhelming and I don't know how to process any of this information. It's all too much.

"What do you mean no?"

"I'm done. This whole thing was a mistake and I hope you and your father go to hell."

"I didn't do anything to you! Why does this all matter?"

"Because you're Madden's fucking daughter!" Ash's jaw clenches as he yells at me from across the room. I can tell standing from here that his whole body is tense and filled with anger. The vein in his neck is prominent. "I wish hell on your family. I hope you all die and fucking join her in hell!"

"So, all of this was basically a waste, right? This whole summer was just meant for nothing?"

"Right."

I turn around and grab the books he bought and throw them all at him. "You're a fucking asshole, Ash! All you do is destroy and hurt! You're filled with it!" I say after throwing each book at his chest. Ash doesn't move from his spot or even flinch. It's like he expected this from me. "You're fucking guilty if you're acting like this!" I yell one last time before Ash finally moves.

He walks up to me and grabs my wrist. "Say that one more time and I swear to god Ariella, I'll fucking ruin you. I'll make sure you are broken down completely and have nothing left in you."

I push away from him and bring my hand across his face. "Don't ever touch me again," I say as tears run down my cheeks. "I hate you."

"I hate you too, Madden," Ash says with a sinister smile, it's anything but sweet and charming like all of the other ones that he has given me.

"I hope I never see you again."

"Hate you too, baby." Ash repeats before he takes a few steps away from me. "Better make sure I never see you again Ariella because if I do you won't be so lucky to make it out whole."

Thirty-Two
Ash

PRESENT

I have deviant tastes when it comes to sex.

I thrive on pain and control. I always have, even as a kid. I just never realized it.

I always had a way to somehow get that pleasure, whether it be from a controlled and safe way with someone I don't know or breaking things in my room. It always makes me feel good.

Having sex with Ariella has always been different for me even when we had just regular, painless sex in the summer. I did smack her ass or grab her neck but not in a way to hurt her. Ever since I came back to LA, Ariella has been pushing my limits and they finally broke last night.

For a good thirty minutes I have been staring at Ariella's back.

She is still sleeping quietly, her chest heaving up and down. She will probably be out for another hour or so. We were up late last night and I would expect her to be tired.

She took everything I gave her like a good girl. She screamed and moaned my name all night and I couldn't stop smiling down at her. Her eyes were filled with lust and seeing her come around me with a face full of ecstasy was one of the most pleasurable things I've ever experienced.

How can someone like her exist and be perfect for me?

I move the covers away from her and my eyes go down to her ass.

It's full of red angry hand prints and then some purple marks on her hips from how hard I gripped her.

She has my marks on her.

She's fucking mine and she better understand that.

I reach out and trail my finger along the marks on her ass. Ariella moans and stirs in her sleep. My eyes go up to the back of her head. Her long brown hair is trailed down her back. She looks absolutely perfect with all of those marks on her.

I slowly move off the bed and go inside my bathroom. I open the medicine cabinet and grab the ointment.

I walk back inside my room and take the covers off of Ariella.

She moans and stirs but doesn't open her eyes. She is still in deep sleep. I grab her waist softly and pull her closer to me, turning her around so that her ass is facing me and she has her head snuggling inside the pillows and blankets.

I put some ointment on my hand and then softly rub it on Ariella's skin. She moans again and I look at her face, seeing her lips part slightly. I focus back on the marks. They are red and angry looking and I feel a wave of possessiveness when my eyes go from the marks to the tattoo we share.

That's just another point that proves she is mine.

I'll kill anyone who thinks otherwise.

After I'm done I put the ointment on my desk and go back into the bathroom to wash my hands.

I look at Ariella one last time before I leave my room and close the door.

When I first woke up, I put briefs on. Ally has the day off because I told her I didn't need her in today. When I walk inside my kitchen, I try to ignore the anger rising up my throat when I notice my father sitting at the kitchen island, looking at his phone.

"What are you doing here? Leave."

"Why did you call Ally off?" my dad asks, still looking at his phone.

Prick.

"Because she needed a day off."

"She has every Sunday off, not Saturday and Sunday. So back to my original question." My dad finally puts his phone down and looks at me. His eyes trail over my neck and my chest. Ariella's marks are on me and I'm wearing them proud because Ariella is mine and I'm hers. "Did you call her off because of the person that did that?" he asks, looking at my chest before meeting my eyes.

"Don't worry about it. Why are you here? Do you need something?" I walk towards the coffee machine and put in a pod.

"Who was the poor girl you damaged this time?"

"Ariella Madden," I state, still looking at the coffee machine and getting it ready.

I hear the chair legs screech against the floor. "What?"

"Ariella Madden. The one I'm supposed to stay away from, remember?" I take a peek at my dad and see his jaw is clenched.

"This isn't what we discussed, Ash. Remember what I told-"

"I remember and I don't care."

"This will ruin everything we have built, Ash. This will possibly land you in fucking prison. I told you to stay away from that girl and her fucking father. Don't test-"

I turn around to look at my dad. "I think you sometimes forget that you and I are very similar." My dad glares at me. "I will do whatever I want with Ariella. Our relationship is none of your business and you have no right to tell me what to do with her. I will do whatever the fuck I want to with Ariella."

"Ash-"

"Did you not listen to a word I said?" I ask, furrowing my eyebrows. '"I said that I will do whatever I want with her and you can't stop me."

"And then what happens when her dad finds out Ash? What will you do then?"

"I'll be happy to expose his side of the case. Don't worry dad. I'm not a complete fool to the whole thing between the two of you." My dad's fists clench and I can't help but smirk. "I know that before I was born, the two of you fought like dogs over women. Who could get the girl first? Come on, everything between the two of you, was always a competition. He got the woman of his dreams and you got a fucked up son and girlfriend who ruined him. It was always a game between the two of you."

I got him.

"I'll take your funds. All of your money and inheritance is still under my name, along with the money Regina left you."

I raise an eyebrow at him. "You really think I give a fuck about that?" I almost want to laugh. "Do that and see if I care. Now get out. I have some things I need to do." I turn back around and finish making the coffee for Ariella.

Eventually I hear my father leave the kitchen and then my door opens and closes.

Fucking finally.

THIRTY-THREE

ARIELLA

Shock rushes through me as I feel my whole body engulf in warm water.

My butt touches a hard surface as water surrounds me. My skin burns where my butt is. But soon, after a few seconds it starts to feel good, relaxing.

My eyes open slowly and I look around. Ash is in front of me, sitting on the edge of the tub and looking down at me.

All of a sudden, I feel so exposed to him. He sees me, everywhere and everything.

Ash isn't wearing a shirt and my eyes go to the tattoo before meeting his eyes again.

"What are you doing?"

"Giving you a bath. You need one."

"I don't smell though."

"Yea but your ass is sore, and I can't have it be sore for next time or else it will just hurt, not give you pleasure," Ash states and I swallow.

Straight forward.

Next time?

"What do you mean next time?"

Ash furrows his eyebrows. "You think I'm going to let you go after last night?" I push my back against the tub as if it will make me farther away from Ash. Ash sighs and he leans in, putting his hand on the edge of the tub near my head. "Answer me. Did you really think I was going to let you go?"

"I thought-"

"No. Obviously you thought wrong." Ash tilts his head to the side and his eyes trail all over my face, lips, eyes, nose, every little detail on my face.

It makes me feel nervous, especially since I'm naked and bare in front of him.

The only barrier between us is his clothes.

"Are you mad?"

Ash sighs and instead of answering he stands up and he starts taking off his sweatpants.

I don't move my eyes away from him as he puts his hand around the waistband of his briefs and pulls them down.

Next thing I know, he is getting inside the tub and he moves me so that he can sit behind me.

His chest is warm when I rest against him. His fingers glide over my arms and his other hand wraps around me and touches the spot where my tattoo is.

I feel his hard cock against my butt making me press my thighs together, reminded of how it was inside me not too long ago.

"I'm not mad," he says in a frustrated tone. He says he's not mad but he sounds and acts like it. "I just don't want you to fall into anyone else's arms, Ariella. Only mine."

I lean my head against his shoulder. "Have you been with anyone else since you met me?"

I don't expect Ash to not be with anyone while we were not talking for the past two months. I would expect him to be with other girls and I know that would hurt me but I still want to know.

Maybe it was stupid to ask and I shouldn't have asked but I just like hurting myself and him telling me has been with other girls makes this whole situation between him and I more realistic.

"No. Have you?" Ash asks.

"No."

"Good. I hate seeing you with someone else other than me."

"I hate it when you talk to other girls and I want to rip

their heads off but I don't go and do it." I turn around so that I can look at him. "You need to stop punching people who talk to me." I say before looking down at his hands. "Why do you always have your hands like this?"

Ash doesn't answer, instead he just stares at me while I'm looking down at his hands. I want to know what he does to make them look like this. It hurts my heart knowing that he hurts himself like this.

He takes his hands out of mine and then he puts one of them on my cheek before leaning in and kissing me.

Ash kisses me and it's almost sweet and soft before it turns demanding, as if he is trying to prove a point. All of his kisses have always been like this. Whenever Ash kisses me, he does it to prove that I'm his and even I can't change that I'm not.

His hand still strokes the tattoo on my side and he bites my lip lightly. "Ash," I whimper.

He removes his lips from mine and then places them on my neck instead.

His other hand starts to trail down my side and over my thigh. "You're a fucking temptation, Ariella. Always have been. I can never get enough of you." His hand is close to the spot between my legs and I want to cross them and make sure his hand doesn't leave. "How can someone like you be so perfect for me?"

"Ash, please touch me," I beg. I want to feel him inside me.

I grip onto his thighs that are surrounding me. "Do you deserve it? I let you come yesterday but didn't even punish you because you liked it?" I don't answer him, I can't. It will make all of this too real. Last night was amazing and I never knew I could like the pain he gives me so much. The rough touches he would give me and the dirty words he spoke into my ear. It all felt so good. "You did. You like being slapped and edged. So, I don't consider that a punishment, Ariella."

"Ash, please. I'll do anything," I beg, while trying to grind my hips against his hand.

His other hand trails up my throat and he stops kissing me. He looks down at me and his eyes are filled with darkness.

"Say you're mine."

I reach up to brush his lips against mine. "I'm yours." Ash smashes his lips on mine and his fingers are now inside me. His mouth on mine isn't as rough, still demanding and possessive. His fingers inside me are rough and fast. I moan and arch my back into him. "Ash," I moan into his lips.

"Say it again," he demands, going faster.

"I'm yours," I breathe against his lips.

He curls them and massages my clit, his touch burning into my soul. I can't get enough. I grind my hips against his hand and moan against his mouth when a wave of pleasure slams into me. I can feel his erection rubbing against me and how hard he is.

"Fuck, you're so perfect, Madden," he says against my lips, giving me a harsh kiss before leaning away. "Get out." He takes his hands off of me, making me feel cold.

I feel like my soul deflates a little and a wave of hurt runs through me. "Why? What's wrong?"

"Get out and you'll see."

THIRTY-FOUR

ASH

From the moment I met Ariella, I always knew she was going to be a permanent fixture in my life. She is someone that just continued to pop up in my head without me even wanting her to. I didn't like the fact that she was always on my mind, even during the months we weren't talking.

I always knew Ariella was going to be mine but it was a matter of how and when. This issue with my father isn't going away. I know that, I'm not stupid.

My father is going to hang my past with my mother over my head to make me do what he wants but I don't want to anymore.

I need Ariella.

"What are we doing here?" Ariella asks, as I get off the bike.

Right now, we are parked in front of a familiar bookstore.

After I got Ariella out of the bath, we stayed in bed for the whole day and then I took her to get some food.

"We haven't been here in a while." I say before taking my helmet off and rest it on the handle.

"I have."

"I mean together." I narrow my eyes at her and her cheeks turn a light shade of pink. "Come on." I grab Ariella's waist and she yelps when I get her off the motorcycle.

I take the helmet off of her and she smiles up at me as I fix her hair.

God she is beautiful.

I wish I didn't fuck things up with her constantly.

I rest her helmet on the handle and grab her hand, pulling her away from the bike.

Last time I was here I bought Ariella so many books she couldn't even hold all of them. She got pissed off at me for spending all of my money but I did it because I knew it would make her happy. She loves books and books make her happy. Seeing her happy makes me happy.

I remember the first time I came in. It was weird how my eyes went straight towards Ariella's when I walked inside the shop. Of course, she caught my eye because of the way she looked at me.

I unlock the door and Ariella furrows her eyebrows at me. "How do you have the key?"

"Lo. He gave it to me a few days ago."

"Why do you have it?"

"Because I want to show you something." I open the door and walk inside with her.

It's dark in here but the moonlight that shines through the window doesn't make it pitch black. I pull her towards the back of the bookstore, where her favorite section is.

I already bought all of the books she wants but I just wanted to bring her here for some peace.

"Why did you bring me here?"

"Why are you asking so many questions?" I look down at her and smirk.

"Because this whole day you've been acting weird."

"Weird how?"

"Nice."

"I'm not allowed to be nice?" I raise my eyebrow at her.

"No, but you're not usually this nice," she states.

"Because you don't like it when I'm nice."

Ariella blushes. "I'm not used to you being nice. If you were nicer then I wouldn't be acting weird."

I put my free hand on her cheek and my thumb caresses her lips, feeling her plump, smooth lips.

"You have such a smart mouth," I whisper. "Do I need

to fuck your mouth so that you understand how to act with me?"

"You like my smart mouth." She smirks and tilts her head slightly while looking up at me.

"Ariella," I warn.

My cock is aching.

It's been aching since the moment in the tub. I have spent the whole day pleasuring her. I don't expect her to give me anything in return but I definitely don't plan on just bringing her here to look at books.

She smirks and lets go of my hand to walk around. The bookstore looks so much different when it's empty and dark. It makes me think of all the things I have wanted to do to Ariella in here.

"You never told me your favorite book," Ariella says as I follow her around the bookstore.

"I don't have one."

She turns her head to look at me. "What do you mean you don't have one?"

"I don't have a favorite book." I shrug.

"Every book lover has a favorite book."

"Wrong. Every book lover has a favorite author. Not a favorite book."

Ariella rolls her eyes and that makes me want to pull her by the hair and slam my dick inside her.

She is so close to making me not give a fuck and push her against the shelf to ram into her.

"Who's your favorite author then?"

"Jameson Hat."

"And what's your favorite book by him?"

"I have too many," I say, but the book called "Only You" pops into my head.

It's about a killer who has to kill a list of people and at the bottom of the list is his wife's name.

She rolls her eyes. "Pick one of your favorite books by him. There has to be one."

"Only You." Ariella furrows her eyebrows and I see a flash of something in her eyes. I don't know what to call it but it makes me feel uneasy. "Why did you look at me like that?" I ask her.

She smiles lightly and shakes her head. "That's my favorite book by my favorite author."

I feel a smile form on my lips and I walk closer to her.

"You believe in fate?" I raise an eyebrow at her.

She shrugs. "At first no, but now I'm slowly changing my mind."

I push Ariella back into the bookshelf behind her. She keeps her eyes on me, they are filled with innocence and wonder.

Fuck my dick.

I'd rather give her pleasure.

I lean down and press a rough kiss to her lips before kissing down her neck and slowly getting on my knees in front of her. I take the sweatpants I gave her and pull them down. Ariella gasps and goosebumps appear on her thighs.

I am faced with her pussy. She isn't wearing anything underneath the sweatpants because her underwear is in the wash. Ariella is swollen and pink. I can see the arousal coating her.

"You're so fucking wet, Ariella," I say, in a husky tone.

I lean in closer and press a kiss to her thighs.

She shakes and shudders when I press my lips there. "Ash."

"What do you want, baby?" I ask, going to her other thigh and pressing a soft kiss there.

"Your mouth."

"Where do you want it?" I feel Ariella's fingers run through the strands of my hair. She pulls me closer to her pussy and she pushes her hips towards my mouth. I press my lips on her and she moans and her legs shake. "Here?"

"Yes," she says.

I flick my tongue against her and she shudders against me. I look up and see her looking down at me with lust filled in her eyes.

Ariella pushes her hips slightly into me. I lick and suck her clit between my lips. I thrust my tongue into her tight hole and she moans, gripping the strands of my hair.

"Grind on me, Madden. I know you want to."

She moans, I grab one of her legs and throw it over my

shoulder. Ariella holds me against her pussy as I lick and continue to suck her.

She is so open to me like this and I like how I can explore every inch of her. She whispers my name and her breathing increases as she thrusts against my face faster.

The fact she is fucking my face for her own pleasure makes me hard as a fucking rock. And when she moans and comes on my tongue, I swear I feel pre cum wet my pants like a fucking teenager.

I lick my lips and clean her up while she controls her breathing or at least attempts to.

"Ash-"

I stand up and hold her waist in my hands. My lips touch hers and I kiss her like she's mine, because she is.

She's mine and she always will be mine.

THIRTY-FIVE
ARIELLA

Usually on birthdays, some people would feel drained or not really excited about what the day might bring them. But this morning I woke up with Ash between my legs, kissing me and murmuring dirty words to me.

He knew how to make me scream and moan his name. He then kissed me and fucked me in the shower. He is insatiable and never knows how to stop and take a break.

After our shower he told me to get ready and that he had a day planned for us. I am surprised that he remembers my birthday but at the same time I can't help but feel my heart beat against my chest from how in awe I am of him.

He knows how to make me feel like I am on top of the

world. He always knows the right words to say to me and how to make me blush.

Bridgette and Jace joined Ash and I for breakfast at the diner and after that, Ash told me that we were going to be going to Santa Monica for the day.

I have lived in LA for all my life and have never been to the Santa Monica Pier which is weird. Ash knows this because I told him during the summer. I remember him asking me questions about things I've done and things I haven't done.

I don't know how to react to Ash acting this way towards me. All I remember is the moment he told me he hated me and that he wanted to ruin me. The Ash I knew from last summer is gone. It was all a facade and how he has been acting for the past few months is who he really is, unfiltered.

Right now, he is nice but still tends to show who he really is from time to time.

I see the dark and dangerous look in his eyes that tells me something isn't right with him and other times I see him give me a genuine smile. It all seems fake sometimes or like it's too good to be true.

His smile and the kind of personality he shows people is fake. When it's just Ash and I, I know it's real. I know he isn't hiding his emotions with me, at least not all of them.

"So, what now?" Bridgette says as we walk through the crowds of people.

We just got finished playing some games. Ash played some games and won me a couple of prizes. I also managed to beat him at some of the games and he rolled his eyes and said he let me win on purpose which I just laughed at.

"Let's go on the ferris wheel," I say and then look at Ash to see what he thinks.

"Yea we can do that." Ash looks at Jace. "You take Bridgette with you."

Jace looks down at Bridgette while she rolls her eyes and crosses her arms over her chest. "If you don't want to go with Jace, I can-"

"No. She will go with Jace," Ash cuts me off and wraps an arm around my waist.

"You know you can't take my best friend everyday, asshole. She loves me more. Remember that," Bridgette says before passing Jace.

Jace laughs and then follows Bridgette.

I narrow my eyes at Ash. "You have been with her all your life mostly. I want to have my turn now." I shake my head lightly as Ash grabs my hand and pulls us towards the ferris wheel.

"You need to learn to share."

"No," Ash says and he pulls me closer to him as we wait in line.

The past few days, Ash has not let me leave his side. He has been up my ass since the bookstore. If I thought he was possessive before, I was wrong.

Whenever a guy looks at me he always glares at them and says he will kill them under his breath. He also sometimes grabs me by my waist and puts his lips on mine and says that I am his.

Ash and I get inside the pod and I sit on the opposite of him.

He smirks and spreads his legs as he sits down, watching me. Once the ride starts, he roams his eyes along my frame, never taking his eyes away from me.

"Stop being a brat and come over here." I smile at him and look outside the window.

The pod makes its way to the very top before it stops. Next thing I know I feel Ash's hands on me and I feel hot everywhere.

Ash pulls me over his lap and I lean into him with a squeal. "We aren't supposed to be sitting like this. That's not how a ferris wheel works."

"I don't care."

I roll my eyes. "You never do."

I feel a slap on my ass making me gasp. Ash's lips lift in a small smirk and his eyes are filled with darkness.

He has that look in his eyes that makes me know he wants to swallow me whole. "Don't make me slap your ass until it's blue and purple," Ash warns. He leans back and keeps his eyes on me. "Did you like today?"

"Yes. Thank you for making it special," I say as my fingers make their way into his hair. "I had fun today."

"Good. I like seeing you smile."

"Then why did you always try to hurt me a few months ago when you came back to LA?"

"Because I needed to hurt you."

I furrow my eyebrows. "Why?"

"Because hurting you was something I needed to do."

"You just said that."

"I can't tell you Ariella, not now at least. Give me a little more time," Ash says and his hand on my thigh tenses before caressing my finger against my skin. "Let's talk about something else. Tell me more about your mom."

I smile softly. I like the fact that he wants to know more about the person who made me so happy I couldn't stop smiling.

"She was amazing. I have already told you about how amazing she was."

"What are some of the reasons why you love her?"

"She always took care of me, no matter what. Whenever we got into a fight, she still said she loved me and would always care for me." I say, smiling at the memories of her and I. "She always made sure I was warm when it was cold outside, she made sure I was doing good in school and whenever I made an accomplishment, she always said how proud she was and then she would have me bake with her." Ash looks almost confused as I tell him these things. It's like everything I am telling him is foreign.

It breaks my heart seeing his reaction of telling him simple things my mother, any mother would and should do with their child. "What's wrong?" I ask, furrowing my eyebrows at him.

Ash looks out of the pod. It's like he is thinking what to say to not make this day ruined.

Please don't ruin this day.

It's been so good and one word from Ash could ruin it all.

I put my hand on his cheek and turn his face to look at me.

I can't tell what exactly he is thinking about as he looks at me. It's filled with a black void that looks almost emotionless.

It's unrecognizable.

It's the same look he has when his hands are bruised and cut.

"Nothing. Don't worry about it."

As the pod makes its way down, Ash doesn't say anything to me.

He doesn't even look at me.

My mind goes into overthinking mode.

What did I say? Did I ruin today? Will this be the end of me and him again?

Ash is different from me and everyone else. Everyday I

am still trying to figure him out and get a deeper look inside his mind.

He is hot and cold and I never know how to act around him sometimes.

I just hope whatever happens between us doesn't bite me back and hurt my heart.

THIRTY-SIX
ASH

After we finished up dinner, Bridgette and Jace said they needed to leave for reasons I don't know but if it gives me time alone with Ariella, I don't care.

Luckily there is a beach next to the restaurant we went to, so Ariella and I decided to just sit down on the beach. Ariella got us a blanket from Bridgette's car.

Bridgette told me we could use it if we didn't had sex on the thing which Ariella blushed at.

She is also wearing my jacket around her shoulders. It's cold at the beach, especially during the winter. Although she is wearing a long sleeve and sweater, I know she is still cold.

When she saw the sweater she blushed and I know it

was because of the many memories of times I have given her my sweater.

It's silent as we look at the waves across from us. Ariella rests her head on my shoulder and I just let my body relax. I don't feel tense, those voices in my head are gone and it's all because of this girl I've spent my summer with.

I just don't know how she does it.

And the fact that she doesn't know how obsessed I am with her is crazy. This feud between my father and Cal is slowly leaving my mind and all I can see when I look at Ariella is her.

"Do you ever wish you could just leave? Forget your name, your life with your parents and who you were with them and just start over in a new town?" Ariella asks.

"Of course. Everyone does," I say softly. "Doesn't mean people do it. Everyone is too scared or they don't have the money for it."

"My dad didn't call me for my birthday."

Not a surprise. Her dad is a jackass and he only cares about himself. I will admit that he was very loyal and very in love with his wife but after she died, a part of him did too.

I think he forgot that he still has a daughter.

"You shouldn't expect anything from that prick."

"Just because you don't like him doesn't mean I can't

stop loving him." Ariella looks up at me and she gives me a disappointed look.

"Yea, but just because you love him, doesn't mean you can protect him. He is a prick for not saying happy birthday to his only daughter. He barely even fucking texts you Ariella," I say. A little too harshly maybe. "If I had a daughter, I would make sure to text her every day to make sure she is okay. I would text her to tell her to have an amazing day and to tell her how beautiful she is because my daughter will be the most beautiful girl in the world right behind her mother. I will make sure to tell my daughter how amazing she will do in school that day or if anyone fucks with her, I'll personally make that little shit's life hell. A father can send a text saying "happy birthday', Ariella."

It's true.

If I had a daughter, I would cherish the fuck out of that girl and make sure she knows how special and worthy she is. I would make sure that she knows she is loved.

And for her birthday, I wouldn't just send her a text.

I would send her pink roses, because only her mother gets red roses from me. I wouldn't just buy a dozen; I would buy hundreds.

Then I would personally write her a note telling her how much she is loved.

It's not hard to send a fucking text and Cal is a prick for that.

"You want a daughter?" Ariella asks, after a little while.

"Yea. I don't want a son."

"Why?"

"Because I'm a fuck up Ariella. I don't deserve to be in this world sometimes."

Ariella removes her head from my chest and I look down at her.

Her eyes are filled with concern and sadness. I know that if she were to see what I do with the mirror in my bathroom she would run away and probably have nightmares about me.

"If I were to ever get pregnant with your kid, I would want a boy. I would be the luckiest girl in the world to have someone like you as a kid. You are so easy to love Ash and you don't even know it." I look at her, all over her face and I can't help but feel in love. She doesn't know this but there is no way I can just stop loving her. I've been in love with her since last summer. I press a kiss to her forehead and make her rest her head against my chest again. "Did I make you mad earlier?"

What Ariella said about her mom made me think of mine. The way Ariella admires her mom makes me jealous of her and the relationship she had with her mom. And the way her mom just died breaks my heart because how could someone take away something so beautiful and meaningful to Ariella?

I wish I had Ariella's relationship with her mother instead of the fucked-up relationship I had with mine that is now tainted with the last memory I have of her.

"No, you just made me remember."

"Remember what?"

"My mother."

"You never talk about her."

"I don't want to talk about her because whenever you are around it's the only time my head isn't filled with her. You make everything quiet."

"Is it quiet right now?"

I wait for a minute to really give myself a moment to think.

It's quiet.

I don't hear the screaming, the yelling, the sound of slapping, or the sound of a cigarettes burning into my skin or glass breaking.

I don't hear the sound of moans or the murmured voices.

I hear waves, Ariella's laughter, moans, the way she yells, argues, and how she breathes. I don't see my mother's face or the way she would make me watch her slowly try to kill herself every night on the couch.

I see Ariella laughing, smiling. I see her fall in love and in awe.

I see Ariella.

I just hear her.

"Yes. So, stop talking and let me enjoy it."

Ariella laughs and she pushes her head into my chest more.

Thirty-Seven
Ariella

I don't like relying on someone. I have never been the type of person to ever rely on someone or try to give my whole heart to someone.

I'm scared of that.

Ever since my mother died, I have never fully given myself to someone with all of my guards down because I don't want to get hurt.

Because what happens when they leave too?

Ever since Ash dropped me off home last night my mind has been in it's own tornado. He told me he would come back later that night and he never did. I was tempted to text him to ask him where he is or if he is okay but I didn't.

That would show that I actually care about him. It's

hard to show my emotions to people, especially Ash because of the hold he has over me.

I'm scared that my feelings for him are growing and it's only a matter of time before they grow into something dangerous that I won't be able to control.

The whole entire day I have been drowning myself into homework and trying to distract myself from Ash. I talked to Bridgette for a little bit and she was complaining about how Jace isn't leaving her alone.

My patience is running thin and I am tempted to call Ash. But instead of being rational, I change into leggings and a sweater before grabbing my keys and leaving.

The drive to Ash's house feels so long and my mind keeps overthinking. All I keep thinking about is how Ash is possibly going to reject me or how he will be condescending and give me his dark, hateful gaze.

I park my car in the underground parking garage and next thing I know I am waiting in the elevator that's taking me up to Ash's floor.

When I am in front of Ash's door, my hands shake as I make a fist and knock on the door. It's quiet on the other side of the door. I knock on the door again and it's filled with echos; nothing.

My eyes drift to the door handle and before I talk myself out of this, I grip onto the door knob and turn it, pushing the door open.

It's quiet and hollow when I walk in. Ash's apartment

is cold and dark. The only light there is, is the one in the kitchen.

But my attention shifts when I hear glass breaking and the sound of grunts upstairs.

My eyebrows furrow and I make my way upstairs, to the direction where Ash's room is. The sound of grunting gets louder and louder as I get closer to Ash's room.

His door is closed and I can't help but feel afraid of what I'm going to find behind the door. I turn the knob and surprisingly it opens.

The sound of glass breaking, and heavy breathing become more clear when I walk inside his room.

The door to the bathroom is closed and Ash isn't anywhere in the room.

I take hesitant steps towards the bathroom door and the nerves I'm feeling are skyrocketing by the second.

I'm about to knock on the bathroom door but then I hear the sounds of more glass breaking and grunting.

It sounds like a pair of fists are hitting glass, over and over and over again.

I open the door to the bathroom and my eyes go straight to Ash who is punching the mirror in front of him.

There is blood all over the floor along with shards of glass. When my eyes go down to his fists, I want to throw up from how scratched up they are.

The cuts he's made are so deep to the point where I swear, I can see the bone.

Ash doesn't notice I see him; he keeps hitting the glass and grunting hard.

His face is red and the veins in his neck are prominent.

"Ash." I walk inside the bathroom towards him, not even caring about stepping over the glass. It's a good thing I decided to wear shoes. "Ash." He doesn't budge, instead he keeps thrusting his fist in towards the broken mirror in front of him. "Plea-" my voice cracks. "Please stop," I say at the same time as I put my hand on his shoulder to push him away from the glass a little.

Ash's breathing is heavy and he looks away from the glass and looks at me with a dark look in his eyes.

This look he's giving me feels familiar, like I have seen him give me before whenever he was really pissed off but even then, Ash didn't have that crazy look in his eyes. My hands shake lightly as I grip onto my sweater.

"Ariella," he lets out before backing away from me, putting so much space between us when all I want to do is cradle him in my arms.

Who hurt you, Ash?

"Ash-"

"Get out. What the fuck are you even doing here? Who let you in?"

"I came in myself. But Ash, what are you doing? Your hands-" My voice cracks again.

I don't even know where to look. All of this is so much to take in and I don't know how to process all of the glass and blood on the floor.

I walk towards him to grab his hands but he pushes away from me and hides his hands from me. "Get the fuck out. Who said you can be here?"

"I'm here because I was worried." My eyebrows furrow. "And I have a right to be after what I've seen." I look around the bathroom again and it pains me to see all of the glass and blood on the floor.

I feel like the food I ate earlier is about to come up.

"You don't need to be. That's not your job. Now get the fuck out and leave."

"No," I argue, standing my ground and not leaving.

Ash raises an eyebrow. "No? What the fuck did you just say?"

"No." I walk closer to Ash. "This isn't okay, Ash. All of this isn't okay. You're hurt, so bad to the point where I can see your bones." I reach for his hand but he pushes me away lightly.

"Get the fuck away from me Ariella, go home. You're not needed right now."

"No. Y-You're hurt. You need to go to the hospital and get stitches or something, Ash," I say, as tears start to threaten to spill from my eyes.

Seeing him hurt like this scares me so much and I

don't want to leave him alone knowing what Ash is capable of.

"Ariella, you're only good for one thing and surprisingly I don't need that right now. So, I'm not going to ask you again. Leave," Ash says, his words are filled with anger and hate.

But I know he is just saying that to push me away.

It's all Ash ever does.

I ignore him and walk closer to him, grabbing his hands to look at them.

Blood falls from his hands and it drips onto mine.

Tears finally fall from my eyes as I inspect the damage he's done.

He definitely needs stitches.

"We need to get you to a hospital to fix your hands." I ignore the pang of hurt and try to focus on Ash and his hurt.

I need to focus on him and how to help him, not the hurt.

"I don't need you Ariella, just leave." He rips his hands out of mine and walks past me. He kicks the glass out of his way and looks in the cracked bathroom mirror. His eyes go to me and the dark look sends chills down my spine. "Why are you still here?"

I slowly make my way to Ash and stand behind him.

His eyes avoid mine when I look at him through the cracked mirror.

Ash is so damaged and I never realized that until now.

Sure, Ash has his issues and he does show how hurt by the dark, sadistic look in his eyes, but I never knew that they went this far.

I place my hand on Ash's shoulder and turn him around to face him.

He still avoids eye contact until I put my hands on his jaw and make him look at me.

"Let me help you, Ash," I say softly and Ash's pupils dilate as he stares down at me. "Let me fix you."

It happens so fast but I feel Ash's rough and demanding lips meet mine.

Thirty-Eight

Ariella

Kissing Ash feels similar to feeling scared. I never know what's going to happen when I kiss but at the same time whenever Ash scares me, it gives me some pleasure.

Or maybe I am just twisted like that and I like the thought of being scared by him.

Kissing Ash has always been something I enjoyed but this kiss he is giving me right now is making me want to give all of me to him. It makes me want to surrender and let him have his way with me.

Ash nips my bottom lip and his hands roam down my body, not leaving one centimeter untouched by him. It feels freeing and euphoric with the way he is caressing me roughly.

So euphoric that I close my eyes and melt into him.

This kiss with Ash is so consuming that I feel like my legs are going to give out, and that's why I'm thankful that Ash reaches down and grabs me by my legs to wrap them around his waist. Ash squeezes my legs around him and he grunts into the kiss.

I feel Ash start walking but I pay no attention to that.

One of Ash's arms leaves me and I hear a door open.

I already know we are inside his shower when Ash puts me down on the floor, still not taking his mouth off of mine. He pushes me against the shower wall at the same time I feel water come down on us. I gasp into his mouth before he pulls away.

I open my eyes and watch him back up to the other side of the shower. He starts to take his shorts off and I can't keep my eyes off of him as I watch him strip in front of me. Ash is long and painfully hard when I look at him. His abs are clenched and I can tell his entire body is tense just from me looking at him.

Ash looks at my body before traveling his eyes back up at me. "Strip," Ash demands.

His eyes are still filled with that darkness but it's so heated that it makes me want to fall on my knees in front of him.

My eyes go to his hands again. "Let me fix your hands first-"

"Strip or else I'll do it. And I won't be nice about it either."

"Can I at least fix your hands, Ash? You're scaring me with the blood. It looks lethal."

Ash walks closer to me, and I press my back against the wall. "I said I don't need someone to help me. I don't need anyone to fix me. What I need is for you to strip or leave."

I know if I leave he is going to go back to the mirror and start hurting himself again.

So instead of leaving like I should, I step closer to him and say, "I want you to do it."

Ash puts his bloody hands on my hips and he pulls me roughly against him. "I can, but I promise you I won't be nice about it."

His hands on my hips go to the waistband of my leggings and he roughly pulls them down. Ash is on his knees in front of me, taking off my shoes and leggings. He throws them outside of the shower. His lips run along my thigh as he makes his way up my legs. I squirm beneath his touch and squeal as his lips make contact with the spot between my legs.

He thrusts his tongue in suddenly and I try to close my legs together but he gives me a disapproving look before diving in again.

"Ash." He removes his tongue from me and then licks his way up my body again while he pulls the sweater off of me and throws it out of the shower.

"Get on your knees," Ash demands and I don't think

twice before kneeling in front of him. I look up at him with innocent eyes filled with wonder. The water running down his hands makes the blood drip down to the floor and towards the drain. As I look up at Ash, I feel hurt all over again. Ash's jaw clenches and his hand reaches down to caress my jaw. "Suck."

I look away from Ash's eyes and instead look at his cock. He is still painfully hard, maybe even harder than before, even if that's not possible.

I open my mouth and Ash threads his fingers into my hair. He makes his way between my lips and roughly thrusts inside me.

Being on my knees for someone like Ash feels good. The way that I can make him hurt and feel pleasure makes me feel powerful and excited. I like the thought of giving him pleasure and being able to control the way he can feel by one single touch.

Ash continues to thrust in and out of my mouth as I place my hands on his thighs so he can go deeper. Water falls from his chest and then makes it's way to my lips as they go up and down his cock. Ash's hold on my hair gets tighter and my eyes travel to his face. His head leans back and his chest rises and falls as he breathes heavily.

The spot between my legs aches, especially since Ash only gave me a taste of what I am probably going to endure tonight.

I gag and moan around him and it isn't sexy or perfect.

The way he's handling me isn't gentle or caring, it is rough and demanding. All he wants to do is take and take and take.

"Fuck," Ash groans before he pushes away from me. "Get up." I stand up and Ash pulls me closer toward him and I feel him hard and eager against me.

Ash pushes me against the wall and his hand cups the spot between my legs. I moan and lean my head against the wall, aching for him. "Oh-" He cuts me off by thrusting two fingers inside me

"Fuck, your moans are fucking heaven, Madden." Ash puts his lips on my neck and he nips and bites my skin.

His fingers keep moving in and out, his thumb tracing my clit. My hands thrust into his hair as I hold him against my neck. His lips and hands on me makes me want to combust. His touch is all consuming and euphoric, I don't ever want him to stop.

I moan into him and come around his fingers. Ash bites down on my neck and I close my eyes and tighten my legs around his hand.

He takes his hand away from between my legs and removes his lips from my neck.

"Come on." He leads us out of the shower and carries me to the room, careful not to step on the glass. Ash leaves me in the middle of his room and then goes back to the bathroom. He comes back with two towels and dries himself off before going to me and slowly drying me off.

When he uses the towel between my legs I shiver and press my legs together. Ash's hand wraps around my throat and he pulls me toward him and presses his lips on mine. His heavy breathing against my lips as he adds pressure to my throat makes me ache and needy. "You're so fucking pretty Ariella, it pisses me off," he says against my lips.

All of a sudden, I'm pushed on the bed and Ash's body covers mine and his lips on my neck make harsh and pleasurable marks.

Ash flips me over so that I am on my stomach, he pulls my hips up to meet his. His cock is hard and hot against me, even after her roughly fucked my mouth.

"Ash, please."

His hands on my hips grip me harshly. "Say the word 'red' when you want to stop."

"Okay." I breathe out before pressing my head against the bed. My hips grind against his and my eyes close right away. I feel his hands grab my hands from each side of my body. He holds them above my head at the same time he thrusts inside me in one go. "Oh my god!" I yell feeling his full cock thrust inside me.

"I'm going to fuck you hard and rough, Madden, and you better count after each one or else we're going to start over. You're not allowed to come until we reach 20."

Each what?

The question leaves my mind when I feel his hand make contact with my ass.

"Ash-" I get cut off with a harsh thrust inside me.

"Count," Ash demands as he starts to move in and out of me rougher. He slaps me again, harder this time. "Do I need to start over?"

"T-two."

Ash smacks me so many times to the point where I almost lose track. "Losing count already, Madden?"

"God, f-five. Please Ash," I whimper as he roughly grips onto my neck and pushes inside me faster and harder. Ash pulls me up and my back connects with his chest, he slaps my ass again. "Six."

Ash's arm wraps around me and he holds onto my neck while pushing his entire cock inside me and pulling out, only to do it all over again.

"This doesn't count," Ash says, before I feel a hard slap on the spot between my legs. I moan and arch against Ash. He covers my mouth with his. I gasp and moan into his mouth as he moves inside me. "Whose pussy is this?"

He slaps me again when I don't answer. "Ash," I mumble against his lips.

"Mine." He thrusts and slaps my pussy again. "It's always going to be mine."

"Ash, please." Ash pushes me back down on the bed and I feel his hand connect with my ass more times than I am able to keep track of. "Oh."

"How many Ariella?"

"Eighteen," I moan against the bed and Ash's fingers

dig into my hips as he pulls me closer to him after each thrust. "I need to come, Ash, please."

"Not yet. Just a little longer." Ash grunts before he grips onto my hips and slaps my ass again.

"Nineteen, oh." My eyes fall closed and I swear I see stars behind my eyelids.

Ash grips onto my neck and pulls me up to hold me against his chest with his arm around me.

I can't keep track because I feel myself come around him. I moan and my legs shake to the point where I am frozen in place.

"Fuck," Ash groans and he's still inside me as I feel his come.

I gasp and my eyes shut as I push my face into the bed as I feel mine and his come fall down from the inside of my thigh.

The rest of the night turns into a blur as Ash turns me over, scoops our come and pushes it back inside me and thrusts inside me again.

THIRTY-NINE
ASH

"If you could read one book for the rest of your life, what book would it be?" Ariella asks, making me look down at her.

"You already know the answer to that."

Ariella smiles before turning around and walking towards the romance section.

We are back at the bookstore.

I thought that taking her here would be fun.

Plus, I want to buy her some more books because it's part of my birthday gift to her. I also have a necklace for her too that I want to give her.

I was going to give it to her the day of her birthday but then she started talking about moms and I needed to be alone that night.

"How many books have you read?"

"More than six hundred," I answer smoothly but Ariella's eyes widen. "You don't believe me."

"It's hard to. Who has read that many books?"

"I'm 19, turning 20 this year. I've been reading since I was 15 years old." I shrug.

We haven't talked about the mirror situation. She tried talking to me about it this morning but I changed the subject and told her to get changed.

When I went downstairs to get water for Ariella, I saw Ally and she looked at my fist and like always she shook her head silently with a disappointed look on her face.

I cleaned up the bathroom before Ariella woke up. I didn't want her to see all of that again.

That should have never happened anyways. My worst fear came true.

She saw me in my worst state and the only thing I can do is make sure she forgets about it and leaves the subject alone.

"I started reading when I was around 16 and I have only read like three hundred books."

"Guess you don't like reading that much," I say, hiding the smile that wants to spread across my lips.

Ariella smacks my arm before turning around and looking at all of the books.

I made the necklace myself and I know it will be perfect for her.

It's hidden in one of her favorite books in the romance section. It's the book where at the end of the book this guy has to kill his wife. "Only You" by Jameson Hat. It's the reason I met her and just like fate, it's both of our favorite books.

I might just be biased because Ariella loves that book with her whole heart but I love that book a lot. It's a thriller romance and usually it's placed in the fiction section of the bookstore because it's like two different genres but I purposely put it in the romance section so that she would pick it up. I asked Lo to put the necklace in the book for me because I knew I wouldn't be able to do it with me being around Ariella.

I watch Ariella look at all of the books while holding four in her hand. I had to get most of them for her because they were on the top shelf.

She doesn't know this but I plan on buying every single book she touches again.

I see her eyes roam over her favorite book and her eyebrows furrow and just like I knew she would, she reaches and takes it out.

"Why is this here? It shouldn't be placed here," she mumbles and it's hard not to laugh from how much I know her. She opens the book like she always does, just to flip through the pages. And when she gets to the middle of the book she stops and furrows her eyebrows again. She adjusts the books in her hand and grabs the necklace. I walk closer to her and grab the necklace from her hands so that I can put it on her. She freezes as I walk behind her and clip the clasp. I stand in front of her and lick my bottom lip as I look at the charm that sits on her chest. "Ash-"

The charm is a book with an A on the front of the cover. It's also a locket so she can open the book and put whatever the hell she wants inside.

"It looks good on you," I say softly as I look at the charm and avoid her eye contact.

I don't like doing nice things. It's rare that I ever show affection to people or show people that I appreciate them. I have never given anyone so many fucking gifts in my life like I have done with Ariella. I swear I would spoil her and give her the world if I could. She is the only person on the earth I have spent a fucking penny on.

I don't like giving gifts to people but with Ariella it's so hard to not give her gifts. She deserves the world and stars.

"Why did you give this to me? Was it expensive?" she asks, taking the charm in her hands and looking at it closely. "It's beautiful. I love it."

She looks back up at me and this time I can't look away from her. She smiles at me and her eyes are filled with so much fucking love and passion. I can feel her love without even touching her.

I just hope I don't fuck any of this up because I like

the relationship I have with Ariella right now. But wherever I'm involved, there is bound to be disasters.

"I got it customized from Tiffany's. It's pure gold because sterling silver tarnishes easily when exposed to salty air, chlorine, sulfur, and a whole bunch of other stuff so gold was the best option."

"Did this cost you a lot?"

I like how that's the first question she asks me. She worries too much.

"Don't worry about the cost. It shouldn't concern you."

"Ash, you don't have to spend this much money on me," she says, trying to prove a point.

"Shut up and go pick out more books to buy."

She shakes her head and mumbles words I can't hear but I just stand there and smile down at her.

FORTY

ARIELLA

Ash is over right now. It's been a few days since the bookstore.

Since the moment I found him in his bathroom and he fucked me hard and rough all night long right after that.

He thinks I have forgotten about it and let it go but he's wrong.

I'm just trying to find the right time to talk to him.

"Pass me the sugar," Ash says before licking brownie mixture off of a wooden spoon.

I hand him a cup of sugar and he pours it into the mixture before mixing it. It's a good thing only Ash and I are eating these because I know that no one would want to have Ash's saliva mixed inside the brownies.

But also, if they were to look at Ash, they would probably rethink their decision and want to lick his whole body while they're at it.

Things for the past few days have been good between us except for the elephant in the room and how I am dying to talk to Ash about that night.

I know he took me to the bookstore to make me forget about it. Although I appreciate the necklace he gave me, I can't stop thinking about him in the bathroom.

All I want to do is ask him about what is going on with him and what is happening in that mind of his.

I wrap my arms around Ash and rest my head against his bare back as he mixes the brownie mix. His body is warm against mine and I feel the way his heart beats rapidly against his chest.

"Your heart is beating so fast," I mumble against his back and caress his chest.

Ash stops what he's doing and he turns in my arms. My arms are resting on his shoulder and his hands go down to rest on my hips.

I swear I think Ash sees the heart in my eyes as I look up at him. "What are you thinking of in that head of yours?"

I feel blush spread on my cheeks. I try to ignore it but it's hard with the way he is smiling at me.

If I tell him what's been bothering me I know he won't be happy in a second.

"I want to talk about that night."

Ash stays quiet for a second. He acts as if I didn't say a thing and I wonder if he actually heard me but then his hands on me tense up and he pulls me closer to him.

"We don't have to talk about that," Ash mumbles.

"Yea but I think we need to."

Ash lets out a sigh and I can tell he is uncomfortable from this conversation but what I saw that night made me so scared and now I can't help but constantly worry about him.

"That night I saw you Ash, I was so scared," I say as I feel my chest tighten. "Seeing you with blood all over your hands," I look down at Ash's hands, which now have stitches on them, that he managed to do himself. "I have never been so scared in my life, Ash." I reach down and hold one of his hands in mine. "I never want to see you in pain like that ever again."

"You were never meant to see that and I'm sorry you did," Ash says softly.

He takes his hands out of mine and I feel one of his hands hold my jaw.

I look up at Ash and he is giving me a soft and almost genuine look.

"How long have you been doing that for?"

I know it's not the first time because I have seen Ash's fists scratched and bruised.

"For a while."

I furrow my eyebrows at him. "Why?"

Ash licks his bottom lip, and he turns his head. I know this is uncomfortable for him and I appreciate that Ash is telling me more than I need to know but I don't ever want to be put in that position again.

Fuck.

Before I can beg him to tell me, the front door to my house opens. I look away from Ash and instead walk out to the dining room and see my dad closing the front door.

Fuck.

I feel Ash's presence behind me and my heart starts racing against my chest.

Double fuck.

My dad turns around and the smile on his face disappears when his eyes move from me and to Ash who is behind me. That smile washes away from his face and he drops his briefcase to the floor.

Triple fuck.

"Fucking Jones!" my dad yells before he rushes up to us and tries to pass me to hit Ash but I cover him and put my hands on my father's chest. "I'm going to kill you. You should have never touched my daughter. You're filled with darkness and fucking poison!" he yells but I push him away from Ash.

Ash starts pushing me behind him so that I can't stop my dad. "Last time I checked, you can't boss her around anymore."

"You're just a little shit. Come over here and say that

to me in front of my face so that I can give you the consequence."

Oh hell no.

I rush to stand in between them and I push my dad away from Ash and vice versa. "Dad, please. Stop, I swear everything is fine."

My father looks at Ash before looking back at me. He has a furious look in his eyes as he looks between Ash and I.

"This is Levi Jones's son, Ariella. You have this son of a bitch in my house."

"My house. You are barely even here to call this place your house."

My dad looks away from me and I see him give Ash a furious and threatening look. "I'm going to give you a minute to put your shirt on, get your shit, and get the fuck out of this house before I rip your head off for touching my daughter with those hands."

"Dad-"

"Not a fucking word, Ariella, I'll deal with you when this son of a bitch is out of this house."

I look up at Ash and see him looking down at me. "I'm not leaving you if you don't want me to."

"I'll be okay, Ash. I know how to handle him."

Ash looks at my dad before looking back at me.

He wraps his arms around me and presses his lips to my forehead. "Call me before you go to bed."

Ash puts his shirt on, grabs his stuff and leaves as my dad glares at him the whole time.

My hands are on my hips as I glare at my dad.

When Ash walks out the door, my dad's eyes travel towards mine.

"Ash, fucking, Jones, Ariella. Are you serious?"

FORTY-ONE
ARIELLA

PRESENT

My father told me to go wait in the office while he turns the car off and gets the rest of his things.

My leg is bouncing up and down from how nervous I am.

I can't help but worry about what my dad will say or think. The way he looked at Ash was scary, he looked like he was seconds away from stabbing Ash in the eye.

I don't know how or when this feud between Ash's dad and my dad started.

I have heard about my dad complaining about Levi Jones since I was a toddler.

I remember my father getting mad talking about him during dinner time and my mother scolded him and said he shouldn't worry about Levi.

I don't know the story behind my father and Levi Jones's relationship but I know it's filled with hatred.

But I also remember my father talking about Levi Jones's son and how the case with him was filled with headaches and how Ash needs to go into a mental institute.

If only my father saw what I saw the other day in his bathroom.

The door of the office opens making me turn my head. My father walks in, he is wearing a usual suit with a tie on.

I know he probably just got back from work and didn't get to change before his flight.

I thought that my dad was supposed to come home in a few weeks because of my birthday.

I didn't know that he would be here earlier, if I knew that I would have had Ash nowhere near my house.

My father sits in the chair behind the desk and then he crosses his hands over one another and looks at me.

"Ash, fucking, Jones, Ariella. Levi Jones's son?"

"It's not a big deal. You are making this thing with Ash and his dad so extreme. I don't get what the issue is between the two of you."

"I told you I don't want you anywhere near that family, Ariella. Did I not?"

"You did but-"

"No buts. I don't want to hear it, Ariella. You disobeyed me. How long have you been talking to Ash?"

"I told you before, we started talking at the beginning of the summer-"

"No, when did you start talking to Ash again?"

My father's expression is serious, and I know that he probably wants to break the desk in half and scream at the top of his lungs yelling, "Fuck you Levi Jones!"

Again, I don't understand what the issue is with Levi Jones. I don't think I ever will because my father probably won't tell me a thing about his past with him. All I know is that he definitely doesn't like Ash because of the case no one will tell me a thing about.

"He moved to LA at the beginning of the semester."

"I'm going to fucking kill Jones."

"Dad, what does Ash have to do with your vendetta against Levi? Ash barely even acknowledges his father. I never once heard Ash speak a word about Levi to me."

"Ariella, if you were there, hearing everything from that trial you would stay far away from him. Ash isn't someone you want to be intimate with. Plus, he is a Jones."

I roll my eyes.

He has such a huge ego.

"Well, no one will even tell me about the trial. If it's so bad, why don't you tell me?" I ask, practically begging.

"No. It's too much."

"So, you don't trust me?" I raise an eyebrow at him.

My father hasn't always been like this. Ever since mom passed away, he has changed drastically and it made me miss him a lot, the old him.

The one who wasn't always so overprotective of his secrets and himself. The one who didn't care about what anyone else was doing, as long as his girls were happy.

My mom made his heart calm and his lips would turn into a genuine smile.

I miss the kind of person he was when my mother was around, but at the same time I didn't pay too much attention to my parents when I was younger. I started paying attention around fifteen years old, around the same time my mom died.

"It's not that I don't trust you, I just think that the subject is very sensitive."

"And Levi Jones? I don't understand what your deal is with him. Why do you hate Levi so much that you don't want your daughter to be happy with someone that she loves?"

I don't know why I said that.

I have never fully admitted it to myself but I feel it.

Deep in my veins I feel like I love Ash Jones because what is there not to love about him? I just wish I didn't sometimes because he can so easily hurt me with just his words.

I have felt something strong towards Ash, since the moment we were chest to chest in the bookstore on the first day of summer. I have always felt something strong towards him. With him I feel like I can be myself with no judgment.

Sure, there are problems when it comes to Ash but no one is perfect.

"You're grounded," my father says, making me look up at him and furrow my eyebrows. "I don't ever want to hear something like that come out of your mouth again. I have never been so disappointed in you."

My jaw fucking dropped.

Last time I checked, I am nineteen years old.

I stand up from the chair. "I turned nineteen a few days ago and you tell me that I'm grounded?"

"I'll be leaving for New York by the end of next week but until then I don't want to see you anywhere near that son of a bitch," my father says, ignoring me.

"You can't tell me who I can't see. You can't control my life anymore."

He rolls his eyes. "Like hell I can." He leans back in his chair and puts his hand on his chin as if he is bored. "We'll talk more about this in the morning. I don't want to talk to you right now, Ariella."

I nip my bottom lip. "I wish it was you instead of her."

I don't wait to see his reaction; I don't want to see the look of hurt in his eyes.

I rush out the door and run upstairs to my room before closing the door and locking it.

FORTY-TWO

ASH

PRESENT

Ariella makes me do things that I never would have thought of doing. I feel deranged whenever I am with or without her. This feeling she gives me makes me feel on edge the entire time.

I never know what will happen next with her.

And I hate how easily she is able to bring down my walls. That's the fucked-up part. Ariella has always been a need since I met her.

So, when her father said to leave, I did the exact opposite.

I walk through her house with quiet footsteps and a rapid heart. Her father is asleep. I made sure before I decided to come through the back door.

When I am in front of Ariella's bedroom door, I

slowly turn the handle and open the door softly. I look through the crack of her door and see Ariella laying on her stomach, reading a book.

Ariella is wearing white lacy underwear and a familiar black band shirt that has rips in it.

Seeing her in that position with clothes that barely cover her skin makes me want to run my hands down her body and make her forget the outside world.

I slowly walk inside her room and close the door. Ariella is so distracted by what's happening in her book that she doesn't notice how I lock the door and walk up to her.

I look over her shoulder and see the page number she's on.

Page 289.

When I put my hands on her hips and turn her around, she gasps and lets go of her book. Her eyes widen and fear flows through her before she realizes it's me.

She smacks my chest. "Ash." She glares at me before turning around and grabbing her book. "You made me lose my place," she says while flipping through the pages.

"289." I grab the book from her and go to 289.

I bend one of the pages before closing the book and throwing it on the floor.

"How did you get in?"

"I have my ways." I get off of her and instead rest my

back against her headboard. I keep my eyes on her, studying her. The holes and rips in the t-shirt confirm it's mine. I remember all of those holes and rips that I have made throughout the years on that old janky thing. Seeing Ariella wear something of mine with nothing underneath makes me feel like a possessive asshole who wants to mark his territory. It's like all I want to do is make sure every person on this goddamn planet knows that she's mine, even her fucking dad. My cock swells as I trail my eyes down her body. "Come here." Ariella complies and she sits herself on my lap. I rest my head against the headboard and place my hands on her hips. "What happened with your dad?" I ask at the same time Ariella squirms against my lap, making me even harder.

If she doesn't stop that right now, I'm going to force her down my cock and make her scream so loud her dad will hear it.

"Do we have to talk about that?" Ariella grinds her hips against mine and I close my eyes.

"Stop. Tell me," I say through gritted teeth.

I feel Ariella's lips on my neck. I turn my head to the side to give her more access.

"You don't need to worry about what he is saying about you," Ariella whispers in my ear before trailing her kisses down my neck. I feel her hands lift the hem of my shirt, touching my stomach before running her fingers across my navel. "Want to know something?"

I open my eyes and see Ariella staring down at me. "What?"

Ariella looks down at my lips before leaning closer. "I think I might love you, Ash Jones," she says as her lips brush against mine.

I kiss her to shut up the thoughts in my head. I take off the stupid ripped shirt to get rid of the all-consuming thoughts. They need to go away.

I don't say anything to her.

Ariella trembles as I glide my fingers down her arm. Goosebumps rise on her skin and she wraps her arms around me.

"Do you understand how breathtaking you are Ariella?"

"Ash-"

"You have the ability to destroy me," I whisper against her lips.

I thrust my hips up to meet her wet, warm pussy. The way both of our parts rub against one another almost hurts. I want to be inside her. I need to be inside her, but the torture is so fucking good.

I slide my sweatpants off and throw them across the room. I rip Ariella's underwear off, making her gasp.

"Please, Ash," she begs before using her hand to stroke my dick. Her hand is tight around me making me close my eyes and rest my head on her shoulder. All of a sudden, I am surrounded by hot, wet walls clenching onto my cock as Ariella pushes down on me, her hand flicking against her clit making her moan and buck against me. "Yes."

"You like being full of my cock, Ariella?"

"Yes." She closes her eyes and begins to move, lifting herself off of my dick before pushing back down. Her fingers grab my shoulders and they dig into my skin, probably drawing blood. "I love it when you're inside me, Ash."

I lean into her chest as she grinds on top of me. My lips wrap around her boob, Ariella moans and pushes her chest into my face more as I lick, bite, and suck. I move onto the next one as Ariella holds me against her chest, moving up and down on my cock.

I trail my hand up her body until it's holding her throat. I don't squeeze but Ariella opens her eyes and looks down at me.

Lust is in her gaze and her eyelids are droopy.

Her thrusts are getting slow and sensual.

I force her down on my dick and lean close to her. "I'm going to ruin you for any other man, Ariella. Strip you bare and fuck you in front of anyone who thinks they will ever get a fucking chance with you. You are mine."

I thrust inside her. "Yes."

"Say it," I demand in her ear.

She stays quiet, eyes still closed as she grinds on me, pleasure consuming her.

I push her off of me and force her on her back. I

spread her legs wide and thrust inside her deeply, to the hilt.

Her walls clench around me tightly and her nails claw my hands. "Ash, I'm close-"

I hold her throat in my hand as I continue to thrust inside her roughly. "Say it."

She moans and bucks her hips against me as her body shakes with pleasure. "I'm yours, Ash. Stop, it's too much."

"Over my dead fucking body."

I thrust inside her, over and over and over. My other hand reaches down and massages her clit making her legs wrap around me, tightly.

I press my lips to hers, muffling her moans.

I don't care if her dad hears or not, but I don't want him to hear the vivid sounds she makes as she comes and squirts all over me.

Ariella freezes up as I spill inside her.

I let go of her neck and rest my hand on the side of her head. My eyes go to our connected bodies. My hand is still rubbing her clit in slow circles.

I pull out of her which makes Ariella moan and shiver.

I kiss my way down her body before meeting her cunt. Her cum and mine are mixed together. I can't help but keep my eyes on Ariella as I lean in and run my tongue down the slit of her cunt.

I lick Ariella clean and she cums for the third time.

By the time I have cleaned her up with a warm towel, she is half asleep and her chest rises and falls. I pull her under the covers, tucking her by my side.

I kiss her forehead and stroke her hair as I watch her.

"Ash?" she mumbles.

"Yea," I whisper, tightening my hold on her.

"I love you."

My heart stops again.

I can fuck her until she doesn't remember what she just said.

But it won't change the fact that I am completely fucked.

FORTY-THREE
ARIELLA

SUMMER

"Ash!" I yell, feeling cold water splash on me.

I splash water back at him and then run in the opposite direction of him. I hear more splashing, making me run faster knowing he is trying to catch me.

He thought that spending the night at the beach again was a good idea. So, we've been at the beach all day in the water, walking around the area. We got ice cream earlier and ate at this Italian restaurant. He also took me for a ride down the Pacific Highway on his motorcycle. It felt freeing to experience that with Ash. He told me that one day he wants me to try and drive it. He paid for everything of course, despite my efforts to pay. This whole summer, I haven't paid a dime because of him. I feel like it's so unfair but he doesn't care.

I feel strong, warm arms wrap around my waist making me squeal. Ash picks me up and throws me over his shoulder.

"Got you," he says, sending a light slap on my ass making me gasp and try to wiggle out of his arms.

Water splashes around us as a wave crashes on Ash and I. I still try to get out of his hold but he has a tight grip on me.

"Ash, let me go!" I laugh and he sends another slap to my ass making me gasp.

"Are you sure?"

"Yes. Please!" Next thing I know I feel my body surrounded by cold water. My eyes immediately close and I hold my breath. It's freezing cold in the water and it's only going to get colder as it gets darker. Ash and I should get out of the water before it gets too dark. I swim up until my head reaches the surface. I open my eyes and look around for Ash only to find him behind me with a smirk on his face. He swims closer to me and his hands hold my waist. I lick water off my lips. "Can we get out? It's starting to get cold," I say, leaning closer to Ash, needing his warmth.

"Yea," he mumbles before kissing the top of my head.

We swim to where the sand meets the water and Ash rewraps his hand around my waist, pulling me into his body. He feels so warm while I am shivering from how cold it is.

When we get to our tent, I grab the biggest towel I brought and wrap it around my body. I get inside the tent and sit down. Ash comes inside a few seconds later with a towel around his body. He sits next to me and pulls me into his chest.

"How are you so warm all the time?" I mumble and rest my head against his chest.

"How are you so cold?"

He got me there. "I wish I knew."

Things with Ash have been good. Since the night we went to his tree house we have been going to the beach, the book store, restaurants, motorcycle drives late at night, sometimes we go hiking and then jump off waterfall cliffs. I have never been so happy and felt so free. Things with him have been amazing this summer.

We have completed all of the bucket list items.

2023 Summer

Go on a date with a stranger.

Kiss a stranger.

Go to a club and dance with a stranger.

Ask a hot person for their number.

Go to New York.

Have sex with a stranger.

Watch the stars.

Watch fireworks on the tallest hill.
Go to the fair
Spend the whole day at the beach.
Sneak into a movie theater.
Get a tattoo with a stranger.

All have been completed. And each one has been one of the best experiences I have ever had. And it's all because of Ash.

I never thought I would have the guts to do something like ask a guy like him on a date. I never thought I would have the guts to even spend time with someone like him.

Ash and I don't talk for a while. I just look down at his hands that are tracing my palm lines. He has little tattoos on his hands that follow up his arm. He also has some on his back and chest.

I've never really asked about his tattoos.

"Do your tattoos mean something?" I ask, tracing a small tattoo on his wrist.

"Most of them do. All of my tattoos have a story behind them but not all of them mean something significant."

The one wrapped around his wrist is a barbed wire tattoo. "What does this one mean?" I asked, stroking that tattoo with my finger.

I feel his head move against mine. "To me it's like suffocation but worse."

"Why did you get it?"

He is quiet which makes me think he isn't going to answer so I move on to the next one. It's a teddy bear holding a paper.

"What about this one?"

"That is a gift I got from one of my friends who committed suicide."

Now I feel bad for asking.

"Can I ask why?"

"She didn't want to be in a world where only cruel things happened to her."

"I'm sorry."

"Don't be. I would have been unhappy if she were still here wanting to kill herself. I'm happy that she was able to find a way to live peacefully."

"No one should face that though."

Ash sighs. "I think that if you truly think there is no other way to make you happy or make you want to live then you should go ahead and do what you want to do. Why would anyone want to stay in this world where you have to pay to breathe or pay to even do anything?"

Deciding to go on to another topic I look at another tattoo on his arm. "What about this one?"

This tattoo is a guy with wings sitting down and

resting his head on the ground. This guy looks desperate and miserable. He looks like he wishes he could stop the voices in his head.

"That's me. A dark angel."

"Why? Why are you posing like that with your face to the ground?" I ask, sadness laced in my voice.

"Because that's how I felt Ariella," he whispers. "Choose another one."

"This one," I ask, scared to hear what dark and twisted thing he tattooed on himself.

It's a sentence, in what looks like Russian, across the side of his tricep.

"It means 'Forever Until The End.' My mom was Russian and she would always repeat this phrase to me."

I hate how his voice cracks a little while saying that. He never ever talks about his mother and I wish I knew why.

Deciding to move on to another tattoo I point to the syringe. "What's this one?"

"It's so that I don't forget."

I feel a small tear fall from my eyes.

I look up at Ash and I see him already looking down at me. "Do I even want to know what the other ones mean?"

"No. And I don't feel like breaking your heart today so don't ask."

I lick my bottom lip as another tear falls from my face.

I nod my head and lean forward to press my lips against his.

As our lips move against one another we fall against the covers and everything disappears into the shadows making it just Ash and I.

FORTY-FOUR
ASH

PRESENT

I jolt awake when I feel a harsh hand grab my shoulder. I open my eyes and look to my left, seeing Ariella sleeping soundly. She looks so peaceful when she is sleeping, especially as she curls into my side.

My eyes go down to her chest which is covered. I turn my head and see her father glaring at me.

His eyes are filled with hatred and he looks like he wants to kill me.

Feeling's fucking mutual.

That asshole.

"Get the fuck out of her bed before I kill you in front of her."

Doubtful.

This motherfucker knows what I have done.

He was in the courtroom that day trying to put me behind bars.

"You get out first," I whisper, not wanting to wake Ariella up.

Cal shifts his eyes to his daughter who has her head curled into my chest with the sheets covering her chest. "You really think I want to see my daughter naked? Get a fucking grip."

"I'm not asking," I say calmly.

Cal looks at Ariella before looking back at me. I see his jaw clench and my eyes move down to his fists that are turning white.

He turns and gets out of Ariella's room, closing the door behind him softly.

I slowly get out of bed without managing to wake Ariella up. I cover her with the blanket before throwing on my sweatpants and sweater.

I slowly get out of Ariella's room. When I turn around, I see Cal waiting for me, leaning against the wall across from me.

"You were supposed to be gone." I shake my head before going downstairs. This asshole doesn't fucking understand that his daughter is trying to sleep. Cal leads me to his office. He closes the door behind me and tells me to take a seat. "Want whiskey?"

I furrow my eyebrows at him.

What is his play?

"No. Stop bullshitting around and tell me why you woke me up?" I lean back against the chair.

"It's no secret I don't like you, Ash," he says while pouring himself a glass of whiskey, at nine in the morning. "You have a very dangerous mind. You are corrupted by your father, who I don't like and you have blood on your hands. It's no secret."

"Then why don't you tell Ariella?" I narrow my eyes at him.

"Because she is sensitive when it comes to things like that. She always sees the good in people. A trait from her mother." He sits in his chair and puts the glass on the desk. "She won't care. She loves you."

I know.

She said it so many times last night while I was inside her.

"What is the point of you telling me all this? I'm not going to hurt her Cal and you should know that."

"Do you love her?" My mind is hollow even though I know the truth. My heart is beating rapidly as I think hard about the answer. "Leave her. It's for the best. You will only ruin her."

Leaving Ariella would also mean bringing back all of the demons inside my mind.

"I think that's up to Ariella."

"Ash, if you don't leave my daughter, I will not hesitate to tell her about what you have done."

"Go ahead. I don't care."

I say that but I'm ashamed of her knowing the truth.

Knowing my past with *her*.

"What about when she finds out what you did to her?"

My gaze finds his and the asshole is smirking at me, thinking he's got me.

Ariella doesn't know how my mother died. She doesn't know that I am responsible for my mother's death. She doesn't know that I am a cold-blooded monster.

My father put me straight into therapy after the accident happened. He told me that I needed to see someone to talk to about what happened and how I can relieve myself from it.

My father says I shouldn't keep worrying about it because the case closed and it was an accident. But I feel awful for not feeling bad.

I didn't feel an ounce of guilt when she died. I was relieved that she died but she still manages to hunt my mind and soul.

When I am with Ariella, I feel relieved, free even. I notice I don't think about the dark thoughts and that my mother's death doesn't consume me.

"No. You can tell her. I was planning on telling her anyway." I shrug.

Cal shakes his head lightly. "You are a hard one to crack, Ash."

"Is this all you wanted to talk about? Because if so, I need to go back upstairs to make sure your daughter is still sleeping." Cal is quiet. He is just staring at me and every few seconds he squints his eyes, thinking hard about something. "Great. I'll be going then."

When I have my hand on the door knob, that's when Cal finally speaks up.

And what he says makes me stop and sit back down.

All I am thinking about is smashing this asshole's desk on top of him and making him cry out for mercy. As he tells me, he demands for me not to see his daughter.

"Ash, it's what's best for her. You really want to ruin Ariella's future?"

FORTY-FIVE

ARIELLA

PRESENT

Bridgette is coming in late today for reasons I don't know.

She told me it was because she went to a party and drank too much but I know it's something more. She has been keeping things from me.

I know it.

When I woke up yesterday morning, I didn't find Ash in bed. His side of the bed was cold when I woke up. I looked at my phone and saw no messages from him.

I didn't text him until last night and I still haven't gotten a text from him.

I know I said that I loved him last night.

I was feeling so overwhelmed and I needed to tell him. It just came out and I saw the hesitance in his eyes. He didn't say it back and that's okay, I just wish I didn't feel this way. I feel ignored and dumped which is stupid because Ash and I aren't really together. We never were.

I just thought our relationship was growing into something more.

When my father saw the frown on my face the morning he left, he seemed very happy, despite my mood. He was acting normal and tried to talk to me about Ash but I didn't want to talk to my father about him. All my father would do is judge me for being with someone he doesn't approve of.

I take my seat in the back of the class where I normally sit. I avoid Liam's eyes on purpose when I pass by him.

As more people start to come inside the classroom, I keep my eyes on the door, waiting patiently for Ash to walk in.

My heart is beating so fast and I can't help but feel nervous. I don't know why I feel so scared. I have talked to him many times before. This time is no different.

All I did was say that I loved him.

But he didn't say it back.

I can't help but feel giddy when I see him walk inside the room.

Today, Ash is wearing light blue jeans, and a gray hoodie with the hood up. As always, he looks good, even when he looks mad or pissed.

Ash always manages to look good. I don't know how

he has this ability to make my heart beat fast and make me want to hold him in my arms forever.

He is so beautiful that it sometimes hurts to look at him.

Ash's eyes find mine and I can't help but give him a small smile. Ash turns his head and chooses to sit down at the end of the row, far away from me.

The distance doesn't seem that far but to me it feels like he is miles away.

I pull out my phone and bring up our messages.

He still hasn't messaged me back. I have only texted him twice since I found out he left me alone in bed.

I stare at the messages and think of texting him. I look at Ash and see him staring at Liam who is talking about some assignment we have.

He looks so destroyed and I can't help but wonder what is going through his head. I wish I could see his hands but he has them tucked inside his pockets.

It feels like it's been hours when Liam says that we are free to leave.

Ash stands up and heads towards the door. I pack my things up quickly before running after him. I catch Liam's eye as I run out the door and catching up with Ash. I grab Ash's arm and bring his hands to me so that I can take a close look at them.

They have bruises and scratches on them, fresh cuts.

"Ash," I say softly but he pulls his hands away from mine.

"Do you need something?"

I look away from his hands and see him raising an eyebrow at me. His expression is bored and he almost seems annoyed while staring down at me.

"Did you get my messages? I've been worried about you?" I furrow my eyebrows at him.

Don't break my heart, please.

"Yea."

"Why didn't you answer me then? Are you mad at me or something?"

"Did you not get the hint or something?"

I look around us and thankfully there aren't many people around. "What do you mean?"

"Do I really have to spell it out for you Ariella?"

"Ash-"

"I only needed you for one thing. I'm over it." My heart breaks, little by little and then slowly my mind just shuts off. Everything around me is blurred and I can only focus on the way Ash is staring at me like I am the bane of his existence. Ash sighs. "Look what we had, it was fun for those few months but I'm bored. You're like every other girl, Ariella."

I ignore the pang in my heart.

My eyes feel watery but I don't let the tears fall. I will not have Ash Jones see my cry over him.

"I thought that-"

He furrows his eyebrows and his lips lift a little. It almost feels like he is mocking me and making fun of me and my feelings.

"Thought that I what? Loved you?"

"I-"

"Why would I love someone like you, Ariella? You're fake. You are like every other girl. There is nothing special about you and there never will be. Why would I want to be in love with you? I mean did say I would ruin you, didn't I?"

And just like that, I snap.

My hand connects with the side of his face and I hear a few gasps behind me.

A tear finally falls from my eye and I nip my bottom lip. "Fuck you." I push him by the chest. "Fuck you, Ash Jones. You're nothing but a heartless jerk. You don't care about anyone but yourself. It was a mistake to fall in love with you!" I yell before turning on my heel and avoiding all of the eyes burning into my back.

Even as I start my car and drive home, I still can't help but feel something strong for Ash. I still can't help but love him.

FORTY-SIX
ARIELLA

PRESENT

"Why does it feel like every time I ditch school, shit goes down?" Bridgette asks as she starts making popcorn.

We are having a movie night.

I'm feeling like shit and having Bridgette here, watching and laughing over silly romcoms will brighten my mood. I have missed hanging out with Bridgette, one on one. I feel like we haven't had a real conversation in a while.

"That's because you are always ditching school and you've been going to parties a lot." Bridgette blushes and now I assume that she isn't really going to parties, she is probably going someplace else. "What's with the blushing?" I raise my eyebrow at her.

Bridgette looks down at her hands. "Well, I'm not just going to parties, per se. I am seeing someone."

My jaw hangs. "Who is it?"

"He's coming over today."

I furrow my eyebrows. Jace is supposed to come over but not until later. My mind starts to piece it all together.

I have seen the lingering looks between Jace and Bridgette a lot lately. They have been hanging out but I didn't think they were hanging out that much. I noticed it after my birthday. I also know Jace has had a thing for Bridgette for a while. It's easy to read him because of how he manages to flirt with her but also tease her. I notice the way he looks at her like she is the only one in the room.

"It's Jace?" I raise my eyebrow at her and Bridgette nods. "You bitch."

"I know." She closes her eyes and sighs. "I feel awful for not telling you. It's just, things between us have been so good. I am really happy with him."

"I can tell." I give her a soft smile. "I know Jace has always liked you."

"Really?" She furrows her eyebrows.

"Yea, it's obvious."

"I never thought it was. I kind of compared my relationship with Jace to you and Ash."

I furrow my eyebrows at this. "How so? If anything, Ash and I were toxic for each other."

"Hell no." Bridgette chuckles and she leans back into the couch. "You guys love each other too much."

My heart breaks slightly once again. "He doesn't. The feeling between us isn't mutual."

"How do you know?"

"Because he told me."

"But you don't see the way he looks at you when you are looking somewhere else."

"What do you mean?"

Bridgette smiles at me like I am playing dumb. "Ariella, that boy is in love with you. He looks at you like you are his entire world. He looks at you like you are the only one who can save him from his demons."

I shake my head lightly.

No he doesn't.

The way Ash looked at me the other day broke my heart. He looked at me like his entire world fell because of me.

The way he spoke to me was filled with hate and I know for a fact that he said all of that because he wanted to hurt me.

The sound of knocking makes me look at the door. Bridgette gets up with an excited smile on her face. She answers the door and I look back at the TV, wanting to give her and Jace some privacy.

"Thank you for coming." I hear Bridgette. "I am really happy you came. I already told Ariella and she actually had a suspicion about you." Bridgette chuckles. Jace says something but that doesn't make me turn my head. The sound of Bridgette cursing catches my attention. "You aren't supposed to be here." I turn my head and see Ash walk through the doorway.

My heart stops and so does time. His eyes connect with mine and I can't stop staring at him.

Ash is wearing a black fitted shirt that shows off his biceps and I can't help but want to run my hand across the muscle. He is also wearing gray sweatpants and my eyes go down to where his hips are. I can see the outline of his bulge making me cross my legs.

"Sorry, I didn't know that the two of them aren't on good terms," Jace apologizes and I start to feel bad.

"It's fine. Ash and I are both adults. We can sit and watch a movie without tearing each other's throats." I joke before looking at Ash. "Right?"

Ash's eyes look empty as he stares at me. "Right." He walks in and seats himself on the couch a few inches away from me.

"What movie are we watching?" Jace asks before sitting on the couch with Bridgette.

"Killers."

"With Ashton Kutcher? Damn if I were to turn gay for anyone, It'd be him. He is a good-looking guy."

"I would probably leave you for him," Bridgette says.

I look away from Jace and Bridgette and look at the

screen. I try not to pay attention to how hot I feel from Ash just being a few inches away from me.

Thankfully my dad left. He said he has business to do back in New York so he couldn't stay any longer. He was going to leave at the end of the week but something with his client came up. We haven't talked that much since I got into an argument with him about Ash.

I don't get why he has such a huge problem with Ash and why he had to ruin everything.

But at the same time, Ash also ruined things as well.

"What's going on in that pretty little head of yours?" I feel Ash whisper against my ear, sending shivers down my spine.

How does he have the ability to make me feel so weak around him? I swear he is the only one.

"Leave me alone and watch the movie," I whisper before looking at Bridgette and Jace who are cuddled against each other, watching the movie.

I feel Ash's warm hand lay on my upper thigh. As I feel him stroke my inner thigh with his thumb.

"You feel warm down there. Are you wet Ariella?" Ash whispers. I try to press my thighs together to not let him get any closer but he doesn't let up. Instead he keeps his hand in between my thighs and spreads my legs. Thank God for the blanket. "Even though I humiliated you, you still manage to spread your legs for me."

God, I want to punch him in the face. "Why do you

always manage to ruin everything?" I scoot away from him but his hand lingers.

Ash smirks and he doesn't move his hand from the inside of my thigh as he says, "Because ruining you is my favorite thing to do."

FORTY-SEVEN
ASH

PRESENT

Some Weekend song is blasting through the speakers. Everyone is either dancing, drinking, or stuffing some kind of drug up their nose.

Jace dragged me here because he thought I needed a night out. He thinks I am pissed off and sexually frustrated.

He doesn't know that I am just aching to punch some glass.

My mind is going in circles and I can't stop thinking about Ariella.

Seeing her the other day, looking so beautifully broken and sad because of me, made my heart ache.

I feel like shit but I have to do this.

It's for Ariella and her future. Her father is a menace who doesn't care about anyone other than himself.

He reminds me a lot of my father which is ironic because they hate one another for reasons I still don't know about.

"Can you wipe that sour puss look off your face?" Nash says, putting his hand on my shoulder. "You look like you want to punch every motherfucker's face."

Because I do.

Nash is someone from one of my classes and I met him on one of the first days of school. I don't really talk to him that much. I'm nice to him when I do see him and I make conversation but that's it. We never hangout.

"Yes, and if you don't stop talking you will be the first," I threaten before taking a sip of my drink.

I just need to quiet my mind and I don't know why Jace bothered to bring me here thinking it would help me.

I don't even know where he is. He told me he needed to go outside because Bridgette was calling him.

I swear since him and Bridgette have started dating, they have not kept their hands off one another.

Whenever Bridgette is with Jace and me, she gives me dirty looks and doesn't speak a word to me.

I know that Ariella told her about everything.

I don't care.

As long as Ariella has her future intact I don't care.

"Whoa, I didn't know Jace had Zoë Kravitz for a girl-friend," Nash's friend sitting next to him says.

I turn my head to the front door and see Jace walking in with his arm around Bridgette's waist.

But I could care less about them two. My eyes go to the brown-haired girl next to them.

Ariella is wearing a black mini dress and her hair is half up, half down.

She looks like a devil sent from hell.

Nash leans back in his chair and I notice his eyes going to Ariella. "Nah, my eyes are on the one next to her." I shove Nash against the wall, keeping my hand pressed against his chest. "Ash, what the fuck?"

"Keep looking at her like that and I swear to God I'll fucking take your eyes out of your eye sockets."

"Dude, it's not even that serious. Calm down."

I take my hand off his chest and walk away.

I can't bother with him. It's like talking to a wall. He is a fucking douche bag who only really cares about himself and who is in his bed for the night.

I walk up to Jace and I can see the guilt in his eyes. "Hey, Ash."

I look away from Jace and my eyes meet Ariella's instead. "You look nice."

To my surprise, Ariella's cheeks turn a shade darker but she doesn't smile.

Ariella ignores me and turns to Bridgette instead. "I'm going to go get a drink. Do you want to come?"

"Sure." Bridgette looks at Jace. "I'll meet up with you later."

Jace nods his head and kisses Bridgette before she walks away with Ariella. Bridgette and Ariella walk past me and go to the kitchen where all the drinks are, purposely bumping into my shoulder making me smirk at Ariella and her attitude.

"Please don't cause any trouble tonight. Bridgette said that Ariella needs a night out and I told them about this party."

"Who said I'll cause any trouble?" I furrow my eyebrows at him. "You bring me to this party to try and have me forget about her yet you decide to invite her?"

Jace sighs and walks closer to me. "Look, I just don't want any trouble tonight. You can keep your distance from Ariella, can't you? I mean, if you didn't want any issues then why are you still talking and flirting with her."

I shake my head lightly.

Jace doesn't know anything and therefore I don't bother answering him or think about what he is trying to tell me.

"Whatever."

I walk past Jace and go towards the bathroom.

As I walk past the kitchen my eyes immediately find Ariella who is talking to Bridgette with a smile on her face.

She doesn't know this but I know that the smile on her face is fake and she is hiding her hurt with fake happiness.

I can tell the difference between her real and genuine smile rather than her fake and filtered smile.

I lock the door behind me and then stare at myself in the bathroom mirror.

"The beach has always been a place I feel safe and secure," Ariella says while playing with the sand.

"Why?"

"Because of my mother. She took me here a lot because I was always stressed out about school and drama."

"High school wasn't the best time for me."

Mostly because of my mother's doing but I don't tell Ariella that.

This thing between Ariella and I is only going to last for a few months. There is no point to opening up my feelings to her because we won't know each other for long.

I do want to stay in contact with her because I like Ariella. I have never felt this way about someone before.

Ariella shuts down all of the horrible and dark thoughts in my head. All of my mothers voices become silent when she is near.

I look down at my hands and see the scars from punching the mirrors.

I clench and unclench my fists, seeing the skin split and blood form.

"These are my friends, Ash. You'll be nice to them, right?"

I look away from them and wash my hands before getting out of the bathroom. When I get out of the bathroom my eyes go to the kitchen where I see Ariella.

What makes me run towards her is Nash who is holding her against the counter, getting way too close for my liking.

Where the fuck are Bridgette and Jace?

My vision goes blurry when I send a punch to Nash's face.

"Ash!" I hear Ariella yell as I tackle Nash to the floor and send more punches across his face.

There are gasps and I don't hear the music blasting through the speakers anymore. "Oh, he is beating his ass!" I hear someone yell.

I pay no mind to anyone, I focus in on Nash's face and the way my fist connects with his nose, over and over and over again.

Everything is blocked out.

All I can see is Nash touching Ariella and how uncomfortable she felt.

"Ash, stop, I can't see him breathing!" I hear Ariella yell.

"Move out of the way!" Jace yells before I feel a hand on my shoulder before someone pulls me away from Nash. My vision comes into focus and I see blood. Blood is on the floor and when I look down at my hands there is blood and the scars fully reopened. Everything is red and my mind turns blank. "Dude what the fuck?" Jace yells and he puts his hand on my chest.

My eyes travel around the kitchen, trying to find Ariella but I don't see her.

I push Jace out of my way and I walk towards the front door where I see Ariella leaving. I push people out of my way and follow her outside.

"Ariella!" I yell but she doesn't turn her head or acknowledge me. "God fucking damnit, Ariella!" When I am close enough to Ariella, I grab her hand and turn her around. I feel a harsh slap on my face. It stings but I know I deserve it after what I put her through. "Are you done?"

"You are awful!" She slaps my chest and shoves me away from her. "You always have to cause trouble!"

"I didn't like how close he was to you. You looked like you wanted to punch him yourself."

"It doesn't mean that you should go and punch him, Ash! You can't keep doing that. You are the one who said this was over. Not me. So fucking act like it Ash. Stop going back and forth," she argues.

"So next time someone touches you like that you want me to turn my eye?" I lean towards Ariella and she doesn't say a thing. "Let me tell you something, Ariella." I walk closer to her and she bumps into a car. I place a hand on the car, next to her head and lean closer until our lips are an inch apart. "Anyone lays a hand on you and I'll fucking end them."

Ariella closes her eyes. "Please, leave me alone. You have hurt me enough, Ash." She opens her eyes and a frown is placed on her lips. Her eyes look watery but I know she won't cry. Not in front of me. "You don't love me, you used me. Please just stick to your word and stop playing with me."

Fuck.

Knowing that she actually believes that hurts me.

She couldn't be more wrong.

If only I can just hold her again. If only I can just have her as mine without worrying about the consequences.

Forty-Eight
Ariella

PRESENT

"I swear I don't Bridgette. He's a fucking douchebag."
I mutter while flipping a page over in the book I'm
reading.

"But the way he looks at you, says something entirely
different," Bridgette argues while I roll my eyes.

Bridgette is such a hopeless romantic. Although she
has troubles, or at least had trouble before getting together
with Jace officially.

"Well, we're done. He never cared about me." I close
the book, not even in the mood to read anymore. Talking
about Ash, being reminded of his heartless words and
heartless self is making my head hurt. "Look, I have to go.
I have a lot of stuff to catch up on for classes."

Bridgette and I hang up after saying bye and I toss my

phone on the side table next to my bed. Goosebumps appear on my skin and I feel the hair on the back of my neck rise. I turn around and see Ash leaning against the doorway.

The last time I saw him was at the party. After I told him to leave me alone he walked back inside the house. I took a few minutes outside to calm myself down and when I went back into the house I saw a girl talking to him.

I felt enraged but also heartbroken. My heart and head are all over the place and I know I told Ash to stay away and just do his own thing, but it hurts seeing him try and move on.

When I saw him with the girl I went to Bridgette and told her I was leaving. We took my car so I left without her because she said that Jace was going to take her home.

When I got home, I spent the night crying and letting myself feel pathetic, only when no one could see me.

"What are you doing here? Didn't you get the hint yesterday?" I ask, sitting up and suddenly feeling insecure with my legs out in the open.

I feel so revealed to him by just wearing this thin tank top and short cotton shorts. Ash's eyes go to my nipples, which I'm sure are puckered and poking through the shirt.

His jaw ticks and he leans off the door before walking towards the bed. "I did but I just wanted to know something." Ash gets on the bed and he leans against the headboard, resting his long, muscular legs on the bed.

Ash is wearing gray sweatpants and then a black compression shirt that shows off his arms beautifully.

"What?" I ask, bringing my legs to my chest, trying not to touch him.

One touch from Ash would ignite everything inside me.

"Come here first," Ash says before his eyes move to his lap and back to me.

Hell no.

He can't just come here and demand things like that from me.

Not anymore.

"No." I get up from the bed and am about to walk towards the door so I can make him get out, but Ash's hand grabs my wrist and my butt is pressed against his hips where I can feel his hardened erection. "Ash," I say, resting my hands on his shoulders, wanting to pull myself away from him.

But being near him, against him, feeling his warmth surrounding me, feels so good and comforting. I feel safe even though this boy has broken my heart so many times.

"When you saw me at the party before you left, were you jealous?" Ash asks, trailing his finger over my arm and along my shoulder.

"What do you mean?" I ask, trying not to shiver from his touch.

Ash stops touching my shoulder and instead, he pulls me closer to him. I refrain from gasping as I feel his erection rubbing against my sensitive spot.

"When I was with that girl before you left, were you jealous?" Ash asks, leaning his face closer to me so that our lips were just a centimeter apart.

It feels like our energy keeps trying to pull us closer and it's only a matter of time before we both do something we regret.

"No," I whisper and I feel Ash's lip brush against mine.

"Say it again. And tell the truth this time."

"I wasn't jealous."

Ash takes my hands on his shoulders and puts them on the headboard near his head. "I want to try something," Ash says while he rests back against the headboard and he rests his hands behind his head. "Let's see who can go the longest without touching one another. If you admit you're jealous maybe I'll let you touch me."

"I'm not playing any of your games-" Before I could finish arguing with him, Ash presses his lips against mine hard.

His tongue glides against mine immediately and I moan against his lips, wanting to kiss him forever.

My mind is long gone and the only thinking right now is my heart and how it feels when Ash holds it gently.

"That girl I was with at the party, she couldn't kiss me like you ," Ash mumbles against my lips, still not daring to touch me. I can't help but grind against his hips. I'm holding myself up by grabbing onto the headboard. "No one could kiss me like you do Ariella."

"Then why were you with her?" I ask before nipping his bottom lip.

Ash thrusts up and moans into my mouth as we lick and suck each other's lips. I feel like I can't breathe but when Ash's lips are on me it's like he's giving me air so I don't need to take a break. I just need him.

And I hate how I do.

"Are you jealous?"

"No." I moan and breathe heavily in his mouth.

"Liar." He whispers.

"Why were you with her?"

"To see if I could feel this. To see if someone could make me feel like I'm about to fucking fly." He takes my lips in his again and I melt immediately. I grip the headboard hard, trying my hardest to not move my hands. He needs to be the one to move first. "Should I go back to her? Should I go touch her like this Madden?"

I try to lean away from Ash but he follows me, still not taking his lips off of mine. "I'll go and find Nash and see if he wants to take a swing-"

Next thing I know I'm on my back and Ash's hands are on me. I gasp and wrap my legs around him as he pushes his hips into me.

"I'll fuck you in front of his swollen eyes and make sure he knows not to touch what's fucking mine." He bites down on my lips and I moan, arching my back. I thrust my fingers in his hair as I kiss him and make inaudible sounds. "I'll make you go crazy Ariella. I'll keep edging you in front of him, so desperate to come in front of him but never let you."

I push him off of me, as much as it pains me to. The spot between my legs hurts but all he's doing is teasing and tormenting me. He's doing all of this on purpose.

"Get out," I say, still sitting on the bed as he gets up.

My eyes go to his hips where I see a noticeable bulge. My eyes go back to his eyes where there is a glint of mischief and a smirk playing on his lips.

"Come on Ariella, I know you like this cat-and-mouse game between us."

"Fuck you. You can't keep doing this. You can't keep changing your mind about wanting me or not. You constantly do this. It's all you have done to me. Don't you think I'm getting tired of it?"

"You don't get it." Ash shakes his head lightly and I can't help but laugh.

"You're insane."

"You haven't even seen insane, Ariella. You seriously don't understand."

"What? What don't I understand? You're not even making any sense. You can't keep going back and forth." Ash doesn't say anything which just happens to make me even more pissed off. I shake my head. "Forget it. Just get out and go." Ash still stands in the middle of my room, waiting for something, as if it will just show itself to him. "All you do is hurt people. Can't you see that I'm hurting because of you?" I ask but he still doesn't say a word.

His jaw clenches before he backs away from the bed and leaves out the door.

FORTY-NINE
ARIELLA

SUMMER

One of the things I've been doing this summer is hanging out with Ash at the beach.

We sit on the sand and watch the stars while talking about weird theories or our life back at home without revealing too much.

I have talked about my mom a lot more with him.

I told Ash all of the wonderful things my mother has done for me and then all of our adventures. I would also smile while talking about her and I swear I saw Ash's eyes glow when he was listening to me.

He listens like everything I'm telling him is valuable and important information that he doesn't want to miss hearing.

"What is going on in that head of yours?"

I turn my head and look at Ash. "I'm just listening to the waves. It's peaceful."

"What do you think is out there?"

I shrug and look back at the waves. "I don't know. I definitely think mermaids are real."

"Mermaids?" I look at Ash and see his eyebrow is raised.

"Yea." I smile. "Only 2% of the ocean is discovered. If mermaids aren't real then something close to them are. How else would people come up with the ideas of mermaids?"

"There is only so much we know," Ash answers.

"What do you think is out there?"

This time he shrugs. "I don't know. I'm not a marine nerd so I don't focus too much on the ocean."

"Can you just entertain me for a minute?" I raise my eyebrow at him and his smirks before looking down at my lips for a second before meeting me eyes again.

"I can entertain you by doing something else," he offers. I can't help but blush and turn my head away from him. How does he have the ability to make me feel so hot and happy so randomly? I've never been big on boys or focused on them too much but with Ash, all I can focus on is him. "Any good books you've read yet?" Ash asks, breaking me out of my thoughts.

"I started reading this one book about a girl who is a killer and an FBI agent. The girl is killing all of these people who ruined her life when she was seventeen and the FBI agent is investigating her case but they fall in love during that."

"What's the twist to this story?"

I love how Ash knows all of the little details about me and what I read.

I always love reading romance books or thrillers. But whenever there is a mind-fucking twist that's when I can't stop talking about it.

"The plot overall was the twist. The experience she had when she was seventeen."

"Did the FBI agent find out who she really was?"

I smile at Ash.

My eyes go down to his lips before meeting his eyes. "I don't know yet. I haven't finished reading the entire book. I'm close to the end."

Ash looks down at my lips before leaning in slowly and kissing me. Ash kisses me like he wants to own my soul and take away all of my fight.

He deepens the kiss and nips my bottom lip making me gasp. He thrusts his tongue inside and I feel his hand on my jaw.

"You are so addicting, Ariella," Ash mumbles against my lips as he starts to lay me down on the blanket. "How do you do it?"

I remove my lips from his, my chest rising as I try to calm my breathing down.

"Do what?"

"Make the demons in my head silent."

I look at Ash with sadness filled in my eyes.

I put my hand on his cheek. "I didn't do that, Ash. You just managed to make them quiet by thinking about something else."

"You're the only one who can do it." Ash rests his forehead on mine.

I wrap my arms around him and pull his body closer to mine.

I can feel his heart beat rapidly against my chest. Even though it's a little chilly outside I feel warm with Ash in my arms. I only focus on the vibrations of his heart beating against his chest.

The sound of the waves are in the background and I manage to close my eyes, falling asleep.

FIFTY

ARIELLA

Liam sent out an email saying he had an important announcement he wanted to make in class today.

I can't help but wonder what it is.

When I walk inside the classroom it's empty except for Liam who is sitting at his desk looking through papers.

The door closes behind me and I grip the strap of my backpack tighter when Liam's eyes connect with mine.

We haven't spoken once since he told me about my grade. I try to never be alone with him because I know what he is capable of. I have heard of the allegations that no one tries to speak too much about.

Liam likes to keep his secrets hidden and away from trouble.

"Ariella." I turn my head to look at Liam who is now

leaning against his desk. "Can you come here for a second?"

My heart starts beating rapidly and the grip on my backpack tightens. I walk up to Liam and stand in front of him.

"What's up?"

"Your grades. I've noticed that they have dropped."

I lick my bottom lip nervously. "I have been super caught up with things outside of school. I couldn't really focus too much on what I was doing in all of the assignments."

"I know but you should have told me, Ariella. I mean final exams are coming up and you need to do your best on those."

I furrow my eyebrows at him. "With all due respect Mr. Locke, I have been preoccupied with other things and you are the last person I would tell those things too."

I see Liam's eyes darken and when I look down at his hands, I see him clenching them in fists.

Liam has always been a calm and steady guy. I have never really seen him go out of control and do things without a plan. Every step he takes, he takes with a plan.

He stops leaning on the desk and now Liam and I are face to face. If he were to take one step closer to me then a paper wouldn't be able to slip through us. Our chests would touch and I would probably start breaking down and freaking out.

Where are all of the other students? Was this some kind of fucked up plan that Liam came up with to get me alone? Where is everyone?

As I am thinking all of this my mind can't help but go to Ash who I am secretly wishing was here with me right now.

I wish I could be in his arms, protected from the world.

"I think you might need some extra credit to help you bring those grades up. Don't you think?"

"I don't like what you're implying, Mr. Locke. I know about your extra credit that you offer."

"Ariella, you're a smart girl." Liam finally takes that step and next thing I know I feel his hand touching my cheek. I try to turn my head away but Liam doesn't let me. "I am trying to offer you something that a lot of girls would take."

"I told you once and I'm not going to tell you again, Mr. Locke. Please take your hand off me," I say softly, wishing he would just step back and leave me alone. Lines form on Liam's forehead and I can tell he is getting frustrated. Then I feel his hand on my cheek grip me tighter. His fingers dig into my jaw and tears start to form in my eyes. "Liam, you're hurting me. Please stop," I say while trying to get his hand off of me.

"You keep fucking pushing and pushing, Ariella. You

know you want me." He pushes me to the ground and I land on my butt. "Why can't you just accept what I am trying to give you?" I get up and don't think twice before running towards the door but I feel a hand grip the back of my neck and pull me away from the door. "You're too good for that little shit, Ariella. I can show you what a real man is."

Liam pushes me down to the floor and he straddles my hips making me feel the evidence of how much he wants me.

"P-Please get off of me. Please," I cry out while trying to get him off of me, bucking my hips up but all Liam does is groan.

"Oh this is going to be so good." Liam groans before holding my hands above my head with one of his before I hear a belt fumbling.

Oh no, please.

"Please, wait wait. Please stop, Liam. Please, I'll do anything, just please get off of me," I say, as tears start to run down my face.

My heart is beating against my chest so rapidly and my mind feels foggy.

I just want to close my eyes and pretend that I am anywhere but here.

"You are going to feel so good," Liam says while using his hand to unbutton my jeans.

I close my eyes and turn my head.

Just pretend you are anywhere else but here. You are anywhere else but here.

I tune everything out.

Just prepare yourself.

You can do this. Just imagine you are anywhere else but here.

I blow out a breath at the same time I hear a door open and next thing I know I feel weight lift off of me.

"I'm going to fucking murder you, you son of a bitch."

I hear a familiar voice say, making me open my eyes and see Ash holding Liam to the floor, punching him too many times for me to even count.

I get off the floor and try to pull Ash off but he doesn't budge. "Ash, get off of him. You're going to kill him."

"Let me fucking kill him then, Ariella," he says while still punching, not even taking a second to take a break. "I'll give him a slow and painful death. He is going to wish he never touched you."

"Ash, please," I beg but he still doesn't take a second to stop punching him. I get out of the classroom and see two male teachers walking in the hallway. "Please help, I need help."

They look at me like I'm crazy but they follow me inside the classroom.

In just a few minutes, police walk inside the room to

get Ash off of Liam. I take that moment to look at Liam and his whole face is bloody and his nose looks like it is about to fall off.

My eyes catch Ash as they hold him by the arms and take him out of the room.

FIFTY-ONE
ASH

"You're a smart kid, Ash. I would hate to see you waste your future on things like this."

I'm in the dean's office now. He has been scolding me for the last hour while Liam Locke is at the hospital.

He fainted and the fucker deserves it.

He deserves worse for touching Ariella.

"Me? You aren't going to thank me for saving a student from almost being raped? You really need to get your priorities straight."

"I know that this whole situation is a lot. I am already getting emails and calls from the school board about this situation," he says, while rubbing his hand against his forehead.

I nod my head. "He better be arrested for what he did.

I know there are plenty more girls who he has tried to do things with."

The dean nods his head. "Yes, I am aware. Ms. Madden spoke to us about that and she even gave us the story of what happened with her."

It's weird how I found her so suddenly.

I was going to class like normal and saw Ariella through the window on the ground. I didn't think twice before I burst through the door and tackled the mother-fucker to the floor.

I wanted to kill him.

But then Ariella got people to stop me.

I never got the email that Ariella is talking about. I never really pay attention to my emails when it comes to school.

"So, what's the punishment then? Expelled? Arrested?"

The dean shakes his head. "No, none of that. We are a school that takes chances on people like you, Ash. I believe you can do amazing things but ultimately, if I'm being honest. I really don't think that you majoring in psychology is what you want."

"Then what do I want?" I raise an eyebrow at him.

"That's up to you, Ash. I haven't contacted your father about this. I know he has helped you get into this school."

"You don't need to do any of that."

"I know but I'm just letting you know." The dean sighs before putting his hands on the desk. "You can go, Ash. But I do want you to think about maybe a different career path."

I don't say anything to the dean about what I am thinking when he mentions a new career path.

Instead, I stand up and walk out of his office.

My mind is in circles as I walk towards the exit of the school.

Between what the dean said and my feelings towards Ariella I cannot fucking think straight.

My mind is being too loud and I want it to just stop.

I need it all to just stop-

"Ash." I look up and see Ariella. She is standing by her car in the parking lot. She walks up to me and I see vulnerability in her eyes. "Why would you do that? Why would you put yourself in that position? Did you get kicked out?"

"No. And don't worry about it, Ariella. It's none of your business."

"It is my business. I was the one who was being held down, Ash. You're lucky you didn't get arrested." I roll my eyes and attempt to walk past her but she puts her hand on my chest. "Are you seriously just going to ignore me? Ash, you're stupid for putting yourself in that situation."

"No I wasn't," I say, almost laughing from how stupid she sounded saying that.

I would attempt to kill Liam a thousand more times if it meant Ariella was safe.

I don't care about her feelings regarding what I do as long as she is protected and not hurt.

"You are. You could have gotten arrested."

"And so what?" I lean closer to her. "I don't care. You are here and safe. He touched you and he shouldn't have. I am glad that I got to beat his ass and guess what? I would do it a hundred more times. I don't care that you don't want me arrested. All I care about is you," I admit.

Ariella shakes her head lightly. "Why would you care about someone you don't love?"

She has no clue how wrong she is for saying that.

Ariella might be the only person I do care about in this fucked up world.

"I'm not doing this with you."

"No." She stops me from walking past her. "Answer the question. Because you can't keep doing this back and forth, Ash."

I look up at the sky, as if I will get a sign from god himself. All I see are birds and clouds forming together. It's probably going to rain.

I notice my mind is finally quiet.

And it's because of Ariella.

It's all because of Ariella Madden.

It's her fault that my mind is quiet and the demons are silent.

I wish it could always be like this.

In the back of my mind, I know it can. But I would be a selfish motherfucker.

I look at Ariella and I see her lips parted.

Fuck.

Fuck feeling selfish.

I'll figure it out later.

I grab Ariella's face and our lips connect.

Little gasps escape from her mouth and I swallow it, wanting more.

Our bodies are crushed together and Ariella's lips move against mine.

I can hear my heartbeat in my ears, beating loudly for Ariella. I can't stop shaking from how good she feels against me.

The kiss spreads into multiple before she opens her mouth to let out a moan. I don't waste any time to thrust my tongue inside her mouth.

Thank God we are against her car because I felt like I was going to faint from just kissing her and being so connected with her.

My hand on her waist slides up to wrap my hand around her throat.

Ariella is so responsive with everything I do to her. She groans which automatically makes my cock get hard.

We are biting and tugging at each other's lips before I hear a whistle from somewhere in the distance.

She takes her lips off mine and her chest rises and falls against my chest. She looks around the parking lot but I can't even keep my eyes off her.

Ariella is so beautiful and I want to stare into her eyes forever.

"Ariella." She looks at me. "Come home with me."

Ariella looks down at my lips and her eyes connect with mine. "You didn't answer the question, Ash."

I lick my bottom lip and hold her face in my hand as I look in her eyes. "I have been in love with you, Ariella Madden since the moment I saw you in the bookstore." I hear Ariella's breath hitch for a second. "I care about you too much to let you go."

"Then why did you say that you didn't love me?"

I rest my forehead on hers. "Come home with me and I'll tell you."

Ariella nips her bottom lip and nods her head. "Okay."

Fifty-Two
Ariella

I walk inside Ash's room with the first aid kit and then sit on the bed next to him.

Ash keeps his eyes on me the entire time, even when I start attending to his cuts. All I am thinking about as I clean his cuts is that he loves me.

Ash Jones loves me.

I just can't help but wonder why he says it now after everything he said to me before.

I still feel Ash's eyes on me when I clean his cuts with alcohol wipes and then put a bandaid on them all.

Thankfully the cuts aren't too deep but I notice new ones that are on his knuckles that I have never seen before. I think from how many times I have looked at his hands, I have memorized every single scar on his knuckles and knowing how he got them breaks my heart.

"Your dad threatened me," Ash says but I still clean his cuts. Only a few more to go. "He told me that if I keep seeing you, he will take away the savings your mother gave you."

I look up at Ash and put the wipes back inside the first aid kit. "What?" I furrow my eyebrows. "What do you mean?"

"I mean exactly what I said. Your father threatened me. That's why I had to stay away from you."

"He said that? Why would he do that?"

"Because he cares about you." He takes his hand away from mine and he puts it on my cheek. "I would do the same if you were my daughter."

"Ash, that isn't for him to decide. I love my mother but money doesn't mean anything to me."

"But it's your mother's money and she worked hard to give you that. You deserve it."

I shake my head and give him a soft smile. "I know she did but I know she would want me to find something more valuable than money and I did. But my father had to ruin it." I lick my bottom lip which makes Ash look down at my lips for a second before looking up to meet my eyes.

"He didn't ruin anything. I still love you. I always have, Ariella. I just have the guts to say it to you." I feel blush spread on my cheeks. "And I hope you still love me."

The smile on my face grows wider.

Instead of answering him I lean in and press my lips on him. Ash kisses me back right away. His tongue immediately enters my mouth making me groan and push my body into his. One of his hands leaves my body and I hear something drop on the floor. I don't pay attention to it because right away Ash pins me down on the bed. His legs are in between mine, keeping them apart.

"I love you," I mumble against his lips. "I'm still so utterly in love with you, Ash Jones."

"Good. No one else is meant to be mine other than you." Ash starts taking off my clothes, piece by piece until I am bare in front of him. The air against my skin is cold and sends goosebumps to my body but Ash on top of me feels like a warm blanket. He feels so strong and warm in my arms. "You're the only person who silences the demons, Ariella." I take Ash's shirt off before he starts kissing my neck making my eyes close and my head turn to the side. "You want to be fucked, Madden?" I shiver beneath him and nod my head. '"Words. I need words, Ariella."

"Yes. I want to be fucked."

Next thing I know, I don't feel Ash's warm body against mine anymore. I open my eyes and sit up as I see Ash get off the bed. I watch his every movement as he unbuckles his belt, making me clench my legs together.

He slowly starts unbuttoning his pants, every movement he does is torture. I just need his touch and warmth.

Finally, he pulls his pants down with his briefs and his cock touches his stomach. The butterflies in my stomach swarm as I look at him.

"Get on your knees for me, Ariella." I do as he says and get on my knees in front of him. "Spread your legs. I want to see what's mine." The butterflies appear again as I do what he says. The breeze against my pussy makes me shiver and groan. "Put your hands on my thighs and if you want me to stop, tap three times." I nod my head and then he says, "Good girl, now open your mouth big and wide for me."

I slowly open my mouth, offering myself for him.

And he takes me violently. He thrusts in my mouth roughly making me choke but Ash doesn't care.

He uses me.

He breaks me.

He makes me close my eyes as I feel the hard ridges of his cock thrusting in and out of my mouth.

"Fuck baby, fuck yourself for me." I use one of my hands and reach down to touch my clit, rubbing small circles. "No one said anything about your clit, Ariella, fuck yourself. Thrust two fingers inside you." Ash shoves himself down my throat over and over again. I gag but he keeps going, keeping a hold on my head, tangling his fingers in my hair as he takes over me. My eyes close and I moan against him as I thrust two fingers inside me. "Such a good girl, taking me so fucking well, Ariella." When I look up at Ash and I see him looking down at me with dark and lusting eyes. His chest rises and falls and I hear how fast and hard he is breathing. I fuck myself hard and faster but I can't help but think about how good Ash's fingers would feel. Grinding myself against my fingers, moaning around him as I imagine it's Ash. "Fuck," Ash says before pulling out of my mouth. "Get on the bed. Ass in the air and open your legs. Let me see how wet my pussy is."

I quickly get on the bed with shaky legs and get in the position he said.

I feel his hips against my ass and I moan with my eyes rolling. "Ash," I moan, pushing my hips against his.

He leans down, his warm, hard body covering me. "Beg for it," he whispers in my ear.

"Please, Ash. Please fuck me." I grind my hips back into him. "I need you."

"Do you love me?"

"Yes."

I choke when I feel Ash thrust inside me harshly. He pounds into me, not wasting a second. "Ariella." My name rolls off his tongue like a sin. "I own you, Ariella. You're mine." *Thrust.* "Mine to fuck." *Thrust.* "Mine to keep." *Thrust.* "And mine to love."

"Yes," I moan as he rams inside me with one forceful thrust after another.

"You are never allowed to get over me. You're mine."

"Yes, Ash." I grab his thigh as he keeps pushing himself inside me, over and over again.

My body feels like a home filled with butterflies, his words and movements make my legs shake and my vision blurry while my stomach manages to feel like it's about to explode. "I'm going to cum," I say, feeling every inch of him inside me.

I feel him pull out of me fully making me scream and my legs press together.

He turns me around and presses my back against the bed. "I want to see you cum." He thrusts inside me roughly, going faster and harder than before.

His grunts and my moans fill the room along with silent 'I love yous'.

I cum with a moan and my arms around him tighten.

Ash keeps moving inside me before he pulls out and cums on my stomach.

Our chests heaving and our sweaty, shaking bodies entangle together before they slow into a steady rhythm.

FIFTY-THREE
ARIELLA

The sound of water from the bathroom is the first thing I hear when I wake up. I hear a few curses and grunts follow, which makes me open my eyes and look at Ash's side of the bed.

His spot is empty and I reach out and feel the sheets.

They are cold which makes me assume he has been out of bed for a while. I sit up and look around the room. The clock on his dresser reads 6:00 am.

We went to sleep just three hours ago. Why is he up?

Ash decided to keep touching me while I was trying to go to bed and we ended up staying up until 3:00 am. He is insatiable and wouldn't stop touching or kissing me.

The way his body felt against mine reminded me of

the days in the summer when he was gentle and caring. When he was in love.

I didn't know if he was in love with me during those days in the summer but it felt like it. The way he held me afterward made me feel safe and warm. I felt like nothing could touch me. He made me feel like I was on top of the world and I had everything in the palm of my hand.

I get out of bed and grab his t-shirt from the floor and put it on. I open the door to his bedroom and I feel tears form in my eyes as I see glass on the ground.

There is blood on the floor and I feel like throwing up and kissing every single inch of Ash's body to make sure he knows how loved he is.

I look up at Ash and see his hands on the counter and him looking down at the sink that is covered with blood.

"Ash-"

"Even though you are here, sleeping with me, I still see her in my dreams," Ash says before looking at me. His eyes are red and puffy which proves that he has been crying. Who in the world could hurt Ash so much that he feels the need to do this to himself? Who would hurt Ash and make him feel this way? More tears fall from my eyes and I don't dare look at his hands yet. I don't want to see what I saw the last time I found him like this. I swallow a sob and start to make my way to Ash but he leans off the counter and makes his way towards me. "I don't want you in here with all this glass. Go back to bed and I'll clean this up."

I look down at the floor and look back up at him.

His eyes are filled with shame and they look so dark and vacant it almost scares me. I put my hands on his jaw and lean closer to him.

"Who hurt you?"

"Ari-"

"Who hurt you, Ash?! Tell me!" I say, tears practically running down my face now. I want to do everything in my power to protect Ash. Seeing him like this breaks my heart and I have never wanted to kill someone ever. I have never wished death on anyone. But seeing Ash like this breaks my heart more than him telling me he didn't love me. I want to kill whoever made Ash do this to himself. I rest my forehead on his. "Tell me, Ash. Tell me. Please tell me. Who hurt you? Who made you do this?"

I hear Ash take a deep breath before he lets out a shaky one.

Remembering him laugh and smile down at me makes me assume everything was fake.

The smile he gave me was fake. That smile that I fell in love with was fake and he just felt like hurting himself. He felt like dying.

That night in the summer when we were on the beach comes to mind. That night when he was telling me about his tattoos.

I didn't think anything of it.

I knew he had demons but I didn't think they were this strong.

"I'm sorry. I'm so sorry, Ariella. I didn't want you to know," he says, moving his head to rest on my chest. I hold his head against my chest and we slowly fall to sit on the floor. My arms are wrapped around him as he cries silently in my chest. "Leave. If you want to, you can. I know I scare you Ariella, but you were never meant to see that again."

I shake my head and I look up at the ceiling.

The only thing that is going through my head is who did this to him? Who would hurt him?

I know Ash isn't a good person. He isn't nice, he doesn't care about a lot of people, he can be selfish sometimes.

But Ash is also the guy who bought me every single book I touched in a bookstore once.

He is the guy who took me to New York.

He is the guy who made my entire summer feel like I was dancing through fireworks and playing with the stars.

He is the guy who would do anything to protect his future daughter and make sure she is getting messages about how beautiful and amazing she is.

Ash is the person to help Jace with his homework.

He saw a man drop a hundred-dollar bill on the street once and he told the man.

He is the guy who tips servers more money than the actual bill.

Yea, sometimes he is an asshole who shows he doesn't care but secretly he does.

Secretly Ash has a heart.

I put my hands on his jaw to make him look at me. His eyes are red and puffy and I look down at his hands and see new fresh cuts that are bloody and deep.

More tears fall down my face. One of his hands reaches up and wipes a tear which makes more fall.

"Tell me. Don't hide from me. I'm not going to leave you, Ash. I promise. I swear on my mom I won't leave you," I beg before looking at him. "Please, I need to know who did this."

Ash sighs and licks the tears off his lips. "My mom."

"What did she do?"

Ash pulls me closer to him and he rests his head on my chest again. I lean my back against the wall and rest my hands in his hair.

FIFTY-FOUR

ARIELLA

PRESENT

"My mom was an addict. Most of the time she didn't even realize she was awake. She was there but she wasn't really there," Ash starts. "She loved drugs. Drugs were her one and only love. She and my dad met at a club and they hooked up. My dad didn't know the type of person she was. Not until it was too late. They saw each other for a few more weeks until she found out she was pregnant and she told my dad she wanted to abort it. My dad didn't want that so he forced her to keep me, but she tried to make herself have a miscarriage. My father made sure she wasn't around drugs or alcohol. He said he didn't want a child of his to be born with any defects. So, he trapped her in a room to make sure she didn't do anything stupid. But one night my dad found her with a hanger between her legs. She was trying to get rid of me herself."

I choke on my tears and it's so hard to not cry, but knowing someone did that makes me sick.

Before I can say anything, Ash speaks again.

"He put her in a mental institution until I was born. My dad took care of me for three years while my mom was still in the mental institution. She eventually came back and said she wanted to meet me. My dad didn't let her meet me until I was five years old. He wanted to make sure that she was okay mentally and wouldn't do anything stupid. He didn't trust her with me. They dated for about two years and my dad made sure to wear a condom every time they hooked up. When I finally met her, I didn't know what to think. I don't even remember that well. My earliest memory of her is smiling at me while giving me a toy truck. Everything before that I don't remember that well. My father said she was normal with me though. But all of the memories after that one were tarnished. They are all dark and twisted memories and I can never get those out of my head."

Ash's finger starts to rub my leg softly and I don't stop touching his hair.

Blood is covering my leg but I pay no attention to that.

"What happened? What did she do to you?"

"She went back into her drug addiction. She didn't

trust some of the drugs that her suppliers gave her so she made me try them. It started when I was six."

The syringe tattoos.

He could've died.

What would have happened if he took the wrong drug or if someone wasn't there to help him?

"Ash-"

"My father was never home around that time. He trusted my mom. She would only test them when my dad went on business trips so she had time for me to act normal around him. She threatened that if I ever told him that she would kill me and make it look like an accident."

What mother would do that? How could someone do that to a child?

My hands in Ash's hair freeze but he rests his hands on mine.

"And then she would force me to have sex with her friends for money. She had to hold me down on the couch and f-force me to stay still as they forced themselves on me." His voice cracks and before I can yell and hold him tighter against me, he continues. "It would happen every Friday because she would buy her drugs on Saturdays. My dad worked late at the office on those days. My mom was a good liar, I'll admit. She hid it so fucking well and I will never know how she did it all." Ash lets out a dark chuckle. "I finally stood up to her when I was around sixteen. I had a car at the time and I would never be home to see her. I would tell my dad I was sleeping at a friend's house. I would call Ally to know when my mom was home and wasn't so that I could get cash and clothes. I would only visit my father's office to see him but I was never home. My dad wondered why but I just said that my friend needed my help. He believed me because he's fucking blind to everything. I didn't sleep in that house for almost two years."

Ash laughs again while more tears just fall from my eyes.

"But one night my mom was home. Ally wasn't home and her cell wasn't working so I thought I would try and see if I could get some clothes and cash because I was running out. I was desperate. So, when I walked inside the house it was empty. I went to my room to get my stuff but my mom was in there. She started hitting me and attacking me. She looked like she wanted to kill me. Our fighting led outside my room to the staircase and it got out of hand. I didn't mean to but it just happened. She was pulling my hair and next thing I know her touch disappears and she is down the stairs with her head cracked and her eyes wide open. There was blood surrounding her head and I was too scared to go downstairs so I didn't. I stayed on the top of the stairs until Ally came home."

I can't hear anything. All I can see and hear is Ash. Seventeen-year-old Ash screaming and yelling, rocking back and forth while looking at his mother on the floor.

I hold him tighter in my arms and cry. I cry for the boy who has had a fucked-up life since he was born. I cry for the boy who has been traumatized and has had demons haunt him since he was just a kid.

He was just a kid.

Six years old.

I cry and sob as Ash moves me so that I am crying into his chest and he is holding me. I feel his lips against my ear but I can't hear a thing he is saying.

I shake my head, it can't be true.

Everything he said can't be true.

"Ariella."

I get out of his hold and look at him.

"You were just a kid." I touch his face and his eyes aren't as dark and vacant.

"Yea, but it's funny how fate works," he says with a lighter mood.

"Why would fate play into this?" I say, tears still running down my cheeks.

"Because the guy who ended up being on the prosecutor's team was Cal Madden and I just happened to fall in love with his daughter."

I didn't fully understand my father and Levi's feud. I knew my father and him have had a rivalry since they were in college but I didn't understand why my father hated Ash so much.

Not until now.

"My dad thinks you're dangerous. He thinks you have violent tendencies." Ash doesn't nod his head or anything, he just stares at me. I put my hands on his face. "He couldn't be more wrong."

"Ariella-"

"No, listen to me," I demand as I ignore the tears still falling from my eyes. "I love my father but he couldn't be more wrong about you. The bitch deserved to die. She deserves to be in hell forever for what she did. You don't deserve any of my father's hatred and I will continue to defend you until my last breath. Do you understand?" Ash's lips lift in a small smile and his eyes are suddenly filled with love. So much love. "Why are you smiling? I'm trying to be sentimental and serious."

"Because I'm in love with you, Madden." Ash simply says.

I shake my head as a small smile forms on my face. It's sad but it's there.

It's a happy, sad smile.

"I'm in love with you too, Ash."

He leans in closer and presses his lips against mine.

FIFTY-FIVE
ARIELLA

PRESENT

I called my father first thing in the morning after Ash told me about my father's threat to him and how my father is connected to Ash. I want to strangle my father's neck and ask him what the hell he was thinking.

I told him that I need to talk to him in person as soon as he is able to book a flight to California.

It's been three days since I called him.

It's been three days since Ash told me the truth, the entire truth and his feelings for me.

Ash and I are not able to keep our hands off one another. I love how he holds me when we are sleeping together and how he touches me when it's late at night.

I love how he touches me like he hates and loves me like I am the only star in his world. His love is all I need and I can't be more grateful to finally have Ash Jones in my arms.

Ever since he told me about his mother and his past in general, I can't help but look at him as that scared six-year-old and seventeen-year-old. It's hard to look at Ash the same way I did before. At night when he is sleeping, I watch him and stroke his hair. I whisper in his ear how much I love him and sometimes I cry. He'll wake up and see my crying and whisper in my ear that he's okay and that he loves me.

Today I told him that I need to talk to my father so he gave me my space and told me to call him after my father and I are done talking. I like the fact that whenever I mention my father to Ash, he turns his head and doesn't care.

I asked him about it and he told me he doesn't really care to hear about anyone else if it doesn't concern me. That is true because when I was talking about Bridgette he didn't even care to listen.

I hear the front door of my house open and I turn my head and see my father walking in. "Hey bug." I give him a small smile as I get up from the couch and go up to him.

He puts his bags on the floor and wraps his arms around me, kissing me on the forehead.

I know my father loves me and cares about me. The problem is that he cares and loves me too much and he feels the need to shelter me which is something I hate. I hate the fact that someone wants to control my life and essentially my decisions.

It's like he is afraid of losing me like he lost mom.

"How was the flight?" I ask, unwrapping my arms and grabbing his bags.

"It was fine." He grabs his bags from me. "Don't worry about those. I'll get them later. Sit in the living room. I know you said you wanted to talk about something urgent and I don't want to waste a second of your time."

I go to the living room and sit down on the couch while my father puts his bags in the guest room upstairs.

He is only staying for two days because he has to go back to work soon.

Earlier today I got an email from the school saying that Liam Locke got arrested for rape charges and other serious charges.

Multiple girls have come forward with the investigation so that just made his arrest quicker.

Thank God he is behind bars.

"So, what did you want to speak about? It sounded urgent."

"It is." I rub my hands against my pants, getting the nerves out of my system. "It's about mom."

My father's eyes soften.

He loved my mother.

When she died, it broke and changed him.

"Okay," he says, wanting me to keep going.

"Well, I want the savings she wanted to give me. I know I'm supposed to get it when I'm twenty but I don't want to wait. I want the money now."

My father's eyebrows furrowed. "What is this about? Why do you want her money now? I pay for almost everything for you? Don't you want to keep that money for when you really need it?"

"No. I want to someday move away from California and get a job. I am looking at paid internships and I want to start being independent instead of being dependent on you. I want my mom's savings so that I can buy an apartment for myself."

"Where do you plan on moving?"

"Manhattan, New York. The internship is there and I want to take it. The pay is good and I know that with my mom's help I can do it."

"You are supposed to be waiting until you're twenty, bug."

"I'm not going to wait until then. Not when you're threatening my mom's savings." I see panic fill my father's eyes. "Ash told me what happened. I'm going to keep seeing him dad, I love him and he loves me too."

"You are making a horrible decision by being with him, Ariella. He is like his father but ten times worse. Did he tell you what he has done?"

Yes, and it broke my heart to pieces.

I hated seeing him cry and in pain. I hated seeing all the blood and glass.

I now have a new worst fear.

Ash told me that he never wants to talk about his mother again but that doesn't mean he wants me to stop talking about my mom.

He said he wants to hear everything about my mom and how much I love her.

I do want to bring him to meet her one day.

"Yes, he told me and it wasn't his fault. If you knew exactly what happened then you would agree. Now, I am going to get mom's savings and if you don't give it to me willingly then I will bring a lawyer in. And you won't like the lawyer I'll be bringing in."

My dad's eyes turn into slits as he glares at me. "You wouldn't."

"I would. I will bring in Levi Jones if I have to."

My father nips his bottom lip. "Just know, if he breaks your heart, the first thing I'll say to you is 'I told you so'."

"Is it a yes, or no?" I raise an eyebrow at him.

My dad's jaw clenches and ticks before he says, "It's a yes. Give me a few days and I'll have all of the money sent to your bank."

FIFTY-SIX
ASH

PRESENT

"So, tell me why you're here today, Ash."

Sitting across from me is my therapist.

Doctor Jameson Cole.

It's ironic how his name is Jameson when Ariella's favorite author's name is Jameson.

He looks like he is in his thirties. He has dark brown hair and dark brown eyes to match. He is wearing black framed glasses. His glasses aren't like the little tiny circle glasses. They are like just normal nerd glasses. Not like the ones from the movies, like the ones that nerds wear in real life.

He is a good-looking guy for someone in his thirties. He probably has a pretty wife at home with a kid who is raised well.

He looks like he is a good guy. The type of guy you would have drinks with and talk shit to when you are just having that kind of day.

"My girlfriend wanted me to come to therapy."

After I told Ariella about everything that happened with my mother, she told me that she wanted me to go to therapy and talk to someone about everything that happened and what I am feeling. We argued a little bit and then we ended up having sex where we were just cursing each other out. In the end she told me to stop acting like a child and just go to therapy.

We both agreed that I would try therapy out for a month and see how it goes and then Ariella said that she would let me try anal with her.

It took a few 'pleases' from her but I said yes. I have never tried anal and with her I want to try everything. I laughed when she said that because, out of all the things I thought she would promise me, it definitely wasn't anal that I thought of.

But her other condition was to take me to therapy and then pick me up. She also thought I should tell my dad but I told her I wasn't going to tell him until I am dedicated.

She also met with my therapist to make sure he is the right fit for me so I am going to try because I don't want to waste Ariella's time.

"How long have you and your girlfriend been dating for?"

"Since the summer."

It's kind of a lie but he doesn't know that.

He and I have a long way to go with this whole fucking life story of mine.

"You love her?"

"Of course. I would do anything for her."

Jameson nods his head. "How did you guys meet?"

"Sorry to go off topic but why are we talking about my relationship with my girlfriend when we probably should be talking about my problems?"

"I like to ease my clients into our sessions. I've met your girlfriend and she seems like a very kind and caring person. She cares a lot about you and I can tell she wants you to get better."

"Did she tell you anything?"

Jameson leans back in his chair. "No, she didn't tell me anything about you other than necessary information. Like if you have a problem with drugs, alcohol, what triggers you, anything I should know before we move forward with our sessions. She answered all the questions and she told me that you are a very hard person to crack and from just talking to you for a few minutes I can tell you are. You are also the type of person to not trust easily."

"Yea, that's my girlfriend for you."

Jameson chuckles. "Back to my original question. How did you and your girlfriend meet?"

"At a bookstore. She asked me out on a date and we kind of just went from there."

"I think there is more to the story there but we'll save that for another time." He writes something in his notebook and I would do anything to read what he is writing. "How is your relationship with your parents?"

I tense up. "My dad is there and we talk sometimes."

"Your mom?"

"Dead," I state, bluntly, trying to show my best that she doesn't mean a fucking thing to me.

"I see. How did she die?" he asks and to that I don't reply. We aren't close enough for me to tell him my fucking deepest and darkest secret. "Back to Ariella. I think we'll be talking about her a lot before we start growing closer."

"What makes you think we are going to grow closer?" I raise an eyebrow at him.

"Because Ash, you remind me a lot of myself. I know we will be getting along just fine as time goes."

———

When I get inside Ariella's car, she has that beautiful bright smile on her face that tells me she is proud.

"So, how was it?" She asks as I close the door.

I throw the journal he gave me in the back and then lean into the passenger seat.

"You're going to be giving me a lot of anal, Madden."

Ariella shakes her head and chuckles lightly. "I only promised you that we would be trying it. That's it."

"It was fucking torture in there. He kept saying that he thinks we will be getting closer and then he made me talk about you a lot."

"What did you say about me?"

"How you're forcing me to go to therapy when I could just fuck you for therapy."

Ariella gasps and she punches my shoulder. "You didn't tell him that, did you?" I stay silent and Ariella shoves my shoulder again. "I can't believe you said that to him."

I chuckle. "He noticed that I love you a lot. He said that every time I would say one thing I loved about you, my eyes would light up and I would smile without even knowing."

"Really?" Ariella's hand makes contact with my hair and she plays with the strands while smiling at me like she's in love.

Because she is.

Ariella Madden is in love with me.

Fifty-Seven
Ash

The waves in the background is calming but I am more focused on Ariella's words and her angelic voice.

She is laying against my chest while reading a book to me. She is like my personal audio book. I've always liked audio books and just listening to her read me what she loves is calming.

Honestly, I'm not even listening to her words. I am just drowning myself into the sound of her voice.

I like how she even says, "Wait, I need to annotate this part," and then she highlights the sentence, tabs it and then continues reading.

I need this to become a regular thing. I like seeing the way her eyes light up when she reads something she likes.

Most of the books she reads are romance but she tries

to always read thriller in front of me instead of romance because of the smut scenes in the books. I can tell when she is reading smut though by the way her eyes turn glossy and the way her cheeks turn red.

"She slowly walks up to me, her breathing, shallow. When I lift her face for her eyes to connect with me, she shivers. I can see the love in her eyes. It's filled with want and need. I like knowing that she wants me, that she needs me to be able to breathe air."

Ariella turns the page and I hear her yawn before she starts reading again. As Ariella keeps reading, her words are getting more and more slurred and I notice how the book seems heavy in her hands.

"Ariella," I whisper in her ear as I take the book from her hands, "go to sleep. We can finish the chapter another time." I bookmark the book and set it down beside us on the blanket.

"But I don't want to leave yet." Ariella turns around and looks up at me.

I tangle my hands in her hair and stare into her eyes. She looks so beautiful right now. Her face is bare, no makeup is on her face, not even mascara.

I love her when she looks like this. I love her even if she has makeup on too.

"We won't. We can stay." Ariella's eyes lift a little before she rests her head on my chest and trails her fingers up and down my chest. "How are things with your dad going?"

"Things are normal. I finally got the money from my mom. I plan on putting down the six months' rent for an apartment in New York that I was telling you about. I think I might be able to move out there this year for sure, maybe in the summer or earlier."

I remember her telling me that. I remember because I plan on moving to New York with her, but she doesn't know that yet.

I know that ever since I saw her at the bookstore I needed to have her in my life but now, after everything I told her about me, my mom, what I have done, my past, everything, I just know she is it for me.

There is no one else like her.

"I remember," I say before closing my eyes and resting my head against the blanket. "I'm moving to New York."

I feel weight lift off my chest making me open my eyes and I see Ariella staring at me with furrowed eyebrows.

She's wide awake now.

"What?"

"I'm moving to New York. I'm getting my own apartment but just know that I will be coming over every single day."

Ariella's lips lift in a smile and it makes my heart fucking pound against my chest to the point I am worried she might feel it.

"Why?"

I shrug my shoulders. I can't believe she is really going to make me say this shit. "Because I love you and I want to be wherever you are."

"What are you even going to do there? Are you going back to school with me?"

"No, but I am for now just going to take a break from everything and find a passion."

Ariella doesn't know this, but that journal I have been writing in since meeting my therapist, I have been writing short stories in and I like them a lot.

I might publish them one day, we'll see.

She tilts her head to the side a little, looking confused. "You'll be okay without a job?"

"I have my mom's money she made from this website and then my dad's savings for me. I'll be okay," I promise her and kiss the top of her head. "What is the internship you have?"

"It's at a publishing house. I think I'll finish my psychology degree and see where the internship takes me." She shrugs.

I can't help but smile at her and lean down to capture her lips in mine. Her nails stroke up and down my arm sending chills down my spine.

This past month has been amazing with her. Things have been going well and things with my therapist have been okay.

I decided I'm going to keep him.

He's okay, I guess.

I take my lips off hers, need to keep my balls intact. "So, me and you in New York? What do you say?"

Ariella nods her head. "I say we're going to have some fun."

I capture her lips with mine and immediately thrust my tongue in between her lips.

FIFTY-EIGHT
ASH

SUMMER

The book is fucking stupid. I don't know why I am buying the second one.

The point that the author makes doesn't make any sense. I mean, it really just ends like that, on a cliffhanger?

What kind of mind fuck did the author want people to have?

And to find out there is a whole series and world connected to those people?

So, fucking stupid.

So why am I choosing to buy a book that feels like lava is melting my brain?

Probably because I am just truly trying to torture myself. I like fucked up books and the way they make you feel things.

They make you so angry to the point where you just want to break everything in your room.

They make you sad to the point where you just want to stop the world so that you can just stop hurting.

But they also make you happy so that when the book ends, you feel a part of yourself just wither away with the characters to live with them.

So that's why I decided to torture myself with reading the second book because well, I like how those things make you feel.

Reading books makes me feel like I'm still there. I am still alive; my heart is still beating and I can still actually feel things.

The bell rings when I walk inside the bookstore and I don't know why but my eyes set on the most beautiful brown eyes I have ever seen. They look like just normal brown eyes but the way she looks at me with parted lips and such innocence, you almost assume it looks fake.

The door closes behind me and I force my eyes away from hers and walk away.

I can't be focusing on that.

But the way she looked at me with pure innocence I know that she is anything but.

I walk towards the Adult Fiction section. I look through the shelves of books. I see a lot of books by Jameson Hat. He is an author who got famous overnight.

I was following him when he only had one thousand followers.

I'm trying to find his newest release which happens to be the book that is the sequel to the one that fucked with my head.

His books are all fucked up but I just can't seem to get enough.

I walk around the rows and rows of books that tower over me. I've never been to this bookstore before. I am spending the week with Jace before heading back to New York.

This was the closest book store I could find near his house and it's a nice area. The beach is ten minutes away and it makes me want to stay in LA longer but I know I have to go back to New York.

When I turn another corner, I end up in the literature section and to my surprise I see the girl with the beautiful brown eyes trying to reach for a book on the top shelf.

A girl like her doesn't seem to be into literature. She seems like a romance girl who reads smutty books.

I walk towards her and my chest presses against her back as I reach towards the top shelf to get the book she is trying to reach.

My stomach dips and I feel a swarm of butterflies in my stomach.

The girl flinches and turns around, staring at me wide eyed. Up close I can see her features more clearly.

She has big doe eyes that look like pure innocence. Her lips are full and they part as she looks over my entire frame.

I don't look at her body because I am too focused on the beauty her face brings. She is absolutely perfect.

How?

I look at the book in my hands. "'Invisible Man.' You seem more like a 'Great Gatsby' kind of girl."

She furrows her eyebrows. "Last time I read Great Gatsby was when I was a freshman. Safe to say that I wasn't interested."

I can't stop my eyes from roaming down her body. She is fucking perfect all over.

How?

I look away from her as my cock starts to harden.

Not now and definitely not here.

My eyes go to the shelf where I grabbed the book from. "Dark romance? That is more convincing," I say with a smirk.

She turns around to look at the shelf and then looks back at me. "I wouldn't be judging my taste in books. I bet you are into one of those boring historical books or something."

Oh, I'm going to have fun with her.

"Now you're judging me." I tilt my head to the side and give her a teasing smile. "I'm Ash."

Her eyes roam over my face again, admiring all of the

small details. It makes me feel good knowing that she likes what she's looking at.

"Ash," she says, testing my name on her lips. "I'm Ariella."

Ariella.

Ariella.

I can't help but smile as I lean against the bookshelf. "So, what books do you read, Ariella?"

She roams her eyes over me again, like she is studying me and seeing if I am good enough for her.

I sure hope to God I am.

"I can tell you about it over dinner?"

I smile.

Yea, we're going to have a lot of fun together that's for sure.

Epilogue

Ariella

Six Years Later

I feel a pair of hands slide up my thighs making me stir in my sleep. Soft lips make their way up my body until finally I feel a single finger slip between my folds.

I moan and my hands reach down towards the person between my legs. His finger puts pressure on my clit making me squeeze his hair in my hands.

"Ash." He does this every single morning and whenever I want to pleasure him back, he always makes me wait until it's night so that he can take over and spank me every time I moan. My eyes are still closed and they feel so heavy every time his tongue licks me from my clit to my hole. "Oh my God," I moan, grinding against his face.

His fingers dig into my thighs as he licks and sucks my clit.

"You like me licking you, love?" he asks and all I can do is moan. "You like spreading your legs for me, huh? This is my pussy, right?"

"Yes," I moan and arch my back, feeling my insanity going over the edge slowly. "Ash, God."

Ash thrusts two fingers inside me and I clench onto them as I come all over hand and tighten my legs around his neck.

"That's it, baby," he mumbles against me, stroking my shaking thighs.

I open my eyes and the sunlight is shining through the curtains. I stroke Ash's hair as I try to calm down my breathing.

Ever since we got married a few months ago he hasn't been able to get his hands off of me. He always makes sure to wake me up with a mind-blowing orgasm and it never gets old. He always has new ways of giving me pleasure in the morning.

Ash makes his way out of the covers and his lips are on mine. I moan into his lips and he trails his hands up to caress my breasts that are aching from what he did to them last night.

He put nipple clamps on them and made me see stars the entire night.

His kisses still stop my world and make me see stars. He makes me feel like the earth is shaking and spinning.

I breathe into his lips and wrap my arms around him

to pull him closer into me. "I can't breathe," I mumble against his lips. "You make me feel like breathing isn't possible."

"Good." He nips my bottom lip and his knee rests between my legs. "I need to get my fill of you before-"

"Daddy!" We hear a little girl scream making Ash and I part.

"Fucking cock blocker."

I laugh as he rests his forehead against mine. "Go unlock the door for her."

He sighs before pressing a kiss to my forehead and getting up.

Alex has school today. She loves school and everything about it. Every morning she is the one running into our room to tell us to get out of bed to have breakfast together. Sometimes Ash wakes up before me to make her breakfast and get her ready but that's only when I'm too tired to get up. Ash always makes sure to tire me out all night.

I am lucky enough to be able to get in to work late. I work for a publishing company as an assistant. I make good income along with Ash's income as a bestselling author.

He has published seven books in the last five years and they have all hit the bestsellers list. He has a very good agent who got him to where he is now.

We had Alex five years ago, a year after we moved to

New York. Alex is the light Ash needed in his life. He loves her so much and you can tell.

Ash would burn the entire world down for Alex and make sure she is smiling while doing all of that. I love watching them sometimes, playing or hanging out. Sometimes he will be in her room reading her a book or telling her how much he loves her before she goes to bed. I love my baby girl but you can tell Ash loves her more which makes me happy.

Ash's therapy is going well. He is still seeing Doctor Jameson. He grew a relationship with him over that first month and Ash decided that he wanted to keep him even when we were moving to New York. So, he has meetings with him either over the phone or video calls. Their meetings happen once a week but when they first started it was three times a week.

Ash is doing a lot better.

Obviously there have been a lot of downs with him where things have gotten scary but there also have been many ups with him. But since we had Alex things with him have been only good.

And our relationship is still as strong as ever.

"Is mommy going to dress me today?" I hear Alex say, making me smile.

I check under the covers to see if I have anything on and I don't. I glare at Ash while he just laughs.

"I will baby, give me a minute and wait in your room

for me." She smiles and runs to her room. "I wouldn't be surprised if she ever catches us again," I tell Ash.

"Don't worry, she thinks it's just us playing twister," Ash jokes before walking towards the bed and laying between my legs.

I rest my hands on his jaw. "How's your mind today?"

"Full of you," Ash says.

He says the same thing every morning I ask him. Sometimes he says that it's full of me and Alex but most of the time it's just me which makes my heart happy.

He presses a passionate kiss to my lips before getting up. "I have a meeting with the CEO today so I have to go in early and I might not be able to pick up Alex."

"It's okay. I'm just spending the day writing. I took the day off so that I can go to Paper Co. and just write."

Paper Co. is a bookstore Ash and I found when we first moved here. We spend a lot of time there and that's where Ash also proposed to me. It wasn't extravagant but it was perfect.

I get out of bed and change into a new pair of underwear and pajama shorts. Ash kisses me one more time before I leave to go to Alex's room.

We live in a nice penthouse in front of Central Park. It's amazing living here and it feels like a dream. Alex's school is less than a mile away so Ash and I walk her to school and then I take a subway to work. Sometimes Ash drives me to work on his motorcycle when I'm running late or on random occasions. Ash walks everywhere when it comes to New York. He knows his way around the area very well. He uses his motorcycle for long drives but he never likes bringing it out of the garage if it's not a must.

I walk inside Alex's room and she is already looking through her clothes.

"Okay, show me what you got." I smile when I see her running around her room trying to pick out a dress.

She only ever wears dresses and I love that about her. Ash always buys her whatever kind of dress she wants. He never knows how to say no to her.

"I want either this pink one or this yellow one but I don't know because I want to wear that white bow."

I smile and point to the pink one. "I think the pink one would look really pretty with the bow." She smiles and jumps up and down. "Okay get changed and I can do your hair baby." She wraps her arms around me and kisses me everywhere on my face. "I love you, mommy," she says before leaving me and going to her bathroom to change.

I look at the clock on her dresser.

Shit, we're going to be late. I really hope that Ash already made breakfast.

"When you're done, come to the kitchen. I'll do your hair while we eat okay?"

She yells an 'okay'. I grab her hair stuff and leave to go to the kitchen where I see Ash, still shirtless and he is preparing eggs and waffles.

"I'll have to eat it on the way to work because right after Alex is done with her hair, she needs to go to school and I need to get ready to take her," I say, walking past him to get water out of the fridge.

"Let me do her hair and then you can get ready." I feel his arms wrap around my waist. "You're stressing out for nothing."

"No, she wants me to do her hair. I'm going to do it quickly and then get ready."

"Ariella-"

"Ash, no. I'll do it," I say, narrowing my eyes at him.

"Ready mommy?" I hear Alex say, making me leave Ash's hold.

"Ten," Ash says with a dark look in his eyes.

I gasp at him. "I didn't even do anything!"

"Don't care. Ten, and if you keep arguing with me then it's going to be twenty." I roll my eyes and he just smirks. "Twenty. Go do my daughters hair."

I laugh and shake my head lightly.

Alex sits on my lap as I do her hair and Ash serves her a plate of breakfast.

This is kind of our morning routine. Then, when we all get home, we just watch a movie and sometimes when I make dinner, Ash and Ariella play or watch a movie in the living room where I have a perfect view of them.

Sometimes my dad or Ash's dad will come over for dinner. Things with my dad have been okay. I had a long talk with him about Ash and he still doesn't fully trust him but if he wanted to come near Alex then he was going to have to be civil with Ash.

Ash met my mom six years ago before we moved to New York. He even told me to leave him and her alone so that he could talk to her. He never told me what he said because he said it was between her and him. I also learned that he asked her if he could propose to me and when he told me that I started crying.

Ash knows all of the right things to do and say and I can't be more grateful to be able to love him so deeply and fully.

And our family is only growing.

EXTENDED EPILOGUE
ASH

ONE YEAR LATER

"How stupid are you feeling today?" Jameson asks over the phone as I shake the milk bottle in my hand.

Right now, I am putting Ariella's pre-pumped milk in the fridge. She plans on going out with Bridgette tomorrow so she pumped milk just in case she drinks. I told her I would put it in bottles so that she can tuck Alex in bed.

She already put Aiden to bed and hopefully he fucking stays there so that Ariella and I can fucking have some time alone together and then sleep a full six hours at least.

Last time I remember, Alex wasn't such a cry baby at night.

Aiden is about three months old and I feel like I'm

going crazy with the constant crying. Most of the time I have to be with Alex and hangout with her because Aiden only likes it when Ariella puts him to bed which I don't know why.

He probably already knows he won't like me.

"Not as stupid as I was feeling seven years ago," I answer.

He asks me the same question every single night when he calls me and every single time I always answer truthfully.

We have one call a week dedicated to me talking to him about my feelings. Before it was three times a week, sometimes even daily when it got really bad, but I've grown since then.

Last time I punched a mirror was before Ariella was pregnant with Alex. It was really bad because when Ariella caught me, we yelled and screamed at each other.

I hated how I was so blind to how much I hurt her that night. She was crying so hard so I left.

I couldn't see her cry like that because of me.

I didn't call Jameson, although he tried to get a hold of me. Jace too and Bridgette.

Long story short I ended up at my dad's house and he let me stay the night. He talked to me and I think that's when our relationship started to change for the better.

I went back to Ariella in the morning and found her cleaning up the glass on the floor while crying. We ended up crying together and I told her how much of a mistake I was and she was being her amazing self. She told me she loved me no matter what and that what happened was just a slip up.

After that night I never punched a mirror. I hated how scared she looked.

That scared me.

Losing Ariella scared me because she was the only one to quiet t5he demons and the voices.

That night I just snapped. I don't know what caused it.

Jameson said it was probably a dream I had or just had the urge to do it.

"Good. You sound tired. Is everything going okay with Aiden?"

"Yea, he just keeps Ariella and I up. We never get time to ourselves that much because, like the fucking cockblock he is, he never lets her and I get a fucking hour together."

"My son was the same way. The second children are always the worst."

"Don't let your son hear that," I chuckle as I put all the milk in the fridge.

"But seriously, everything is okay?"

"Yea. Everything is good besides that. After I'm done with you, I'm going to go see Ariella. She is putting Alex to sleep right now."

Even though Alex is six, she loves her bedtime stories.

She is a reader like me and Ariella. She is always saying how much she wants to read my books but she can't just yet because she needs to at least be sixteen to read what I write.

Most of my books are psychological thrillers but I have some romance books because Ariella demanded that I need to write one so that she could read it and I could be her favorite author. They aren't just romcoms, they are darker romance and Ariella said that's okay.

She isn't scared about what I write. I'll admit that all of my books are twisted and fucked up. They are so fucked up and with the kind of shit I write in them, you would think I'm in a crazy hospital.

Writing is a way for me to be able to put all of my thoughts down without saying or expressing anything out loud.

It's because of Jameson that I'm an author. During our first month together, I decided to write in the notebook he gave me and I wrote everything I was feeling in a story format.

"Give me three things."

Jameson asks me to give him three things I loved about the day or the week.

He already knows the two things.

I sit down on the barstool and rest my elbows on the counter. "My kids. Ariella, always Ariella, and this new book I'm writing."

"What is it called?"

"I don't know yet. It's a story about Ariella and I."

"You're finally writing one, after how many years?" Jameson laughs.

"I've been thinking about it since I started writing but I couldn't actually put it all down in words."

"Well, I'll be buying the first copy."

"As will Jace and Bridgette and Ariella," I laugh.

All of them always say that. Ariella is always the one to read it first because I can't say no to her. Plus, I have to give it to her so she can send it to her boss to read.

"Well, it sounds like things are good."

"Yea they are. I mean kids aren't easy, who said they would be?"

"I know you won't self-harm, Ash. You have grown and if you do that you know that Ariella will be scared and I think that's what stops you most of the time."

He's right.

Scaring Ariella is the last thing I want to do.

"Yea. Plus, I don't want the kids to see their dad like that. They can't see their parents in that state."

"Exactly, and I think that is great motivation for you to keep doing better." I lick my bottom lip and nod my head, as if he can see me. "I'll let you go. I can tell you want to go to Ariella."

"Yea, I'll talk to you later."

I hang up and put my phone in my pocket before

getting up from the stool. I make my way towards Aiden's room to go check on him. He is still sleeping soundly.

I go to Alex's room and the door is cracked open slightly.

"And then what happened?" Alex asks.

I peek inside and see Ariella laying in Alex's bed and her arms are wrapped around her.

"Your dad then told me he loved me."

"And how did he say it?"

I hear Ariella chuckle softly. "I have been in love with you, Ariella Madden since the moment I saw you in the bookstore. I care about you too much to let you go," Ariella says, quoting the exact thing I said to her seven years ago.

"He loves you a lot, doesn't he?"

"Yes, he does." Ariella laughs.

"And you love him?" Alex questions.

"I do. I love your dad a lot Alex. He is the only man I've ever loved."

My heart swells and I feel so much whenever I look at Ariella or just hear her say that. Despite all of the shitty things I have done to her, she loves me like I am the one who saved her when it was the complete opposite.

"Can I hear more?"

"Not tonight. It's late and you have school."

"But mom-"

"Tomorrow."

I leave before Ariella can catch me watching her. I go to our room and wait on the bed for her.

I hear a door close and then soft footsteps walking closer and closer. The door to our room opens and she walks in.

She is wearing my sweatpants and shirt and I swear my dick swells when I see her in my clothes. It's always a turn on seeing her dressed like that.

When she looks at me, I can tell she loves me. I don't even need to question it.

"Come here," I say as I spread my legs a little for her. Ariella smiles, like she always does whenever I tell her this. She walks towards me and sits in my lap, wrapping her arms around my neck. "I don't think you realize how much I love you."

"I do, Ash. I can see it." She smiles and caresses my jaw softly. "I know you're in love with me. I can see it. Trust me."

I don't say anything, instead I press my lips against her and she tightens her arms around me.

THANK YOU

If you enjoyed this book please feel free to leave a review as it would mean a lot to me.

I always enjoy reading good reviews and I always love reading reviews that have criticism in them. Criticism makes me a better author and I always love knowing what I can work on as a writer.

A simple, "Great Book" would be amazing.

Appreciate your love and support so so much!

ACKNOWLEDGMENTS

Wow this book was hard to write but it was all fun. This book was one of my darkest stories ever and because of that it was extremely challenging to write but also fun. It's definitely one of my top three favorite books I have written and I think it's because of Ash's character mainly.

I loved Ash's character so much. I think towards the ending he grew so much from his past and he all did that for Ariella. He wanted to be better for her and his children and I think this ending was perfect for him, especially with his talk with Jameson at the end.

I wrote this book because I wanted to explore how dark I can write books and towards the ending it started to turn out to be a story I want people to read and remember that there is always someone there to help you, no matter what. There are people that love you and care for you. If anyone is going through anything serious like Ash or feeling the way he felt, please talk to someone about it because there will always be someone there to listen.

Now onto my appreciation towards the people who made this book better!

To Antonia, you are such an amazing editor and I appreciate all of your help and advice while editing this book. This was such a hard book for me to write and you definitely helped me in ways some people couldn't so thank you.

To my Beta Readers, I am so thankful to be able to have your guys support and help. You made this release and publishing process so much easier than my last release so thank you guys so much. The advice you all gave me was perfect and it made this story even better in my opioid so thank you for your critical and honest advice.

To Sonali, Amanda, and Mae, who I love with all my heart. You three have just been my rock since I started and some since like last year. I appreciate you guys always supporting me and giving me the advice I need. You three have just been the best of friends I could ask for in this community and I can't describe how grateful I am for you guys.

To Lila, who helped me last minuted with proof reading. I had to put you in the acknowledgments because you saved me even though it may have not seemed like it, you did. So thank you, thank you, thank you!

To all of my favorite bookstagrammers, which are WAY too many to name, thank you all for being apart of this amazing community. You make the bookish community such a positive and fun place. I love what I am doing thanks to all of you.

And finally to my readers, thank you for being here with me since day one or since today. I am lucky to be able to publish books and make amazing content for you all. I am able to do what I love every single day thanks to all of you. I can't express how much I thank you all. I appreciate every single one of you.

About the Author

Jaclin Marie is a Self Published Author who lives in Southern California. When she isn't writing a compelling story or reading, she either spends her time at the gym or watching Disney Animation movies.

Jaclin started writing at the age of sixteen but she has always been a book lover. She started writing on this writing platform called Wattpad before she decided to publish her debut, Ace De Luca. Although that was her first published book, it wasn't the only book she has written. Since she started writing, she couldn't seem to stop and just like she found her passion.

Darkness evades Jaclin's mind and it demands to be heard. Writing darkness down on paper is something she loves doing. She makes her readers not only think about her plots but completely sob over them.

Her current works published are just a taste of what goes on inside her head.

Printed in Great Britain
by Amazon

39392388R00233